WIND RIVER

TOM MORRISEY

A NOVEL

WIND RIVER

BETHANYHOUSE
MINNEAPOLIS, MINNESOTA

Published by Bethany House Publishers
11400 Hampshire Avenue South
Bloomington, Minnesota 55438

Bethany House Publishers is a division of
Baker Publishing Group, Grand Rapids, Michigan.

Printed in the United States of America

Library of Congress Cataloging-in-Publication Data

Morrisey, Tom, 1952–
    Wind river / Tom Morrisey.
        p.   cm.
    ISBN 978-0-7642-0347-3 (pbk.)
    1. Iraq War, 2003—Veterans—Fiction. 2. Fly fishing—Fiction. 3. Wyoming—Fiction. 4. Psychological fiction. I. Title.

    PS3613.O776W56   2008
    813'. 6—dc22

                                                                    2008014233

To Terri and Ken Blackstock,
Athol and Sue Dickson,
and Angela and Gary Hunt:
friends across the time zones.
"I thank my God upon every
remembrance of you. . . ."

When Gaal saw them, he said to Zebul,
"Look, people are coming down from
the tops of the mountains!"
Zebul replied, "You mistake
the shadows of the mountains for men."

—JUDGES 9:36

WINDRIVER

CHAPTER
ONE

Wyoming—sixteen years ago

THE MORNING SUN HAD JUST CLEARED THE SUMMITS TO THE EAST, and the grass in the small valley was still thick with dew, wetting the boots and the shins of the man and the boy.

The man, tall and unstooped, wore bib overalls over a flannel shirt, his feet shod with cream-soled tan work boots, white hair crowned with a faded green John Deere ball cap. Carrying a heavy Kelty backpack topped with a rolled tent, he walked confidently. His oaken walking staff, gripped just beneath the fist-size burl at its top, seemed to be more for cadence than support. The whiteness of his hair, his wire-rimmed bifocals, the crow's-feet next to his eyes, and a longish nose, just beginning to thicken, were the only hints that he was well past his middle years.

The boy wore a hooded sweatshirt and blue jeans bought too long and cuffed short so they wouldn't drag. His pack was little more than a rucksack, and in his right hand he carried an Orvis split-bamboo fly rod, fully assembled and bobbing before him like a slender, overlong divining rod. Like the man, his blond-streaked light-brown hair was also topped with a John Deere cap, only his cap was still brand-new.

A small movement in the woods high on the hill to their right brought both hikers to a halt. They stood there, silent, for a moment, the bright mountain sun reflecting off a thousand beads of water on the foliage around them. Then the man made a sound halfway between a cough and the *caw* of a crow.

Up on the slope, a deer stepped out from the trees, velvet nubbins of horn sprouting on his tawny head. The deer stared at the man and boy, took a tentative step in their direction, then turned and bolted back uphill, his white tail upright in alarm, the snapping branches marking his flight for several seconds after he had vanished back into the forest.

The man tamped his staff on the ground and chuckled. The boy looked his way.

"Why'd he come out like that?"

"I called him," the man said. "That sound I made? That's the sound his mama made when he was just a fawn, how she told him to stop doin' whatever he was doin' and get over to her. They hear it when they're growin' up, and they never forget it. Even if you can't bring a deer to you with that, you can freeze 'em in their tracks for just a second when they hear it. It's how they was raised."

The boy made the sound, a tenor echo of the man's warm baritone.

"That's it," the man told him. "You've got it."

They walked on in silence for the next few minutes, the trail winding down to the valley floor where it paralleled a small, clear creek.

The boy slowed, stepped nearer to the creek bank, and then looked back.

"Look." He pointed to the water, where several sleek brown shapes hovered in an eddy, a stray shaft of sunlight picking out the bright red patch just behind the upstream end of one undulating form. "There's cutthroat in there."

"Always have been," the man said. "But if you're thinking what I think you're thinking, then you may as well just give it up. Black bear fish this creek all the time, and them trout are way too skittish. I've seen lots'a folks fix to hook one, but fixin' is all they ever done. You can't catch 'em; they're too wild."

The boy scowled and looked back at the creek. He turned to the man again.

"Well, can I try, at least?"

The man looked around and then walked to a half-buried gray granite boulder sticking out of the purple mountain heather just above the trail. He shed his backpack and sat. "Sure," he said, leaning back against the rough rock. "I could use me a breather. But you're wasting your time, boy. Them trout are just way too wild."

The boy set his pack down next to the man's, opened the flap, pulled out a small aluminum fly box and selected a mosquito-size dry fly, an Adams pattern. He held it up to the man, who shrugged and said, "Good as any, I suppose. But I don't suspect they'll be buyin' what you're sellin'."

Scowling, the boy took pliers from his rucksack and bent the fly's barb flat to the bend of its hook. He pulled the tippet from the fly reel, threaded it through the rod guides, and tied on the fly with a practiced clinch knot. He glanced at the man, who said, "Gift-wrap it if you want. Won't make no difference."

Then the boy pulled nail clippers from his pocket, snipped off the tag end of the tippet, and returned the fly box and pliers to the pack. He glanced up at the man, who had taken a small black book from the chest pocket of his overalls. The man read, looking up every moment or two. He appeared to be following a distant snowcapped skyline with his gaze.

Lips set thin and straight, the boy stepped toward the stream, stopped, backed up, then stooped close to the heather and approached the water again. He moved stealthily, setting his feet without so much as a sound, and stopped completely once he was within sight of the stream's far bank. Slowly lowering himself to all fours, he looked back at the man, who met his gaze for just the tiniest fraction of a second before resuming a leisurely inspection of the distant ridge.

The boy reached the bank and parted the grasses. Near the center of the water, a large trout rose, its brown back bowing the surface before it dipped back down and resettled to the gravel streambed. Tapping his fingertips against his thigh, one beat to each second, the boy watched, and when the big trout rose again he resumed his count: tapping, tapping, tapping.

Five times he watched the big fish rise and fall. When it sounded for the sixth time, he pointed the rod tip through the parted grasses, keeping his thumb on the reel and pulling the tiny fly back toward him with his other hand, the way a prankster might pull back a rubber band in school. The rod tip bowed upward from the pressure, and the boy's lips moved, silently forming the numbers *one, two, three . . .*

Then, just as the fish was due to rise again, the boy released the tiny fly and its hook.

The fly shot out and up on its spider thread of tippet. Then the minuscule ruff of fur around the shank caught air and the dry fly slowed and settled toward the water.

In the creek, a brown shape began rising.

There was a swell of crystal water, a splash, and the fly was gone, the tippet pulling tight and yanking the bamboo rod tip downward.

The boy fed line off the reel, letting the fish pull until the tippet had completely cleared the guides and a foot or two of pale yellow fly line was clear as well, pointing this way and that as the trout raced to and fro in the pool.

Standing, the boy held the rod high, clear of the shrubs near the creek bank, and glanced back at the man, who was slapping his thighs and laughing with delight.

The boy straightened up and did his work, cupping the rim of the fly reel with his hand and letting it run a little. When the fish turned, he took line with it, keeping tension on the barbless hook. He did this three times. Then the fish seemed to tire and the boy stepped down the bank and into the water, gasping as it reached his knees.

He kept the rod high, turning and guiding the fish until it drew next to him. Still keeping tension on the line, he dipped his free hand beneath the surface, cupped the fish behind its pectoral fins and lifted it free of the water. The red mark behind the big trout's gill plate gleamed fiercely in the bright mountain sun.

"Whoo-eee!" The man was standing on the creek bank now, a black Vivitar camera in his hands. "That fella's two pounds if he's two ounces. Hold him up and turn a little this way, Tyler."

Tyler trapped the fly rod between his arm and body and held the fish out with both hands, displaying it like the prize that it was.

The man took one picture, then another. He glanced at the sun and said, "Breakfast was kind'a on the light side this morning. Want me to break out the stove and fry that fella up for you?"

The boy shook his head. "I just wanted to see if I could catch him. Let's let him go."

The man crooked an eyebrow. "That's no rainbow, you know. Cutthroat are smart. They remember. You won't be pullin' that prank on him twice."

Tyler laughed. "Then I'll just have to come up with a new prank."

He cocked his head. "Don't you think I should put him back?"

The man held up an index finger and then opened to the front of the little book he'd been studying. He leafed forward a few pages.

" 'And God blessed them,' " he read, " 'and God said unto them, Be fruitful, and multiply, and replenish the earth, and subdue it: and have dominion over the fish of the sea.' "

He closed the book and looked at the boy. " 'Have dominion.' You know what that means?"

Tyler shook his head.

"It means you get to decide. That may be a fish of the creek instead of a fish of the sea, but it's close enough. You still get to call the shots. Cook him or set him free, God says you're the boss. Sure you don't want him for lunch?"

The boy shook his head again. "I want to put him back."

"All right. Turn him loose, then."

The hook came free with one turn and a pull, and the boy lowered the fish belly-first into the stream, moving him back and forth in the cold clear water until the trout's brown body quivered and it swam from his hands and shot for an undercut on the far side of the stream.

The boy handed the fly rod up to the man and clambered out of the water. The man had put the camera away and held out a dry pair of boot socks. Tyler nodded and accepted them, sitting down on the warm, rough surface of the boulder to pull off his sodden boots. A soft breeze ruffled the hair above his forehead as a yellow butterfly flitted nearby among the heather.

"Is that really true what you told me? That nobody has ever caught one of those trout before?"

"Not in all the years I've been comin' here. And I've been comin' here since before the war. Seen folks try it. Lots of folks. You're the only one I've ever seen do it."

The boy beamed, and the man seemed to dim a little, his smile straightening, eyes moving back to the jagged edge of the distant ridgeline.

"What are you thinking?"

The man smiled at him. "About how much I love coming here. About how I like being here with you."

"Then why did you look sad there for a little bit?"

The man cocked his head and studied the boy a moment, then turned his attention toward the ridge again, tucking the Bible back into his bib pocket and buttoning the pocket shut.

"I've been coming into the Wind River Range for more than fifty years, Tyler. Started when I was barely shaving. And now . . . well, now I'm old."

"You're not old."

The man took his cap off and his white hair shone in the sun.

"There's snow on the mountain," he said, laughing.

"But you're still strong."

"Am now." The man nodded. "But I won't be forever. And I was just thinkin' that there'll come a day when I won't be able to do this anymore. When I won't be able to just pack up and go."

The boy looked at the ridge as well.

"Then I'll bring you," he finally said.

"How's that?"

"When you can't come on your own. I'll come and I'll get you and I'll bring you. I'll come to your and Miss Edda's house, and I'll put you in my truck and I'll bring you."

"You have a truck now, do you?"

Tyler shook his head. "Not yet. But I will when I'm a man. And I'll come and I'll get you and I'll take you into the Winds, just like you take me now."

The man smiled, tan skin crinkling more deeply behind his glasses at the corners of his blue eyes.

"Well, I'd like that," he said. "You wouldn't have to do it

all the time. Who knows? When you grow up, you might live somewhere way across the country. But maybe when I'm too old to come up here all by my lonesome . . . maybe you can come get me sometime and bring me back up for one last trip. Could you do that?"

"I'll do that."

"You promise?"

The boy spat on his palm and held his hand out.

The man spat on his own and they shook. No laughter. No jokes.

"It's a promise," Tyler told him.

"All right then." The man looked around the valley and took the boy's wet socks, putting them under the straps that held the tent on his pack so they'd dry as they walked in the sun. "One last time. One last trip into the Winds."

"When you're too old."

"That's right. When I'm too old."

CHAPTER
TWO

Iraq—three years ago

TY PERKINS BENT DOWN AND WIPED A STRAY BIT OF SAND FROM the toes of his tan suede combat boots, then tugged at the bottoms of his trousers, flaring them where they tucked into the boot tops. Opening his locker, he took out the combat-uniform blouse with the buck-sergeant chevron on the sleeves and put it on, not bothering to check his reflection in the single, small mirror on the inside of the locker. He left his body armor where it was for the moment, and glanced at the watch on the inside of his left wrist.

"Roll in five," he said to the three other men in the big, hut-like, canvas-walled tent. "You good to go?"

"Hewh." The men grunted as if they'd been lightly punched— the Marine Corps version of a "yes." Ty put on his body armor, flicking sand from the fuzzy parts of the Velcro straps and then holding the central part—the part with the biggest ceramic plate—over his chest as he smoothed the hooked ends of the straps into place. He quickly assembled the rest of his gear: an assault rifle and sidearm, a field-dressing kit, extra ammunition, a flashlight, a two-way radio with earpiece, a CamelBak hydration system, and a knife—a short-bladed Ka-Bar, the butt of which was chipped and scratched. He topped it off with a pair of shades: Wiley X combat goggles with metallic blue lenses.

After it was all on, he glanced at himself in the mirror and shrugged at his own reflection.

The other three men were dressed more or less identically, the color and shape of their eyewear the only real difference, and the private in the group, the new guy, added a pair of fingerless leather gloves before lifting the SAW—the squad automatic weapon. The big gun in the group.

All four men grabbed their helmets and, without a word, headed for the door where they stepped out into the windless heat and stink and distant noise of Iraq.

Ty ran his helmet under a water spigot, put the thick pot on his head and cinched the chin strap, blinking as a stray bead of water rolled down his temple and onto his fresh-shaven chin.

"Okay. Rock and roll." Climbing into a Humvee, rudimentally armored on the inside with ballistic vests pop-riveted in place, Ty groaned. "Man, thing's like an oven already."

The driver, a sweating young private, nodded. "The body armor holds the heat in. Won't stop an RPG. Won't even stop a good rifle round, but it'll sure hold the heat."

Ty nodded back, tapped on the laminated surface of a folding map.

"Where we left off yesterday," he told the private. "Six streets in from the last place we started. But come in from the north this time. We don't want to follow the same route two days in a row. You start doing that and these guys'll line the street with Fiats full of C4."

He keyed the button on his shoulder mike.

"Okay, Marines," he said. "Same mission as yesterday. Hand out the flyers about the town hall meeting at the civic center and use the interps to repeat the information verbally. Do not speak to a woman unless she is accompanied by a man, and do not enter a mosque unless I tell you to. Any questions, comments, domestics?"

Fingertip to the headset beneath his helmet, he listened for a moment and then nodded. "Okay. Let's roll."

The three-vehicle convoy moved out, through the double gates and sandbag fortifications at the entrance to the compound and down a short road into the city proper.

Fallujah engulfed and surrounded them. Jacketed men sat at wooden tables and sipped coffee from demitasse cups as they talked to one another, gesturing to make their points. A few street venders grinned and waved, their expressions seemingly too innocent and childlike for full-grown men. Women moved like burkhaed ghosts along the sides of the streets, veiled heads bowed, gripping baskets with bread poking from the tops.

A small boy looked up from where he was making a kickball out of plastic bags and tape, and tracked the Humvee with somber eyes as it passed. Ty smiled and waved at him. The kid's face remained expressionless, but he nodded slightly before returning to his task.

The three vehicles pulled up next to a crowded market across from a mosque. Within seconds everyone except the drivers was out, assembling into four-man fireteams, fanning out across the marketplace, smiling and keeping their weapons lowered. Ty lagged behind the central fireteam just a bit, where he could keep an eye on all twelve of his marines. He keyed his radio and called his platoon commander, reporting the squad's location and status. Then he took off his helmet, brushed a hand back through his close-cropped hair and put the helmet back on. He wiped his hand on his BDU, the moisture evaporating from the desert-camouflage fabric like fog from a breath on glass.

Ty refastened the chin strap on his helmet and inspected his fireteams. The first team was doing exactly what the mission called for: handing out pamphlets about the council meeting while giving the recipients the information aloud just in case they couldn't read.

The second fireteam was doing the same as the first, except the private with the SAW had a gaggle of children around him; he was handing out pencils and little paper tablets.

The third fireteam was a different story altogether. Two of them stood guard at strategic positions in the marketplace, scanning the crowd and looking for potential threats, while the other two and the interpreter were gathered in front of a wool-jacketed man who was gesturing with his arms as he spoke rapidly.

Ty straightened up and moved forward. As he got closer, bits of a British-acquired accent became intelligible. Both the Iraqi and the fireteam leader were smiling, exchanging banter.

"Do you know how many Frenchmen it takes to defend Paris?" the Iraqi was asking the marines.

The two men and the interpreter shook their heads.

"Neither do they," the Iraqi said. "It has never been attempted!"

All four men roared with laughter. The Iraqi glanced Ty's way as if to include him in the joke. Then the man looked past Ty, and his eyes widened. He began to wave his hands back and forth, and shouted in Arabic, "*La! La! La!*"

Ty spun to his left, his right hand going to his holster as he turned, the sidearm pulling cleanly into his hand. He raked the pistol with his thumb, and the safety went off with a soft *snick*.

A turbaned old man was moving toward the squad from the mosque across the street, running faster than any man his age should ever have to run. He was holding something aloft, a small, winged box of some kind, and it had a black wire that ran back into the folds of his tunic-like robe.

He screamed as he ran: "*Allahu akbar! Allahu akbar!*"

Ty swung the pistol up, pulled the front sight down onto center-of-mass on the old man's chest, squeezed the trigger once, let the front sight come to a rest on his target again and squeezed a second time. The loud bark of the .45 echoed back from the stucco walls, and in the deafening silence that followed, he heard the old cleric's body hit the cobblestones of the ancient street, the *th-thump* too small and light for the enormity of what had just happened. Off to the right somewhere, Ty's spent brass shell casing rang as it bounced off something hard.

There was the distinct *chrr-ick* of the SAW being racked, and that brought Ty's head up. Still aiming his pistol at the downed man, he shouted, "Hold your fire. Call 'em out."

A babble of voices rose up across the marketplace—Arabic cries of alarm and fright. But over the din, the fireteams answered, "One, no threat here, Sarge," and, "Two, all clear," and, "We're good. Three secure."

Ty nodded as the two men who'd been talking with the Iraqi moved forward, rifles ready and at their shoulders. The cleric lay on his back, the device he'd been holding now at his side on the street. Still aiming his rifle at the cleric's head, one marine placed his boot on the man's wrist so he couldn't grab the box again, with the other marine kneeling to feel for a pulse at the base of the man's neck. He moved his free hand back and forth, palm down.

"Clear, Sarge."

Ty lowered his pistol, holstered it and walked forward. Both of his marines began examining the dead cleric. One of them cursed in exasperation.

"What have you got?" Ty said, joining them.

"The thing he had in his hand—it's just an old Xbox controller. And look at this. . . ." The marine moved the cleric's robe to reveal where the wire from the control ended in a single silver plug. "We got hosed, Sarge. It wasn't connected to anything. This old boy was bluffing."

CHAPTER
THREE

"The field report says that you employed your sidearm, Sergeant," the JAG colonel began as he looked down at a photocopy of the report. "Were you carrying your M16?"

"Yes, sir," Ty said. "I was."

"Why not use that?"

"Sir, my rifle was hanging by its sling, and I had civilians to either side of me. The pistol was easier to bring to bear, sir."

"But your target was twenty yards away. Your rifle would have been the more accurate weapon."

"True, sir, but I wasn't worried about missing."

The officer put on reading glasses and, squinting, spent several seconds looking at another photocopy. He then set the paper and the glasses aside.

"Your squad corporal said you made both shots offhand—one-handed. When I learned small arms in the Corps, they taught us to use the Weaver stance, Sergeant: holding the pistol with both hands."

"Sir, I was on the pistol team at Quantico after my tour in Afghanistan. I competed at Camp Perry, summer before last. Conventional pistol is shot one-handed; it's against the rules to touch the pistol with your free hand. So that's how we practiced. I got comfortable with it, sir."

"And why the two shots?"

"It looked as if I was dealing with a threat to the squad and the civilians around me, sir. I had to make sure I neutralized it. So I double-tapped."

The officer nodded and made a note in the report's margin. He glanced up.

"May I see your sidearm, Sergeant?"

Ty removed his pistol from its holster, extracted the magazine, racked the slide to extract the round in the chamber, locked the slide open and handed it, grip first, to the officer.

"Beretta nine is standard Corps issue these days, Sergeant," the colonel said, turning the Kimber .45 over in his hand. "Your platoon commander know you carry this?"

"Sir, would I get him in trouble if I told you that he does?"

The colonel shook his head. "Jarheads love their .45s. We all know that."

"Well, sir, the 1911 is what I shot with during full matches. The last rounds have to be shot with a .45, and we shot the second round—the center-fire round—with the .45 as well. That way you don't have to learn three different guns. I got used to it. And when I got orders to come over here, our armorer built me this gun. It's not a target pistol like the Springers we used on the team—those are way too tight for the field. But Kimber was building some of these for the Corps' special-ops detachment to use over here. Our chief armorer got one, changed the barrel and did some basic accurizing and trigger work on it, and the team gave it to me as a going-away present. I asked my platoon leader for permission to carry it, and he cleared it for me with the battalion."

The officer made another note.

"Sir, is that going to be a problem? The gun?"

The officer picked up the round Ty had ejected and shook his head. "These are full-metal-jacketed rounds, completely kosher according to the Convention. No worries there, Sergeant. You're legal. And your general orders call for you to use deadly force at your discretion to protect your unit and the civilian population. You were doing both."

He made another note and looked up.

"I think we're finished here, Sergeant. I'm sorry to have put you through this. I know you were asked a lot of this already, and I know it's been a long, hard day. But Battalion wanted a legal report, and they wanted it right away."

Ty nodded. Then he cleared his throat.

"Sir? May I ask a question?"

The colonel squared his papers. "Fire away."

"Sir, the man I killed: how old was he?"

The officer folded his arms.

"Does that really matter? Nineteen or ninety-nine, he was still an imminent threat to the security of your people."

Ty didn't say anything.

"Well," the colonel said, glancing at the report. "I imagine it will be in the papers anyhow. He was seventy-eight. An imam, not at the mosque there across from the marketplace, but from the other side of town. A Sunni, same as most of the people in Hussein's old government. Looks as if this fellow came there this morning just to do what he did."

"To make us kill him."

"You had to. If you'd used less force, you would have been exposing the civilians around you to additional potential risk. People would have been asking why you didn't take more aggressive action to protect them."

"But tomorrow the papers are going to report that a marine shot an unarmed old man."

The colonel initialed a buck slip and bundled it and the slim stack of papers together with a silver banker's clip. He looked up.

"That's how our enemy does their fighting, Sergeant. Maybe they told this old guy that they'd pay his family big bucks if he did this. Maybe he thought this was going to be his guaranteed ticket to paradise, his personal jihad. Maybe he was doing it to goad some younger guys into doing the same, or maybe he was getting ready to drop dead of cancer anyhow—if so, the autopsy'll show it. Who knows? It might be all of the above."

"Doesn't matter. I did exactly what they wanted us to do."

"Sergeant, you defended your position with force commensurate to the threat. The enemy took advantage of that. And yes, the papers will scream bloody murder. But on the upside, Iraq is now short one nutjob. Maybe that squares it." The colonel put the report away in his briefcase, then looked Ty straight in the eyes. "Sergeant Perkins, do you think it might help to review this with a doctor?"

"A shrink, you mean, sir?"

"Or a chaplain. Or both. Or at least request some leave. Send your wife an e-ticket and have her meet you in Germany. Nobody would fault you for it."

"Well, sir, if it's up to me—"

"It isn't. But I'll listen to what you have to say."

Ty accepted his pistol from the officer, reloaded the magazine, racked the slide, locked the safety and returned the .45 to its holster. "Sir, if I take time off, it might send the wrong message to my squad. Next time something happens, someone might hesitate. Our people could get hurt."

"A cogent argument for keeping on keeping on, Sergeant." The colonel closed his briefcase. "And if that's how you really feel, then go ahead. My report will show that there's no legal reason you shouldn't continue in active duty. You reacted quickly, responsibly and as trained. If that imam really had been packing HE explosive, you'd be up for a commendation right now. If Battalion has any guts, you still will be."

The officer stood and Ty stood with him.

"You did the right thing, Sergeant," the colonel said, reaching out to shake Ty's hand. "I'd go in the field with you any day of the week. Don't you lose any sleep over this. That's what your enemy wants. Deny him."

"Yes, sir. Thank you, sir." Ty shook the officer's hand, then saluted, turned and stepped out of the air-conditioned hut and into the sweltering afternoon sun.

"Brother. Would you look at that—the Corps will let just about anything wear the uniform these days, won't they?"

Scowling, Ty pivoted on the ball of his foot. The scowl left his face as his eyes widened. "Gunny?"

Hulking and stocky, the man grinning back at him was dressed in the same desert-camouflage battle dress uniform as just about everyone else in the compound, only his was newer, more neatly pressed. His sleeve bore the chevrons and rockers of a Marine Corps gunnery sergeant, and he had an olive-drab satchel over his shoulder. He grinned even more broadly, warping the pale trace of a scar that ran down his left cheek.

"What's the matter, Perkins? Cat got your tongue?"

Ty came out of his lethargy and gripped the older man in half a bear hug.

"What are you doing here, Gunny? Aren't you still on the team?"

"Captain of the pistol team and co-captain of the whole shootin' match, if you'll excuse the pun. Which is what I'm doing here. Seeing as we beat the pants off Army and Air Force at the championships last July, and the Navy never could hit a backing board, the forces-that-be in the Commandant's office decided it would be good for morale to show me around over here. You jarheads are supposed to look at what an extraordinary specimen of ten-X manhood I am and fall all over yourselves to be first to reenlist."

Ty laughed. "Don't hold your breath."

Gunny checked his watch. "Sun's over the yardarm, Perkins. You all have a source of adult refreshment here?"

"Only if you consider Coca-Cola an adult refreshment,

Gunny." Ty quirked an eyebrow. "Combat zone—no alcohol allowed. Even if you leave the base, you're out of luck. It's a Muslim country."

"And this here's the Tennessee remedy for that." The older man lifted the flap of his satchel, revealing the brown, paper-taped necks of three whiskey bottles. "I promised two of these to some old buds from El Toro, but the other one's just for contingencies, and this here's a contingency. Let's go."

Ty looked around and pulled the flap down on the satchel. "Not so brazen, man—that's an Article 15 if you get caught with it. Besides, I really think I ought to just go . . ."

The older man held up his hand. "Perkins, I know what happened when you were out with the squad this morning. Heard about it as soon as I choppered in. So I took advantage of my celebrity status and checked around. Found out from the mortuary docs that neither one of the wounds you put in that old geezer bled all that much, which means you can still shoot; you stopped that man's heart with the first shot. If I ever get it, I hope my enemy extends me the same courtesy. But I figured you'd be torn up about it, your kill being some geriatric religious freak and all. So I found out where JAG was giving you the third degree and came over here. What—you think this was some kind of coincidence? And you *are* going to help me get rid of the evidence of this here potential Article 15 violation. No arguments. You think you're torn up over plugging that old man, just wait and see how you feel when *this* old man kicks your backside."

Ty held his hands up in mock surrender, and the gunnery sergeant grabbed him by the elbow. The two of them swung by the recreation hall and picked up a two-liter bottle of Coke. Then they went back out into the heat and started walking toward Ty's tent.

"So, Perkins, how you feeling?"

Ty shrugged. "The day I joined the Corps, it was the week after September eleventh. . . ."

"I was working enlistment back then," Gunny said. "Best week I ever had in that job. Made my numbers for the year. No sweet-talkin' or hand-holdin' necessary. Man, we had people lined up out the door. You dropped out of college to enlist, didn't you?"

"Not really 'dropped out.' I talked to the dean's office and got them to give me credit for the classes I was in; they'd just started. I figured I'd finish up when I got out of the Corps."

"That still your plan?"

Ty shrugged.

"What year were you in school?"

"Junior."

The gunny spat in the dust and shook his head.

"Don't be an idiot, Perkins. Finish up after you're out. Uncle Sugar will even pick up a bunch of the tab. Believe me, I've seen too many jarheads who got their discharge papers and then just stumbled around, workin' nothing jobs and spending Friday nights in a Legion hall, remembering when they used to be somebody. You're better than that. Finish school."

"Yes, Dad."

If the older man heard the jibe, he didn't show it. The pair crossed paths with a major, saluted him, and got a salute in return.

"I think I can tell you the rest of your story, Perkins,"

Gunny continued. "You signed up after 9/11, all full of Pine-Sol and vinegar, thinkin' you were gonna hunt down Osama bin Laden—"

"Not just thinking, Gunny. When I deployed to Afghanistan, we were actually *looking* for the guy."

"But now you're over here, and they got you playin' policeman and public-relations man, and wet nurse and who knows what else, and you're wondering what this all has to do with fighting terrorism, right?"

Ty nodded as they came to a stop in front of his tent. Gunny shook his head.

"Perkins . . . Ty. There's one thing you've got to know about the Corps, son. You don't get to pick your wars. Other people do that for you. They pick 'em, and you fight 'em, and as long as they don't tell you to do anything that's truly and blatantly illegal, you do it. Washington runs the wars, Sergeant. We run missions. That's where your focus has to be. Succeed. Accomplish your mission. If you think of anything bigger than that, it'll just make your head hurt."

Ty nodded as the older man opened the door to the tent. "C'mon," Gunny said. "Time to give this soda some backbone."

When Ty woke up, he was on the cot in his tent and sunlight was spilling through the one window in the door. His boots were off and his cover had been hung up, but other than that, he was still in his BDU. He sat up and groaned as his head caught up with him. Right hand to his temple, he looked at his watch.

"Oh, man!"

Ty jumped out of bed and put a hand to his head again. Then he saw the Post-it note stuck to his locker.

PERKINS—
COOL YOUR JETS. I'M TAKING
YOUR SQUAD OUT. SQUARED IT
WITH YOUR LT. YESTERDAY—
I THINK I STILL REMEMBER HOW
TO WALK AROUND AND LOOK LIKE
I'M IN COMMAND. GET YOURSELF
SOME RACK TIME AND I'LL SEE YOU
AT THE REC HALL LATER ON.

At the bottom was the gunny's clear, bold signature.

Blowing his breath out in a long, slow half whistle, Ty sat down on his cot. He stretched out and fell back to sleep.

Waking half an hour later, he grabbed his shaving kit and a clean uniform and went over to the showers, where he stood under hot water and soaped himself for a good ten minutes. Then he dressed and got to the mess hall just before they were about to stop serving breakfast.

He was walking across the compound on his way to the library when he heard helicopters coming in fast from the east. At about the same time he saw the front gates open, and two armored troop carriers and a Humvee came racing in, heading toward the helipad.

Ty began running that way as well. The vehicles came to a stop just as he got there. Two corpsmen were helping a man out of the Humvee. His head was bandaged, but there was enough showing to make the man recognizable. It was the private who carried the SAW in Ty's squad.

"Riccolo!"

The man looked up.

"Sarge? How the . . . ? Oh that's right, you were—"

"What happened?"

The private's face seemed to clear.

"IED. Car bomb, Sarge."

"You the only one hurt?"

The man shook his head. "I think everybody's hurt, Sarge. And the people in the first Humvee, that gunny and them . . ."

He trailed off, as if he'd lost his place.

"What, Riccolo? What about Gunny?"

"He's dead, Sarge. All them guys are dead."

CHAPTER

FOUR

Stafford, Virginia—present day

FROWNING AT THE MIRROR, TYLER PERKINS BUTTONED THE
uniform shirt and tucked it into his trousers, straightening everything so that the button platen of his shirt front and the fly of
the brown trousers lined up perfectly. He threaded the web belt
through the belt loops and tightened it, ran a finger tentatively
along the neat edge of his day-old haircut, and then stepped
back for the overall view.

"It's going to be hot today. Wouldn't you rather wear your
walking shorts?"

The young woman who'd entered the room was wearing a
robe several sizes too large for her slim frame, her shoulder-length
chestnut hair still disheveled by the pillow. She was carrying
two mugs, the coffee in them tinted tan by the milk, and as she

handed Ty one of the mugs, the front of her robe fell open a bit and she smiled. She reached up to give him a kiss, and he turned a little. It landed on his cheek.

Ty took a sip, set the mug down on a coaster atop the plain oaken dresser and fetched his ankle-high boots from the side of the bed.

"No," he said. "I think I'll stick with long pants today."

"You never wear the shorts."

"It doesn't look right. I take a handcart full of packages into some of those offices up by Alexandria, and I walk it back to the mail room, and everybody I pass is in shirts and ties, and then there I am, the UPS guy, dressed like he's just back from summer camp."

The woman laughed and then sat on the bed next to him, her expression suddenly turning serious. "Ty, you don't have to be the UPS man if you don't want to."

"Nothing wrong with driving for Brown, Angie. Brown pays good money."

"I know they do, and you do a good job of taking care of us. But I was just thinking that, if you wanted an office job . . ."

He glanced her way, just with his eyes, not turning his head. "You're not going to start with college again, are you?"

She moved nearer to him.

"Well, Ty . . . it's been almost ten months since you got out. And you only have a little over a year left of school. The government will pay for it all. Most of it."

He stiffened a little when she said that.

"That'll last for a while," he said, tying his left boot. "It's not like there's a clock ticking or anything."

"But . . ." Angie began. Then she fell silent, the word dissolving in the air between them. She reached over, took his hand and slid it into her open robe, holding it there. "Coming straight home tonight?" Her voice had just the slightest bit of husk to it.

Ty slid his hand out and tied his other boot.

"I can't," he said. "I promised Harry I'd help him put that drywall up in his family room."

"But it's Friday."

"That's why he wants to do it tonight. So we can run late if we need to, and neither one of us has to drive a route tomorrow."

Angie sighed.

"Ang." Ty looked at her. "We've only got the pickup. Your car won't be out of the shop until next week. Harry's been running me in to work for three days now. I owe him."

"You can take the truck." Her voice was small. "I don't need the truck. I'm not going anywhere today."

"I don't want to leave you here without wheels." He stood up and got his sunglasses from the dresser.

"Ty . . ."

He pocketed his wallet, a key ring, a white cotton handkerchief, ironed flat.

"Ty . . ."

He turned and, as he did, Angie opened her robe and hugged him, wrapping the big bathrobe around the two of them, pressing the length of her body against the brown fabric of his uniform. Her left cheek was against his chest and her long hair covered her face.

"It's been months, Ty." Her voice was smaller still. "Months and months and months and months and months."

He leaned forward and stopped when his lips were almost but not quite touching the top of his wife's head. He straightened up, stroked her hair and said, "I think I hear a car, Ang. Harry's waiting."

She released him and then followed as he walked down the hall and into the kitchen, where his lunch was waiting in a brown bag. He picked up the bag, turned and said, "Listen. Barbara's going to be over there tonight. Why don't you give her a call and set something up? Maybe get us all some steaks to grill? That way we can eat together, and you and she can visit while Harry and I work. Would you like that?"

Angie wiped her face with her sleeve and she smiled. But her eyes still glistened from the tears.

"Great," Ty told her. She held her arms out to him and they hugged. Ty looked to the front door. "I gotta go."

Harry handed him a Krispy Kreme cup as Ty climbed into the Dodge van and Ty smiled his thanks. Both men waved to Angie, who was standing in the doorway with the robe clasped closed with one hand, waving with the other, the tousled sleep still in her hair.

"Tyler, my man," Harry said, "that is one outstanding woman you married. My, my, you are one fortunate son of a gun."

"I know." He waved again and Angie closed the door. "I know."

He leaned back and sipped his coffee, grimacing just a bit. "Still hot," he said. "You must have just picked this up."

"Habit from the Corps," Harry said. "I never was much of a breakfast eater. Got one of those slow metabolisms. If I eat too much, all I want to do is get fat and sleep, like some old bear. But coffee? I like the jump start. Need it, at this point. About a year ago, Barbara put me on one of those diets where I couldn't have coffee. I made it three days before I threw in the towel. Gave me this splitting headache."

He turned out of the darkened subdivision onto a county road. Up ahead, a pair of red taillights disappeared around a curve.

"You were in Desert Storm, right?" Ty asked.

"That's right. We started the business, and y'all finished it. I was at battalion, waiting to drive my colonel back to our company when word came down that we couldn't go all the way to Baghdad. *That* was a cuss streak. Sounded like a hundred carpenters hit their thumbs with the hammer, all at the same time."

A light rain sprinkled the windshield, so Harry put the wipers on.

"But you were married," Ty asked, "before you deployed?"

"Yeah. Barbara and I tied the knot right after I got out of basic training."

"What you saw over there—did it change anything between you?"

"What I *ate* over there made me appreciate that woman's cooking. That's for sure." Harry laughed. Then he stopped and looked over at Ty, his brow furrowed in the light from the instrument panel. "What're you saying, man? You gettin' the bejeebies from what you saw when y'all were overseas playin' cowboys and Muslims?"

Ty shrugged.

Harry put the defroster on.

"Don't you be livin' with that stuff, Ty. Ain't no need. The VA's got all sorts of docs for that kind of noise."

"I know. I saw one for a little while. He put me on some sleeping pills that made me feel stoned until noon the next day."

Harry turned onto a main highway—early morning headlamps and taillights in both directions.

"Well, then you need to find you a different doc or a different pill. That is one pretty little young wife you got there, Perkins. I kid you not. She's a sweetheart too. Doesn't want nothing more than the white picket fence and the chance to give you a houseful of babies. And that's a very good thing, brother. You don't want to be messing that up for yourself. You know?"

"I know." Ty looked out the window at a Krispy Kreme doughnut shop, the HOT NOW! sign lit up in red neon in the front window. "I know."

CHAPTER

FIVE

THE ROOM HAD BEEN SET UP AS A STUDY, BUT IT WAS ACTUALLY more of a catchall. It had a desk, as well as a Dell computer and a couple of file cabinets, but it also contained fly rods and fishing vests, framed photographs of mountains, a small table with a fly-tying vise and a lamp, and a shadow box that held Ty's Marine Corps medals and his ceremonial sword. In the closet, there were two kinds of chest waders—the regular kind and the thinner nylon foldable sort that backpackers used—a little-used Osprey internal-frame backpack, a three-season mummy-style sleeping bag hanging loose in a mesh storage bag, hiking boots, a down vest and mountain parka, and a tan fishing vest with a tuft of lamb's wool above the left breast pocket. Far to the side of the closet, where they were barely visible, hung his dress blues and the faded blouse and trousers of his battle dress uniform.

Ty was sitting at the desk, but the computer was turned off. The keyboard had been pushed forward under the flat-screen monitor to make room for a pile of mail that he was sorting: bills to the left, personal mail to the right, junk mail into the trash can at the side of the desk.

He tossed away a circular from a lawn-care service and one advertising a local pizzeria, and stopped at a smaller card-size envelope addressed to him in thin, reedy handwriting.

Ty looked at the return address: *125 Bridger Street, Pinedale, Wyo.* Just that. The street address, the town, the old-fashioned state abbreviation, and no zip code.

He opened the envelope and pulled out a picture postcard: Gannett Peak in the Wind River Range, topped with its bread loaf of corniced snow. He flipped it over; both the message and the address portions on the back of the card were covered with the same thin handwriting:

Dear Tiger,

Your Aunt Betty told me that you got back from overseas safe and sound, and I thank the good Lord for that. Edda prayed for you every day that you were over there. I had hip-replacement surgery 2 years ago in February, and am now walking pretty good on my own. Was cleaning up my fishing things in the garage this morning and that got me thinking about you. I know that you are far away and busy, but I sure miss you.

Come see me sometime if you get the chance.

Your friend always,
Soren

Ty turned on the computer and keyed in the address for *ZabaSearch.com.* He typed *Soren Andeman* into the search line and selected Wyoming as the search state.

A moment later, a listing popped up. The address matched the return address on the envelope, including a phone number as well. Ty reached for the cordless phone, then glanced at the clock: it was just after eight in the morning, eastern time. He put the phone back on its charger.

"Ty? Are you ready?" Angie's voice was close, in the living room. "The flyer said the contemporary service is at nine. The eleven o'clock is traditional, organ music and robes. I don't want to go to that."

Ty slid the postcard into his blazer pocket.

"I'm good, babe. We can leave right now."

The church was in what had once been a Home Depot, its ceilings and columns painted flat black, a raised platform set up near the center, brick-red carpeting over the concrete floor, with theatrical-type light fixtures hanging from the steel bar joists above. When they pulled in, the people walking in were in jeans and khakis, and some even wore shorts. Angie glanced at Ty and he nodded and took off his necktie, leaving his collar open and stashing the new silk tie in the console of the F-150.

Inside, they got greeted three times on the way to their seats—modern-looking bent-wood folding chairs—and as soon as they sat, a young redheaded woman came by with bulletins and a couple of pencils—the little stubby kind, like the ones they hand out at golf courses.

"First time here?" Her voice had just enough drawl to show that she was that rarest of rarities in the Quantico area—a native Virginian.

Angie nodded.

The woman smiled, first at her and then at Ty.

"Well, don't you worry when the offering basket comes by;

TOM MORRISEY

you're our guests. But if you'd like to fill out a card ... we aren't going to come by and knock on your door or anything, but we'd love to have you on our mailing list. We do lots of events—concerts and things."

"She was nice," Angie said when the woman had left. She opened the bulletin and offered Ty a pencil. "You want to fill one out too?"

"No. That's okay. You can fill one out for both of us."

Angie looked him in the eyes for the smallest of moments, then nodded and began filling out the bookmark-like form.

Two minutes later, the lights dimmed and a spotlight came up on a single guitarist at center stage. He began playing—slow at first, holding some of the notes in a riff that sounded vaguely Latin at times. Then the tempo quickened, the auditorium erupted in music, the lights came up to reveal that a bass player, another guitarist, a drummer and a saxophone player had joined in. A large screen descended from the ceiling as a young woman with short blond hair entered, half skipping and half dancing from the back of the stage, bringing her hands together in an exaggerated motion over her head and encouraging the crowd to clap. As she did this, everyone around them rose to their feet, clapping in time, and the guy sitting in front of Ty and Angie was doing a little jig in place. Angie rose as well and, after a second, so did Ty.

The woman onstage was at the keyboard now, adding its music to the swell of sound, and she adjusted a boom micro-phone with one hand and began to sing. Angie was singing and moving her head so her long hair brushed to and fro. Her eyes and Ty's eyes met, and she exaggerated her clap, nodding. Ty

48

clapped as well, and kept it up for four or five beats. Then he stopped and, after a moment, clasped his hands behind his back. Parade rest.

Another song followed that first one. Then another, and another after that. And finally the band ended with a wall of noise followed by applause and more than a few whoops and whistles. The woman at the keyboard welcomed everyone to the service, playing softly, one-handed, on the keyboard as she spoke. Then she and the music stopped at the same time, the lights dimming once again.

A film clip began to play on the screen: Robin Williams and a pale young woman in the ruins of a gray house. She was talking in a half-dazed voice about how she had destroyed her family and he was telling her it wasn't so. Then, as Robin Williams stood up to leave, the clip ended. A spotlight came up on a man onstage, a slender guy in his late thirties or early forties. The house lights came up as well and the screen showed a scene that played over and over again: a drop of water hitting a still pond, ripples spreading in the golden light of sunset.

The man onstage was dressed casually in jeans and a light sweater. He had gold highlights in his brown hair and a deep tan, and he sat on a tall stool and took a sip from a bottle of Aquafina. He turned a page on a silver music stand that sat to his side and began to speak.

Everyone was sitting now, and Ty patted the pocket of his jacket and then took out what had been in there: the postcard he'd received in the envelope in the weekend mail. He looked at the photograph on the front of it—the mountain in bold relief against a sky robin's-egg blue, the snow white yet with just enough of a pinkish-gold blush to it to show that the photograph had been taken only minutes after dawn.

Ty turned the postcard over, held it at an angle so the light from the stage would catch it, and read the block of text at the upper left corner of the card:

Gannett Peak *(13,804 feet)*, *highest mountain in the state of Wyoming and monarch of the Wind River Range. Photo by Soren Andeman.*

The man onstage continued to talk in a conversational guy-next-door baritone. Ty tilted the postcard again and a stray beam of light from the fixtures overhead highlighted two words: *fishing things.* He moved the postcard a little more, and now an entire sentence was illuminated:

I know that you are far away and busy, but I sure miss you.

Ty sat quietly, tapping the postcard noiselessly against his fingertips. He looked at it again and this time the light fell on the next sentence down:

Come see me sometime if you get the chance.

Ty closed his eyes and sat very still, the rise and fall of his chest nearly imperceptible. Then he opened his eyes again and looked once more at the postcard.

Come see me sometime . . .

Now the man on the stage was saying something about

prayer, and heads were bowing all around the auditorium. Angie bowed, and Ty bowed as well. He ran his thumb along the edge of the card.

"Wow. Great service, huh?"

"Yeah." Ty nodded as he turned the key in the ignition. "It was different. What do you think, the Sunday brunch at Peppino's? It's close."

"That'd be nice. So . . . what did you think of the pastor's message?"

Ty gave a wave and a nod to the orange-vested man directing traffic out of the parking lot and turned north on the main thoroughfare in front of the church.

"It was . . . good."

Angie tucked her church bulletin into the pocket of the truck door.

"I thought what he had to say about parents and their kids was right on target, didn't you?"

Ty nodded as he changed lanes.

Angie smiled and stroked her husband's arm as he drove. "What was your favorite part of the message?"

Ty glanced at the rearview mirror and said, "I guess that was my favorite part."

Angie stopped stroking his arm.

"Ty?"

"Uh-huh?"

"Look at me, Ty."

"I'm driving, Angie."

"We're at a stoplight. Please, look at me."

He looked at her.

"What was the message about today, Ty?"

He glanced away for a moment. "It was about . . . God. God's love."

The light changed and they began moving again. The silence in the cab was so thick that you could clearly hear the thrum of the off-road truck tires on the pavement.

Finally, Ty glanced at Angie. "What?"

"You didn't even listen."

"I heard it. Some of it. And then I . . . zoned out. Sort of."

He made a right into a parking lot in front of a building with an Old World wood motif.

"You didn't fall asleep, did you?"

He shut off the engine. "No. I absolutely was not asleep."

"Well, if you were awake, I think you would remember that the pastor spoke on the opening of the fifty-first Psalm."

Ty looked at her, his face neutral, expressionless.

"Tyler Perkins." Angie took his Slimline Bible out of the center console pocket and held it up between them. "Have you even opened this up since you got back from Iraq?"

He shrugged. "Truth told, I never opened it up all that much while I was *in* Iraq."

Angie lifted her shoulders and then settled them. "And you call yourself a Christian."

"I am. Or I was . . . I am."

Angie leaned back against the door panel. She opened his Bible, placed the ribbon bookmark at the fifty-first Psalm and, closing it, handed it back to him.

"Well, maybe you should be reading this. Maybe you should

be reading *all* of it, but you can start here. It's just the first four verses. It's about . . . well, Pastor Ron was talking about how most of the great men of the Bible overcame guilt to become true leaders. Moses after killing the Egyptian. David after killing his most loyal general. Paul after persecuting Christians."

No glint of recognition showed in Ty's eyes.

"And I would have thought you needed that, Ty, because . . ." Tears began to well in Angie's eyes. "Ty. What *happened* to you over there?"

He said nothing, and she closed her eyes. A pair of tears trailed down her cheeks.

"Ang, I can't . . ."

"I know. I know. You've told me that before. But whatever it was, it didn't just happen to you, Ty. It happened to us. It happened to *me*. And I'm paying for it. I'm paying for it every single day."

She sniffed and pushed her hair back with her hands. Out on the street, a motorcycle went by, discharging a deep staccato thunder.

"Ang, I'm sorry."

She breathed deeply. "I know you are. I just . . ." She shook her head and opened her eyes. "Just what were you doing in there if you weren't sleeping?"

"Thinking."

"Of?"

"Remember I told you about Soren?"

Angie pinched her fingers to her lips. Then she nodded. "The man who used to take you backpacking and fishing when . . ." She left the sentence hanging unfinished.

"When my mother was staying with my father while he was in the VA hospital in Salt Lake City. While he was dying."

"Yes." She was looking her husband right in the eyes now.

"Well, this came in yesterday's mail." Ty handed her the postcard. "It was in an envelope. I didn't see it until this morning."

Angie looked at the card and touched the thready script lightly with her fingertips.

"You want to go see him." There was no question in her voice, but there was no accusation either.

"Well, I do . . ."

"But?"

"But Soren is not a young guy. He's not even a late middle-age guy. He's old. Really old. I remember sending him a card for his eightieth birthday, and I was in Afghanistan then. It was a while ago."

"That sounds like all the more reason to go see him."

Ty pursed his lips, then shook his head. "You don't understand, Ang. He doesn't want me to just come see him. He wants me to come take him—to take him up into the Winds."

Ty reached out and turned the postcard over.

"Even today, when you stop in a souvenir shop or an outfitter and you buy a picture postcard shot in the Wind River Range—that general part of Wyoming, really—Soren is probably the guy who took the photo. He keeps boxes of 'em at his house and he uses them instead of stationery. I've never gotten a note from him that wasn't written on one of his postcards, and if it's a letter he's sending instead of a note, he just uses several. Over the years, I've noticed that the pictures are clues as to what he's thinking of when he writes. If he's reminiscing, he sends a sunset. If he's feeling like sharing some thoughts, it'll be a mountain lake. For family stuff he sends one of my mom riding a horse on a trail when she was a girl. That's how she knew him; he was friends with her father back when he was still alive."

Ty tapped the photo. "But Gannett Peak? I've never, ever gotten a Gannett Peak shot from Soren unless he was thinking of making a trip in. Believe me. He wants me to take him into the mountains."

Angie looked at the picture.

"Do you think he could make it?"

"I just . . . don't know."

"Well, there's one way to find out."

Ty looked down at the truck console. "I . . ." He looked up. "No, that's just . . . I have some vacation coming. But I promised you we'd go to Orlando next winter, Ang. We have reservations."

She put her hand on his. "And Orlando will be there next year, Ty."

He looked up. "You don't want our vacation?"

"I do." The tears were gone from her eyes now. "But I want to make that trip *with* you, not just *along* with you. And if you won't talk with me about what happened . . . over there, then maybe you'll talk about it with Soren."

Ty was quiet for a moment. He looked his wife in the eyes. "Angie, I don't even know if he can travel."

She squeezed his hand, then moved to open her door. "Like I said, cowboy, there's one way to find out."

CHAPTER
SIX

Little America, Wyoming

TY STARTLED AWAKE WHEN THE CELL PHONE BEGAN RINGING. He fished it from the console of the Ford Ranger and opened it. *ALARM 1* was spelled out on the tiny color screen. He pushed the button on the top left of the keypad, just under where the word *DISABLE* showed on the screen.

Yawning, he closed the phone and squinted at his surroundings: parking lot, semis, some pine trees on a hill on the side away from the highway, barely visible in the predawn gloom. He peered at the digital clock on the outside of the phone's cover: 5:01 a.m. glowed bluely back at him.

He glanced at his watch, still set to eastern time: 7:02.

Flicking the key in the ignition, Ty pressed the buttons to lower both windows. Birdsong and cool air flooded in. He stretched, put the windows back up and turned the key off. Then he opened the phone and speed-dialed the top number.

Angela stopped spooning ground coffee into a filter basket and turned toward the ringing, flashing phone in its charging cradle on the far end of the counter. She took a step closer, squinted at the pale digital numbers and then made a little gasp as she scooped the phone up and thumbed the Talk button.

"Ty?" She pushed her free hand back through her hair, preening just a little, and then she smiled, shook her head and stopped. "Where are you? . . . Wyoming? Already? Baby, have you been stopping to eat and sleep? . . . Wow—how fast have you been driving?"

She listened, head cocked, while she sidled down the counter and resumed measuring coffee into the filter basket. Nodding once, she kept the phone to her ear with an uplifted shoulder as she returned the measure to the coffee canister, shut it and put it away.

"Little America? Sure . . . like a big truck stop and a motel, in the middle of nowhere, right?" She put the canister next to its twin on the counter. "What time is it where you are? Five? Honey, you should still be sleeping."

She pushed a button on the coffee maker while continuing to listen. After a pause, the black machine gave a hiccuping gasp.

"How soon do you get to your friend's place?" she asked. Then after a moment: "And then the two of you are leaving straight from there?"

The coffee maker gasped again.

"Yeah. I didn't figure you'd have cell phone coverage all the way to the mountains." She was holding the phone with both hands now. "No, no. That's okay. You don't have to try. I just want to know if you're ... okay. That's all. This is your time with your friend; don't call unless you need me."

Dark brown coffee began dribbling into the glass carafe.

"I will," she was saying into the phone. "And Ty? I love you, honey."

The inside of the carafe steamed over as more coffee dribbled in.

" 'Uh-huh?' What's 'uh-huh,' mister? Don't you know you're supposed to say, 'I love you too, Angie?' "

She hugged herself with her elbows as she said it, the smile on her face at odds with her moist brown eyes.

"Yeah, but I had to ask you to say it. No. Don't listen to me. You know me; it's early and I'm stupid before my first cup of coffee. And of course I know that you ..." She looked up at the blue sky in the upper part of the kitchen window and wiped one cheek with the side of her hand. "Just you be safe, okay? It's a good thing you're doing with your friend. But you come back to me safe, you hear?"

Her elbow bumped the coffee mug as she turned, moving it just a little.

"That's not supposed to mean anything. Just that I miss you, you know? And I *do* love you. Have a good time, honey. Catch a lot of fish. I'll see you in a couple weeks."

Angela held the phone for a long time before she wordlessly put it back on the charger. She was sniffling, and she got a Kleenex from the box on the counter, blew her nose, wiped her eyes and tossed the evidence into a trash can in the cubbyhole under the sink.

She straightened up, said "It's fine" to no one in particular, and poured herself a cup of fresh-brewed coffee.

Ty put the phone back on its charger cable. It made a little chirrup as the power trickled into it. When he set it into the console, the numerals on the phone's cover were still illuminated, the backlight glowing blue in the small, oblong compartment.

He flipped down the visor and took something out from under the elastic band that encircled it. It was a pair of wallet-size photographs, laminated back to back under clear plastic. On one side was a picture of Angie, planting peonies in the flower bed next to the walk at her mother's house, and smiling up at the camera with the tiniest smudge of dirt on her cheek. On the other side was a snapshot of the two of them in sandals, walking shorts and Hawaiian shirts, posing like the tourists they were in front of Shades of Green, the military-only resort at Walt Disney World.

Ty flicked the edge of the pictures with his thumb. He put them back behind the visor, closed both truck windows and got out. Over in the direction of the highway, a semi was slowing down, its Jake brakes throbbing in decrescendo and drowning out the birdsong. Ty stretched once and thumbed the remote, the pickup's lights blinking once as the doors locked. He turned, took one step, stopped and turned back to the truck.

A second push on the remote. There was a dull click as the doors unlocked and the interior light came on. Ty opened the driver's door, sat, and took the Slimline Bible out of the console and unsnapped the travel cover.

The ribbon still lay in the book of Psalms, chapter 51. His finger traced the first four verses as he strained to read the fine print under the pickup's dome light. He read them a second time, then took the pictures from behind the visor and stuck them in the Bible beteween the front cover and flyleaf. Leaving the ribbon where it was, he snapped the cover shut and put the book back in the center console. Then he got out of the pickup and thumbed the remote twice, getting a flash of the lights and a horn chirp as the doors locked and the antitheft system armed itself.

Ty slid the remote in his jeans pocket and, shoulders hunched against the morning cold, began trudging across the half-empty parking lot. On the far side of the asphalt a café was open—people going in and out of the front doors, waitresses in white uniforms moving back and forth with coffee carafes behind big plate-glass windows. In one of those windows, a neon sign was burning, its large red letters spelling out a single word: BREAKFAST.

CHAPTER
SEVEN

Pinedale, Wyoming

"Oh no you don't, mister."

One flour-dusted, age-spotted hand reached to the side and slapped. The hand it slapped—more of a tap than a slap—was age-spotted as well, but larger. Its owner put the back of it to his mouth and feigned injury.

"What's that for? I thought you was making those for me."

"I was. I am. But this is trail bread. It's for the trail, not the kitchen. And it's not all for you, Soren Andeman."

"Why? You coming along?"

"I am not." The woman, stooped and round-shouldered, her head still erect, like a turtle's head held upright from its shell, opened an ancient Tappan oven and took out four small pans of bread, setting them gently on the shelf of a sideboard.

"You don't go in the mountains no more. I don't think you've gone since we sold the lodge. Why would you want to go with me now?"

The woman opened the oven door again, put four fresh pans on the center rack, and closed the door. She turned toward the old man and raised an eyebrow. One eyebrow.

"Mister, if you think you're going to trick me, you'd better get yourself some fresh material, 'cause that stuff's getting old."

The man shrugged. "For a minute there, I thought we was going to have to run down to Green River, to the Wal-Mart, and get you a new pair of boots."

"Soren—"

"Oh, Edda. I was just having some fun with you. I know it ain't you that's coming . . ."

His voice trailed off.

Edda glanced his way and then returned to her baking.

"What time," she asked, "did Tyler say he was going to be here again?"

"Tyler?" Soren blinked. "He . . . said it would be early afternoon sometime. I figure we'd pack up the truck, get to bed early tonight, and then head up to Big Sandy tomorrow at first light. You ain't gonna need the truck, are you?"

Edda tipped a bread pan on its side and tapped it on the bottom, dropping a loaf out.

"Tyler's a grown man now, Soren. You're going with him. He's coming to get you in his truck."

Soren's eyes opened wider. "Yes. Sure. Of course. That's what he said. In his truck."

"That's right, dear."

Soren tapped on the table.

"Hmm?" Edda arched her eyebrows.

"You're sure Tyler's still coming?"

"We both talked with him."

Soren nodded at the cooling loaves.

"I'd better try one of these, then." He smiled, crow's-feet fanning out from the corners of his eyes. "Wouldn't want him eating none if it ain't done right."

CHAPTER
EIGHT

"WELL, WELL, WELL. LOOK AT WHAT THE CAT DRAGGED IN."

"Hello, Miss Edda."

"Oh, just listen to you, 'Miss Edda'-ing me." The short, plump woman held the door open wider and looked up, offering a tissue-paper cheek for Ty's kiss. She squeezed his hand and looked back into the house, her movements slow, done in stages.

"Soren? Tyler's here."

The old man appeared in the kitchen doorway, squaring a feed cap on his head, as if wearing a ball cap when receiving visitors was something the etiquette books recommended. He looked Ty's way, and for a brief moment his face went completely blank. Then his smile erupted, a double row of perfectly even, too-white false teeth, and he made his way across the kitchen, using first a chair back and then the counter for support. He held out a hand.

Ty shook it. "You're looking good, Soren."

"This hip's acting up again." Soren kept Ty's hand in

his, not shaking it—just holding it. "Went to see the doctor yesterday. . . ."

Edda shook her head. "It was last week, Soren."

"Well, went to see him, and he said I was doin' too much walking. I asked him why in tarnation he give me a new hip if he didn't want me walkin' on it. Anyhow, I think he ought to give me a better one, and I asked him about that and he said I'd have to wear this one out first. So I'm fixin' to wear it out." He was still holding Ty's hand, holding it with both of his, and he tugged on it. "Come on in, Tiger, come in. I'll tell you what: it is good to see you, boy."

Edda smiled and put her hand on her husband's wrist. He released Ty's hand.

"You hungry, Tyler?" Her eyes, clear and brown, examined him kindly from behind her glasses.

"I'm fine. I stopped this morning and had a pretty big breakfast."

"Breakfast! That was hours and hours ago. You sit yourself down, right here."

Ty started to protest, but Soren touched him on the shoulder and shook his head. "Won't do you no good. When this woman gets it in her head to feed you, you're gonna get fed. Sixty years we been married—"

"Sixty-four," Edda corrected him.

Soren cast his eyes skyward. "I was just countin' the happy ones." He pretended to flinch as Edda slapped him on the shoulder. He chuckled and pulled back a chair. "Anyhow, sixty-four years we been married, and while this little woman here might have gave me plenty to worry about in that time, dying of starvation ain't ever been one of 'em. So you may as well sit, boy. I'll even join you. Wouldn't mind a little spot of dinner myself."

An hour later Ty stood at the sink, hands wrist-deep in soapy dishwater. He took a heavy glass tumbler from the water, rinsed it and handed the glass to Edda, who wiped it dry and put it away.

"Tell me something," Ty said. "Do you think he's ready to do this?"

"Do what, dear?" Edda asked without looking up from her work.

"To go into the mountains." Ty turned and faced her. "To make this trip."

"Well . . ." Edda paused as she wiped a plate, one with a Blue Willow pattern, turning it slowly in her hand. "He's not going to be *more* ready if you wait," she finally finished.

Ty laid a hand on the sink. "Edda, for a second there, when I walked in here, he didn't even know who I was."

"Oh, it's been years and years since he's seen you, sweetie. And he's old. He'll be eighty-seven come September. I'm six years younger than Soren is, and I barely recognized you at first. I don't know, but . . . well, the Marine Corps changed you, Tyler. I have to tell you that. It took the joy right out of your face."

Ty exhaled, almost a sigh.

"Tell me the rest," he said.

She glanced up at him.

"About Soren, I mean."

"The hip is like he said. It pains him something awful,

especially if he's cold. The doctor thought he might have had a stroke—just a small one—about two years ago. And he's been on heart medicine since forever. . . ."

The way she paused told Ty she wasn't done talking. He waited.

"The memory problem isn't Alzheimer's, Tyler. His doctor gave him a bunch of tests and checked him for that. No, he said it was early dementia—what they used to call *senility*." Edda set the plate away.

"Edda, for pete's sake . . ." Ty glanced at the living room.

"Don't worry; he can't hear. He always takes a nap after dinner. And even if he wasn't napping, he can't hear most things unless he's in the same room with you."

"Edda . . ."

She set her towel on the countertop. "Tyler, I fell in love with Soren Andeman when I was fourteen years old. Not that he knew I was alive back then, mind you. He was twenty, and working on the railroad, and my but he was handsome. And strong? Like an oak tree, that man was. So I told my mother what I was thinking of, and she told my father, and he invited Soren to the house for my sixteenth birthday. Now, I suppose today that might seem scandalous—sixteen and twenty-two falling in love. But those were simpler times, and that's what happened. Anyhow, we were married the following Christmas, sixty-four Christmases ago."

Edda looked out the kitchen window, where the shadows were lengthening. She shook her head slowly.

"For most of those sixty-four years, that's what Soren was to me: the strong one. The man who could do anything. When the war ended and he talked about starting that fish camp up at Big Sandy, the idea was too big for me; I couldn't get my head around it. But he could, and he did it. *We* did it. And then when we retired from that, and some of his friends wanted him to run for Sublette County Sheriff . . . did you know that he was sheriff here once?"

Ty nodded.

"I didn't know if you would. It was before you were born. But anyway, when he was talking about that, I just didn't know—we'd never, ever done anything in politics before, and there was this rancher, a man named McLane, who would be running against us, and he had deep pockets. But Soren ran, and he won, and when he finally retired from the Sheriff's Department, well, I just lost count of all the people who told us that he was the best sheriff this county ever had."

Edda patted the counter softly. "All those years and he was the strong one. Now that's going away, Tyler. Going, and it is never, ever coming back." She turned to face him again. "I don't want to put you on the spot, dear. Soren would never forgive me if I did. But he's been talking and thinking about nothing but this trip since you called us. It's his chance to go visit something he thought he'd lost forever. And to answer your question, no—he probably isn't completely up to this. But in my heart I know it would hurt him far more if he didn't go."

Ty washed a plate. He washed it again.

"Did he tell you?" Edda asked.

"Tell me?"

"About what the Forest Service is doing. Doing for *him*. Tyler, it took an act of Congress."

"Act of . . . what are you talking about, Edda?"

She tsked. "He asked me not to tell you. Said he wanted to. I'd best hush. Don't let him know I said anything."

Ty looked down at her. "I don't think you *have*, Edda."

She raised her eyebrows.

"Okay," Ty said. "I won't say anything. I'll wait for him to tell me. But what does this have to do with this trip?"

Edda took the plate from his hands, dried it and put it away. Then she reached out and lightly set her hand on Ty's forearm. "You're too young to understand this yourself, but once a body gets to be a certain age, just living is not enough. You get to the point where you just feel like something that's set on the shelf long past its season. You need a reason to keep on going."

She sniffled and wiped her cheek with the back of her hand.

"This is terribly unfair. Unfair to you. But I love him, Tyler. Love him more than life itself—my life, or his. And being with you and going on this trip is what's keeping my Soren going right now. It's his reason."

She looked down.

"Am I asking you for too much?"

Ty covered her hand with his.

"No, Edda. Of course not. You never have."

CHAPTER

NINE

Ty PRESSED THE OLD PUSH-BUTTON WALL SWITCH, ILLUMINATING the antler-shaded ceiling fixture in the center of what Edda called Soren's office.

It barely merited the title. It did have a desk, but it was being used more like a shelf—covered with notebooks, topographic maps, leaves and flowers pressed between wax paper, and box after black-and-yellow box of Kodachrome slides. Behind the desk was a leather chair, filled to its brass-tacked arms with *National Geographic* magazines, back issues of *Reader's Digest,* and sheaf after sheaf of opened correspondence, some of the envelopes bearing stamps that had not been issued in years.

Ty found what he was looking for by the door: Soren's old Kelty backpack with a tarp rolled and folded on its top and a summer-weight mummy bag strapped to the bottom. On the pack's side was an Orvis fly-rod tube with *Zero Grav* engraved on its top. Ty grabbed the pack by its straps and glanced around the tiny room.

"You looking for that old Orvis split cane?"

Soren stood in the doorway, dressed exactly as he'd been dressed at dinner the evening before, right down to the feed cap.

"Well . . . yeah. Actually, I was."

"Up there, on the rack."

Ty followed the old man's gaze to where the rod rested in its two pieces on the crooks of a rifle rack, the grain of the bamboo honey gold in the incandescent light, the freckled cork of the grip dark in spots from the decades of hands that had held it.

"You don't use it anymore?"

"Me? No. That new one's made out of astronaut stuff, boron or whatnot. Light as your kid sister's kiss. And I'm at the age where I cut half the grip off my toothbrush, just to save the weight. 'Sides, I'm saving that old cane rod. Gonna give it to somebody when I'm gone. You want to use it?"

"If you're saving it and *you* won't use it, it doesn't seem right that I should."

"Don't see why not. You're the one I'm saving it for."

Ty moved his lips to speak, but nothing audible came out. He cleared his throat.

"Don't be that way, Soren. Fish your rod."

"I am. I just ain't fishin' *that* rod."

Ty folded his arms. "Well, then I'm not either."

Soren chuckled. "Stubborn streak, huh? Wonder where you got that from. Suit yourself. But we better get this stuff out to your truck. Road to Big Sandy's worse than it ever was; county don't want to spend no money on it. It ain't a real far way out there, but it's a *long* way, and that's for sure."

They carried all the gear out, Ty taking the backpack and letting Soren follow with his walking sticks: the long burl-topped oak staff he'd carried when Ty was a boy, and a newer one—fiberglass by the looks of it, topped with a strapped grip like a ski pole.

"If you're so worried about weight, why do you carry two of those?" Ty nodded at the new pole.

"This one's got some history to it." Soren tamped the wooden staff's bronze-shod tip on the pea gravel of the drive as he stepped off the back stoop. "I carry it so as I can remember."

"Remember what?"

"Can't say."

But the old man's countenance seemed miles and miles away from the joke.

"We got two bottles of white gas?"

"That's right." Ty patted the outside pockets of his backpack. "That, plus what's in the stove."

"Good. Good. May as well leave the water bottles empty for now. It'll just taste like plastic if we ride water up there in this heat. Besides, Big Sandy water's better than Pinedale water any day. You and Miss Edda wax those eggs this morning?"

"Dipped 'em in paraffin and then put 'em in the cooler. If we have the lodge keep them in the icebox tonight, they should be good for a week or more out on the trail."

Soren lifted the lid of the cooler. "Got the trail bread in there too. That bacon won't be good but one morning, but there ain't no better way to start a trip. You remember how to make camp coffee?"

Ty grinned. "I think I about threw the billy pot halfway across the lake, first time I tried. Yeah. I remember."

"Good man."

Ty lowered the hard-shell tonneau cover on the back of the pickup. After he'd turned the latch and pressed it into its recess, he glanced at the old man.

"Soren, you sound . . ." He stopped himself.

"What? Sharper in the morning? That's 'cause I am. Doctor says it has to do with how I use oxygen. Get more out of it when I'm fresher. You want me to do your taxes, you'd best get hold of me well before noon!"

Ty laughed. Then he sobered.

"You know, where we're headed—the high country—there's not as much oxygen up there as there is down here."

"True enough." The old man paused for a moment, then shrugged and said, " 'Course, how sharp does a body have to be to *fish?*"

Soren made one last trip into the house to collect his trail book—a dog-eared, water-spotted composition booklet with black marbling on the cover and a faded ribbon marking a place in it.

"Just that? You don't want your maps?"

The old man's feed cap bill moved: left, then right. "Not unless they've been movin' stuff around up there. No. I'm fine."

Ty smiled as Soren shuffled out to the truck. He turned when he felt a hand at the small of his back.

"Sweetie, could you take this for me?" Edda held a small black book in her right hand.

"His Bible? How'd he forget that?"

Edda shook her head. "He doesn't forget it, honey. I set it out for him. He just leaves it. He's been leaving it behind for years now."

"Never did that when I was walking with him."

She shook her head again. "Not then. But the last eight or nine years, ever since you got out of high school and started college, when he leaves for the mountains? He goes without. Even if I put it in the bib pocket of his overalls, when he's gone, I look on the kitchen table and there it is. He's taken it out and left it. Give it to him when he's up there. But wait until you're in the mountains, all right?"

"Sure." Ty opened the breast pocket on his khaki shirt and tucked the little book in, buttoning it away. Soren was just turning around at the truck.

"We better go, boy. Gotta get moving soon, or I'm gonna have to stop along the way to pee."

Ty laughed. "I can stop all you want."

"Don't want. Just do. You got a little something for me to travel on, Miss Edda?"

Soren's wife put her hands on his shoulders, and they kissed— an old people's kiss, with the pout of their mouths exaggerated, as if they were straining to reach one another across a tall fence. Then Edda turned and kissed Ty on the cheek, pulling him down by his shirt front so she could reach him.

"Soren's right. You'd best go."

She stepped back onto the stoop as Ty got in and fired the engine.

"Good-bye," Edda told the two of them. She looked at Ty and smiled. "Bring him back to me. Either that, or come back and tell me where you left him."

CHAPTER

TEN

THE DRIVE IN TO BIG SANDY WAS ALL JACKRABBITS AND ANTELOPE, sagebrush and prairie grasses, the backdrop of the Wind River Range purple with the morning sun behind it, and seeming to grow higher by the minute. Ty stopped three times for Soren, and the third time, the old man seemed to forget what he was there for. He wandered off a ways from the dirt two-track of the road, examined a twig of sagebrush, glanced around and then stood with his hands on his hips, examining the brightening line of peaks to the east. Finally, Ty walked over, put his hand on the old man's shoulder, and reminded him why they'd stopped. That brought Soren out of his reverie; he attended to his business and they drove on.

When the rooftop of the big log lodge at Big Sandy came into view, Soren seemed to revive a little.

"Looks as though they're keeping the place up," he said. He removed his hat, took a comb from the bib pocket on his overalls, made a few passes through his thin white hair and put the hat back on.

Ty stopped the truck at the bottom of the broad steps, under the weathered, carved sign that read WIND RIVER MOUNTAIN LODGE in gold, square, no-nonsense letters against a brown background. Soren clambered stiffly out.

"You comin'?" he asked through the open window.

"You go on in. I'll park the truck and be right in after you."

Ty drove the truck past an empty hitching rail, stopped at the end of the log building and got out, taking the green and white Coleman cooler out of the back of the pickup and setting it on the kitchen stoop. Then he got back in and drove the truck onto a grassless patch of ground crisscrossed with tire tracks. A big Dodge SUV already occupied the shade from the only tree in the parking area, so Ty just parked where the walk would be shortest, fished a collapsible sunshade out from under the seat, opened it up and set it in the windshield.

He sat for a moment, his fingers drumming the console. Then he lifted the padded cover and took his Bible out. The pictures were still in there, but he didn't look at them. Instead, he turned to where the ribbon marked its page, twisted and tugged off his wedding ring, threaded it onto the ribbon, and reclosed the slim blue-covered book. The ring made a bright metallic *clink* as he put the Bible back in the console. Then he killed the engine, got out and, pocketing his keys, walked across the hot, dusty ground toward the lodge.

Even with the curtains pulled back on its windows, the

interior of the lodge was dark, a marked contrast to the brilliant mountain midday outside. Ty stood there for a moment in the entryway, letting his eyes adjust to the difference, the details of log walls and kerosene lanterns in sconces emerging slowly from the gloom. Across the lobby, a grandfather clock ticked steadily, but that was the only sound—there was no hum of air-conditioning, none of the background noise associated with the modern indoors.

"Tyler?"

Ty turned toward the voice—young, female. A glimmer of recognition lit his face, and as he walked toward the ponytailed woman behind the desk, he cocked his head. "Kathy?"

She came around the counter, arms out, and gave him a hug—quick, stiff, as if she wasn't sure about it.

"Wow," she said, keeping her hands on Ty's shoulders, looking at him from arm's length. "This is sure a . . ."

"I know. I didn't know you were up here."

"I didn't know you were even—" She stopped, shook her head. "Three years now. Abe hired me after Darcey moved back East. You come up with Soren?"

"I did, just now." Ty looked around the big log lobby, but there was no sign of the old man.

"Saw him. Asked me for the restroom as soon as he got in. You bring him up for a visit?"

"No. We're going in."

Kathy let her hands slip from Ty's shoulders. She glanced down the lobby and, lowering her voice, said, "Into the backcountry?"

At the far end of the lobby the grandfather clock groaned

to life, whirred and sounded a single chime for the half hour. It resumed its sonorous *tock, tock, tock . . .*

"Yeah. And I know, but he's . . ." Ty glanced behind him to make sure the lobby was still empty. "Listen, I was thinking on the way up. Any chance I could hire a horse-packer to take us in?"

Kathy nodded, her chestnut ponytail mimicking the movement. "Hanson's headed up in the morning. I can have him add a couple, three horses to the string. What do you have, just the two backpacks?"

Ty nodded.

"Okay. Won't need but one for that. And a saddle horse for Soren. You walkin' or ridin'?"

"I'd better ride or he won't want to."

Kathy smiled, thin-lipped, and shook her head. "You're right about that."

Ty reached for his back pocket. "Can I settle up with you now?"

She stopped his hand with hers. "No settling to it. Soren and Edda started this place. Way I see it, they deserve all the free visits they want. Besides, Hanson was going up in the morning anyhow; got some camps to resupply in the backcountry. And those three horses can use the exercise."

She was still holding his hand, and she seemed to realize it just then. The shadow of a blush crossed her face as she released it.

"I'll set you two up with a couple of rooms for the night."

"We can share one."

"Two's no trouble. Had a FedEx this morning from a doctor

in Salt Lake City. He and his son had a reservation for this week, but now he's covering for somebody else in his practice and had to forfeit his first night's deposit. So I've got the rooms, and they're already paid for. You and Soren'll be more comfortable this way."

Ty nodded. "Well, thanks, Kathy. I appreciate that."

She gazed at him for a moment, and then, just as her eyes seemed to well up, she glanced down.

"Don't mention it."

CHAPTER

ELEVEN

THE TABLE WAS SET WITH CANDLES; THE SCONCES ON THE WALL reflected the light of half a dozen oil lamps. Except for the waning red glow of twilight, the tiny flames were the only light in the large dining room, but if the seventeen people sitting around the long maple table—the guests of the lodge and its staff, right down to the wranglers—if they thought the rustic surroundings unusual, they did not show it. The banter was what one might expect from a group made up mostly of male company: laughter, questions, affirmation. Near the center of the table, two guests—one in a brand-new Columbia fishing shirt, the kind with the Velcro rod holder, the other dressed from the L.L.Bean catalog—talked a little more loudly and a little more often than the rest of the group: the behavior of men in unfamiliar circumstances.

"Well," Soren said to no one in particular, "Edda will be happy to know that her standards are being respected at this table. Although I'd best check again, just to make sure. Could somebody please pass the taters and the gravy?"

"Sure thing." The man at Soren's left, the fellow in the L.L.Bean outfit, reached across the table, lifted a large ceramic mixing bowl and held it out to Soren.

All conversation around the table ceased. Soren did not accept the proffered bowl.

L.L.Bean blinked. "What?"

At the head of the table, Kathy, chestnut hair up in a bun, smiled an amused apology. "This is Wyoming, Mr. Witte. We go by bunkhouse rules here."

"Bunkhouse rules?"

"No passing except to your left. Otherwise, all the food winds up on one end of the table and somebody goes to bed starving."

"Oh. Well, sure." The tourist handed the bowl to his left and it made its way around the table, past Kathy and down the other side, making the turn at the end and finally coming back to Soren, who grinned and helped himself. Then he nudged the fellow in the L.L.Bean and held out the bowl.

"You want some?"

Dutch apple pie came and went, and Ty quietly excused himself from the table. The rest of the men had all turned their attention to Soren, who was telling a story about a bear.

"A last year's cub, it was," Soren was saying. "You know, a sow will sometimes nurse and root for a cub two years, unless she gives birth to another, in which case that last year's cub gets the boot. I mean, he's a full-grown bear, but he ain't hunting like one, and more often than not he takes to mooching if he's wandering near a trail, and sometimes they'll get downright pushy. Well, every time I'm 'bout to lay my head down to sleep, this little ol' black bear is sniffin' round my tent flap and I've got to get up and chase him away. Finally, I'm sittin' there outside my tent with a piece of wood and a pile of rocks, and every time he comes close enough to see him in the light from my campfire—'cause I've fanned the campfire back up by then—I toss one of those rocks up in the air and I'm battin' 'em straight at this bear. . . ."

Ty stepped out onto the lodge's long porch and patted at his empty breast pocket, the habitual gesture of a man who once smoked and has momentarily forgotten that he's stopped. He dropped his hand to the porch rail and gazed south, where a single star had appeared in the darkening sky.

"Well, I'd say that Soren is most definitely in his element."

Ty turned. Kathy was stepping onto the porch, an enameled mug in her hand. She nodded at the mug. "Coffee?"

"No. Thanks. I'm good."

She nodded over her shoulder at the lodge. "Don't you think you ought to be in there, listening?"

Ty smiled and slowly shook his head. "I've heard most of Soren's stories before. And he knows that, so if I'm in there, he'll try to shorten 'em up. Either that or ask me to chime in, as if I was there when it happened, which I usually was not; I wasn't even *born* when most of his stories happened. So it's better I'm out here; Soren's at his best in front of a fresh audience."

Kathy brushed a stray hair from her eyes and looked up at the evening sky. A second star had joined the first one, both of them close to the southern horizon. Off to the east, the dark, torn-paper edge of the Wind River Range was fading into a cobalt blue.

"You know they're naming a lake after him up there?"

Ty looked at her. "Say what?"

She nodded. "A lake. Cirque Lake, up in the high country. They're renaming it Lake Andeman."

"I thought they couldn't name lakes and mountains and things like that after a—"

"Living person? No. They can't. Not usually. But they're making an exception in his case. It took an act of Congress."

Ty tapped his palm against the railing. "So that's what Edda was talking about . . . or wasn't, really."

Kathy glanced at him.

"I think," Ty said, "that Soren was saving the surprise."

"I'm sorry. I just assumed . . ."

"It's okay. You didn't know."

"Actually, there's people here who'd like to name the entire range after him. In Sublette County, in this whole part of the state, he's half patron saint and half local hero."

Ty nodded. "I can understand that. He's quite a man." He looked up and saw that a third star had appeared, then a fourth.

Kathy sipped her coffee. "Yeah? Well, if you think he's so great, why are you trying to kill him?"

He turned to face her.

"Tyler, when Soren got here this afternoon he didn't know who I was, and he's known me since I was a baby."

"But you've changed. You're grown up now—"

"Later on, he had to ask me where the restroom was."

Ty said nothing.

Kathy shook her head. "You know as well as I do that Soren built this place, Ty. And I don't mean he wrote the check or handed stuff off to a contractor. He *built* it. He and Edda and a couple of men he hired from down off the reservation. They made the foundation, they set the walls, they put the slate on the roof. There isn't a hat peg or fireplace stone here that wasn't put there by Soren Andeman's own hand. He should know this lodge better than anyone. Yet today, he shows up here at his own door, the place where he lived every summer for twenty-seven years, and he can't even find the restroom. Now, what business does a man like that have going up into the mountains, and what business do *you* have taking him there?"

Ty drew closer to her, lowered his voice to a near whisper. "I'm not planning on taking him that far in. Just as far as Jenny Creek Pass, probably."

She nodded. "That's good. But why are you taking him in at all?"

"He wanted to go. And he won't be able to go much longer. He's an old guy, Kathy—it's now or never."

"If you want to be frank about it, it's really *then* or never. His mountaineering days should be over." Kathy set her mug on the porch railing and, turning, leaned back against one of the tall roughhewn logs with her arms crossed, her face barely visible in the deepening twilight. "Is that all this is about? Nothing else?"

He cocked his head. "What do you mean?"

"Do I have to go there?" Kathy shrugged. "Ty, I don't hear

word one from you for two years. Next thing I know, my daddy's cousin tells me you've joined the Army—"

"Marines." Ty began to raise his hands, but put them back on the railing.

"Whatever, and that you're getting *married*. Did I have to hear it that way?"

He squeezed the railing. "Kathy, I thought we agreed—"

"To back off a bit? Not to rope each other into a geographically undesirable relationship? Sure we did. I didn't want you to think you were tied up while away at college, but I never thought you'd go and get . . ."

Even in the dim light, Ty could make out the twin tracks of tears glistening on Kathy's face. Ty started to extend his hand to her, but then stopped and reached into his right hip pocket instead. He came out with a red bandanna, which she accepted with a sniff.

"And now . . ." Kathy wiped her nose. "Just about the time that a whole month has gone by without me thinking about you, here you are showing up on my doorstep. What's that about?"

Ty pressed his hands together as if he were praying, put his fingers against his lips and nose and exhaled. "Kathy, I didn't know that you—"

"Yeah. You told me. Give me your hand."

He raised his head a bit. "What?"

"Your hand." She held her right hand out. "Give me your left hand."

Ty reached to take her hand, but she ignored the gesture. She took his left hand by the wrist and turned it over, palm facing down. With two fingers of her right hand she gently traced the backs of his fingers.

"I didn't think I saw a ring earlier," she said. "But I can feel it: where one used to be. And not too long ago either."

She released his hand and straightened up. "What's going on, Ty?"

He touched the place where his ring had been, cleared his throat. "My ring's in my truck. I don't wear rings in the backcountry. Don't wear any jewelry, except a watch. Habit I got into in the Corps."

"So . . ." Kathy smiled thinly. "Everything all right between you and the little missus?"

Ty said nothing.

"Uh-huh." She nodded. "And here you are."

"Kathy, it's not like that."

"What'd she do? Give you the boot?"

He shook his head. "Nobody gave anybody the boot."

Kathy moved her hands to her hips. "So why the silence when I asked you? Why not say, 'Nope—everything between my wife and me is just great'? Because it isn't. Is it?"

Ty returned both hands to the porch rail, looked at the sky again, now thick with stars. "It's complicated, Kath."

"That I believe."

"What can I say that will make me sound like less of a jerk? What we had was, well, it was in high school. And it was here, in Wyoming. I was out East, I met somebody, I fell in love . . ."

The slightest bit of a sob escaped from Kathy.

"I did, Kath. And then I enlisted, and high school seemed far away. Wyoming seemed far away."

"To you maybe. But from where I am, Wyoming's all I can see."

Her tears were back, and Ty put a hand on her shoulder.

"I'm sorry, Kathy."

She looked up. "Are you? Well . . ." She sniffed. "Sorry's a good start. It's better than what I had, by a long shot." She turned and started walking across the porch toward the lodge, letting his hand slip off her shoulder.

"Kathy, I—"

"I've got to go. Good night, Ty." She hurried away, past Soren, who was just coming out onto the porch, his tall walking stick in his left hand.

Soren turned as Kathy passed, then looked back at Ty. "Why, that girl was crying. Is she hurt?"

Ty nodded.

"What happened?"

Ty stared at the empty doorway. "Looks as if I broke her heart."

"That all?"

Ty stared at Soren, his brow furrowed.

"You break your arm, that's four, maybe six weeks of mending," Soren said. He was walking to the railing, his staff making irregular thumps as he shuffled across the broad wooden porch. "Break a leg, it's eight weeks. Sometimes more."

He glanced back. "But a broken heart? Right thing happens, that can be plumb gone by morning."

CHAPTER
TWELVE

TY WOKE THE NEXT MORNING WHILE THE SKY WAS STILL A DEEP gray outside his window. He blinked, felt on the bedside table for the lamp, found it, felt until his hand landed on the keylike knob, and turned it.

Nothing happened. Ty scowled and patted the tabletop until his hand landed on a box of farmer's matches. Then he sat up, struck a match, blinked again and lifted the lamp's globe with one hand while he lit the wick with the other. He lowered the globe, turned the wick up until it began to smoke and then lowered it, white light flooding the tiny pine-paneled room.

Ty stood and was just reaching for his jeans when his cell phone began to beep. He opened it, shushing the alarm, and thumbed the menu button, bringing up the home screen. Next to the little antenna icon, not a single bar glowed. He pressed the red button and held it, shutting the phone off. Pulling on his jeans, he picked up his shaving kit and stepped out into the hall, padding stocking-footed down to the bathroom at the end.

A lamp was burning low in there, and he turned it up before closing the door. Next to the sink was a placard that read, *Our water is solar heated. Please keep your showers brief.* He undressed, turned the water on and held his hand beneath the spray, feeling for the temperature.

Soren was already in the dining room, a half-finished stack of flapjacks in front of him, a link of sausage on his fork, when Ty made his way downstairs.

"Get some grub in you, boy." Soren wagged the fork in Ty's direction as he spoke. "We got us a walk up to Clear Lake today."

"Clear Lake?" Ty helped himself to flapjacks off the sideboard. "I thought we'd just head up to Jenny Creek Pass."

Soren shook his head and wiped a drip of maple syrup off his chin. "Jenny Creek's for greenhorns and honeymooners."

"It's got trout." Ty put a couple of sausage on his plate, then hesitated before adding a third.

"It's got a few rainbows." Soren nodded. "But we want to get up to where the educated ones are." He winked at a fisherman down the table, who laughed.

Ty sat next to Soren and poured himself coffee from the carafe on the table. "Maybe we should wait until we're on the trail to make that decision. Once we get to the pass."

Soren poured himself some coffee as well. "If you want. What—you breakin' in a new pair of boots or something?"

He winked at the fisherman down the table, and the fisherman laughed again.

"Morning, gentlemen."

Kathy's greeting was bright, cheerful—not a hint of the pain of the evening before, and Ty turned in his seat to face her.

She was on the arm of a man about his age: clean-cut, medium height, Forest Service uniform, turning his ranger hat in his hand.

"Soren, I'm glad you're still here. Got somebody who's been wanting to meet you. This here's my fiancé, Bob."

"Bob Bridger, sir. Please, don't get up." The ranger shook Soren's hand.

"Bridger? That's a right famous name in these parts."

The ranger smiled. "I don't think old Jim and I are any kin. My family moved to Jackson Hole from Vermont when I was about two—my father came out to manage a guiding business. I worked that for a while when I was in high school. Used to use your guidebook as my bible when I came down here into the Winds."

Soren laughed. "Hope I didn't get you too lost."

Ty dabbed at his mouth with his napkin and set it next to his plate.

"Oh." Kathy touched the ranger's arm. "And this is one of our local guys, come back for a visit, Ty Perkins."

Ty stood and shook hands with the ranger.

"I've heard a lot about you," Bob said. "You were in Iraq, weren't you?"

"There, and Afghanistan."

"Well, my hat's off to you. I'm afraid all my time in uniform has been devoted to telling people not to build campfires except in designated rings."

Ty grinned. "Sounds as if it's probably been a lot more productive than mine."

Kathy stepped forward. "Bob's taking the management exam next month. They're going to be making him assistant manager of the whole district."

Bob looked up at the ceiling. "Kath, that's putting about seven carts ahead of the horse."

"Maybe so, but you're going to make it." She gripped his arm and smiled at Ty. At least her mouth smiled at Ty. Her eyes told another story.

"Best of luck on that," Ty told the ranger.

"Thanks, man. Please, sit. Finish your breakfast."

After breakfast, Ty carried his and Soren's overnight bags out to the truck and set them in back, under the cap. When he returned to the lodge, Soren was waiting for him on the big front porch.

"Got our packs?"

"Around the side, over here."

Soren stepped down off the porch, taking the steps methodically—staff first, then his right foot, and then his left, and so on from one stair to the next until he was on the hardpack. He rested one hand lightly on Ty's shoulder as the two walked around the corner toward the barn.

Soren stopped.

"We're takin' horses?"

"If that's okay with you. I did me a lifetime worth of walking overseas. If a ride's available, I'd just as soon take it."

Soren studied him. "So we're doin' this for you, huh?"

Ty looked at the distant mountaintops, at the corral near the barn, and finally at Soren. "That's right—we're doing it for me too."

Soren worked his lips. "You tell me somethin'. Miss Edda put you up to this?"

"No way. Only instruction I had from her was to either bring you back or tell her where I left you."

Soren thought about that and then he laughed. But after a moment his face straightened. "Well, we're payin' for our share of the pack string, ain't we?"

"You most certainly are not."

Both men turned. Kathy was behind them, hair back in a ponytail, dark Ray-Bans hiding her eyes.

"Soren," she said, "you ran this place before I was even a glitter in my daddy's eye. You know as well as I do that you got to put a saddle on your stock every once in a while or they get all stupid about carrying a rider. And we haven't had all that many people wanting to horse-pack this year. I'd feel obliged if you'd just ride them a while. Fact is, I ought to be paying you."

Soren looked her over, head to toe and back again.

"Call Ireland," he said. "Someone's stolen the Blarney Stone and brung it to Wyoming."

Kathy laughed; it sounded positively girlish. She struggled to find a straight face. "Besides, Soren, Hanson's got some high camps he has to resupply. It'll be right on his way to drop you two at Jenny Creek Pass."

Soren shook his head. "We're goin' to Clear Lake. Upper end."

Kathy looked at Ty and then back at Soren. "All right. Then

he can drop you off at the upper end of Clear Lake. Same difference. It's still on the way. That way my stock doesn't go all saddle-stupid."

"Well, okay. But only because the boy here did so much walkin' when he was overseas in that Iraq."

Soren set off toward the corral, his staff thumping a quicker tempo on the bare trampled ground between the lodge and the barn.

"Clear Lake?" Kathy said to Ty.

"Yeah. He sprung that one on me at breakfast. I'm hoping I can talk him into Jenny Creek once we get up there."

Kathy put her hands on her hips, gazed up at the distant mountaintops. "Jenny Creek Pass is almost four miles in—more than far enough if you've got an eighty-six-year-old man with a gimp hip to take care of. And Clear Lake's a good hard four miles beyond that."

She turned and looked at Ty. "I just hope you're a lot more persuasive than you used to be."

Hanson, the wrangler, was in his late teens or early twenties, smooth-skinned but with a prodigious mustache, a veritable Marlboro Man in training. He wore a straw hat that might have once been a Stetson and a flannel shirt with the sleeves cut off. On his right arm he had the sort of tattoo one would get during a trip to Cheyenne Frontier Days—a buffalo in profile against a Lakota dream catcher. On his left, there was an intricately shaded heart with a scroll flowing over it. No name was on the scroll.

"Had me a girl when the studio started that one," he told Ty when he caught him looking. He pushed his hat back on his head. "Didn't have her when I went back for the shading; that was when they were going to put the name in too. And that got me thinking—made me gun-shy about putting anything in there at all. Don't want to have to get one of them dopey cover-ups later on."

"You could always go with *Mom*." Ty said.

"The thought has occurred to me."

They shook, exchanged names, and then Hanson glanced at Soren and led a stocky sorrel saddle horse over to a stile made of halved logs.

"It's a privilege to be taking you in, Mr. Andeman," Hanson said. "My papa was one of your deputies—Earl Winslow. Told me enough stories about you to fill a book."

"Earl Winslow?" Soren thought a moment. "Sure. Sure: peppermint candies!"

"That's the one."

"How's he doing?"

"He passed last year, sir."

Soren looked genuinely distressed. "I'm sorry . . . I didn't know. I should have gone to the funeral."

"He passed out East, sir. Ohio. He was living with my aunt after they found the cancer. All things told, it was just easier to have the funeral out there."

"Well, I'm sorry for your loss, son."

Soren shook his head and looked at Ty.

"Don't get old," he said. "Half the time these days, I ask after a friend and find out he's gone. Don't think that doesn't get to you."

He shook his head again and stepped onto the stile, using

his staff for balance. Two-stepping each riser, he got to the top, leaned over the saddle, and shifted himself onto the horse, taking a couple of tries to find the stirrups. He handed his staff to Hanson.

"Put that someplace safe, all right? I've had it so long it's almost part of me."

"Understood," the wrangler said. He laid the long wooden staff lengthwise on one of the horse packs and lashed it down with two lengths of manila twine. Then he glanced at Ty. "You ride much, sir?"

"Don't 'sir' me—I work for a living." Ty kept a straight face for a moment, then grinned. "As for the riding, I grew up out here."

The wrangler nodded. "Just wanted to check for the return trip. Headed out, these girls are gonna be slow and steady as a union work line. But when they know they're headed back toward the barn, they tend to get a tad rambunctious."

"Horses haven't changed much."

"They never do," Hanson agreed. "That's why I like my job."

They mounted up and Ty looked around.

"Forget something?" Hanson asked.

"Thought Kathy was right here."

"Saw her headed back to the lodge. We can hang tight here a minute if you need to talk to her."

"No, I was just going to tell her . . ." Ty shook his head. "That's all right. It's getting late. Let's move out."

"You bet, boss." Hanson made a *chick-kick* sound with his tongue and cheek, and the pack string started forward.

The next hour and a half was all pine air and dappled shadows, the steady *clop clop clop* of hooves against the stony trail, distant birdsong, a light breeze and the occasional snort from a packhorse the only other noises. Then they rounded a bend and the world opened up in front of them: the horizon was filled with snowcapped peaks, the relief of the shadows so sharp that it belied the distance. Down at the bottom of the bend, a small silver creek meandered through a soft green meadow. Ty let loose with a low whistle.

Hanson laughed.

"I top this rise three, sometimes six times a week," he said. "And it gets to me exactly the same way. Every single time."

Ty turned in his saddle. "Jenny Creek, Soren. Look good to you?"

The old man straightened up. His face looked pale, his mouth straight. "Looks fine. But we ain't stoppin' here. Not till we get up to Clear."

"We can take a breather if you want," Hanson said. "Them high camps are probably gonna be empty until late afternoon, anyhow—everybody's out fishing or climbing."

Soren shook his head. Under his John Deere ball cap, the white hair was damp with sweat. He patted his mount's neck.

"I get off this here lady, we're gonna need us a ladder to get me back on. And I peed before we left. I'm fine. Let's go."

Ty studied him. "You sure?"

"Don't baby me!" Soren's voice was exasperated, almost sharp. He glanced ahead, at Hanson. "Can we just go?"

"Boss?" Hanson was looking Ty's way.

Ty studied Soren again and then nodded. "Okay," he told the wrangler. "Let's go."

The country got steeper, the uphill sections rising so quickly that the men had to lean forward, over the horses' withers, to help them to keep purchase on the slickrock trail. There was less shadow now, the soil too stony even for pines, and Ty glanced back at Soren frequently to see how he was doing.

"Don't need to keep looking back here," Soren grumbled. "I ain't about to fall off. You need to be keepin' your eyes on the trail, before you ride that animal right off an edge."

"It's a packhorse, Soren. It's going to follow the others no matter what I do with the reins."

"Well, then let him follow 'em with you lookin' forward. You don't need to be glancing back my way every five minutes. I ain't no invalid."

Ty huffed and turned back toward Hanson and the head of the string.

They all rode in silence for the next thirty minutes. Then the country flattened, the pines came back and the horses' hooves fell softer on the trail. Off to the right, through the pines, a swatch of blue glistened in the noon sun.

"Big Sandy Lake, Soren," Ty called. "See it?"

No reply.

"Soren?"

Ty looked back. Soren was hunched forward over the pommel, nearly falling off the left side of his horse.

"Hanson!" Ty yelled, jumping off his horse. "Stop the string. We need help."

CHAPTER
THIRTEEN

THE WRANGLER GOT TO SOREN AT THE SAME TIME AS TY. THE old man didn't wear a belt, so they just grabbed fistfuls of his bib overalls at the waist and pulled.

"Ah! Ohh!" Soren pressed a hand to his hip as they half-caught him, half-lowered him to the ground. Working together, Ty and Hanson maneuvered him over to a flat-topped boulder at the edge of the trail and set him on it. The wrangler ran to his horse and came back with a flannel-sided canteen, which he raised to Soren's lips.

"Thanks," Soren burbled, the water falling out either side of his mouth.

The wrangler lowered the canteen. "Heat get to you?"

"Not the heat." Soren shook his head. "It's this stinkin' hip them doctors gave me. It don't sit a saddle worth beans. It's just . . . man. Hurts like a son of a gun." He looked up at Ty. "I'm sorry, boy."

"Don't be." He glanced Hanson's way. "Let's look for a fire ring. We'll make camp right here."

"No, no, no, no—no!" Soren struggled to his feet, tears coursing down his dusty cheeks. "Not here. We ain't staying here. I want to get to Clear."

"Soren." Ty put his hand on the man's shoulder. "You're in no shape to ride."

"Don't need to ride," he said, brushing Ty's hand away. "I'll walk it. Fetch me my stick."

Hanson looked at Ty, the question obvious in his face.

"Soren," Ty said. "I don't think you can—"

"Can and will. I can walk from here to Jackson Hole and back again. Won't set no speed records, but I can make it. I may not sit a horse no more, but if there's one thing I still am, it's a walker. Now, you gonna get me my stick or am I gonna have to hobble the whole way?"

Ty closed his eyes, opened them. "Okay. We'll walk to Clear Lake. But can we rest here a little bit?"

"Rest? Not camp?"

"Just rest."

Soren nodded and sat down heavily on the boulder.

Hanson stepped nearer to Ty. "What we doin' here, boss?"

Ty looked skyward and then put his hands on his hips. "Let's get my pack off the horse, and I'll take the tent off and strap Soren's sleeping bag up top. That way, if we need to bivouac for the night anywhere between here and Clear, we can do it."

Ty glanced over at Soren. The old man said nothing, sipping at Hanson's canteen and resting. Ty turned back to Hanson. "Listen, I hate to ask, but can you run up to the upper end of

Clear Lake, find us a campsite and cache the rest of our gear? That, and hang our provisions in a bear bag?"

"No problem at all, boss. I do that for half the people I bring up here, and most of them folks are with me when I do it."

"Yeah, but we're not tourists."

"I know that, boss. But like I said, it ain't no problem. It's a privilege, in fact. Mr. Andeman's a man I've admired all my life."

Ty glanced at the old man and then nodded at the wrangler.

"Me too," he said.

"Then let's fetch your backpack, okay?"

Together they pulled Ty's gear from one of the heavy canvas horse packs, swapped Soren's backpack with the tent, then shifted some things around to balance the weight of the double-sided horse pack. Ty opened their food sack and took out two quart-size freezer bags, one full of trail mix and the other beef jerky. As Hanson unlashed Soren's staff from the second packhorse, Ty reached into the deep center pocket of his pack and opened up a travel-size shaving kit. He found his money clip, counted off a few bills, and returned the clip and kit to his pack.

When Hanson handed him Soren's staff, Ty handed him a twenty and said, "If you're coming by Clear later on in the week, can you run us up a dozen eggs, a pound of bacon and a stick or two of butter?"

"Sure thing, boss." Hanson tucked the bill into his left breast pocket and buttoned it. "I've got to run in on Saturday. That's four days from now. Oh, and you'll have some change coming."

"No I won't. And I'd like you to have this too." Ty held out two more twenties.

Hanson shook his head. "That's way too much, boss. Fact is, anything's too much. Years from now, I'm gonna be able to tell my grandkids that I got to take Soren Andeman, the mountain man, on a trip up into the Winds. That's reward enough in itself."

The twenties still in his hand, Ty crossed his arms and cocked his head at the wrangler. "Tell me something, Hanson. You got a current candidate for that blank spot on that heart on your arm?"

Hanson chuckled. "Besides *Mom*? Yes, sir. I suppose I do."

"Well, memories aren't going to buy her a steak and baked potato in Pinedale. Take the money. You're going way above and beyond here."

"Boss . . ."

"Not for you. For your girl."

"All right." The wrangler accepted the bills and tucked them away in his pocket—the right breast pocket this time. "You sure you two are gonna be all right?"

"I'm sure. If it looks like Soren's too tired, we'll just stop and bivvy for the night and then walk the rest of the way to Clear first thing in the morning."

"Okay, boss. Your gear will be waiting for you when you get there. Upper end of the lake, off the trail a bit. I know a spot."

"Appreciate it."

Hanson nodded, tied the two packhorses into the string and got on his mount. He glanced back at Soren. "Pleasure meeting you, Mr. Andeman." Soren grinned weakly and waved. "You too, boss." Hanson tipped his hat at Ty, then clucked twice as he and the pack string moved on down the trail.

Ty brought the trail mix and jerky over to Soren.

"Now's as good a time as any to have some lunch."

"What time is it?"

Ty checked his watch. "Just coming up on noon. Good time for a breather—no use walking in the hottest part of the day."

Soren nodded, gnawed on jerky, and ate a couple of handfuls of trail mix. Then he stretched, took his trail notes out of his bib pocket, and leafed through the worn little notebook.

"Clear Lake's only about two miles from where we are right now. Pretty steep, but I used to make it in an hour. Suppose we'd better double that just to be safe. And if our gear's gonna be at the upper end of the lake, we'd best add another hour to get up there. Still, that's only three hours, and it's just noon. Mind if I close my eyes for a bit?"

"Sounds like a great idea, Soren." Ty took a fiberfill vest out of his pack and handed it to Soren, who nodded his thanks, slid down the boulder until he was on the ground, legs splayed out in front of him, and then fluffed the thick vest behind his head as a pillow. In less than a minute he was sound asleep.

The old man slept for five hours. After two hours, Ty had stooped over him and extended a hand to shake Soren awake, but he'd stopped before he touched him, listening to his deep, rumbling, steady breathing. Instead, Ty walked to the lakeshore, searching it up and down, and in just a couple of minutes he found a flat spot with a fire ring. It wasn't the best campsite in the world; the trees were too close around it, blocking the breeze,

and if Big Sandy Lake was buggy this late in the summer, they'd
be bothered by insects all night. But it was a place to spend the
night if they needed to, a good Plan B. And with that, Ty went
and sat down near Soren and closed his eyes, breathing in the
good pine air, both men shielded from the sun by the green
canopy of trees.

When Soren finally awoke, he muttered, "Oh-oh," lumbered
to his feet and, with the old knurled walking stick in one hand
and the new carbon-fiber pole in his other, shuffled off into the
woods above the trail. Ten minutes later he was back. His face
had color in it again, and he looked happy.

"Man. I sawed the logs. What time is it?"

"Five," answered Ty. "I found a place we can spend the night
just over there a bit. I have the stove and the cookware with me.
We can catch a couple of trout with my rod and have us some
supper."

"No, no. No need to do all that. Let's get going up to
Clear."

"Be close to dark by the time we get there."

"I'm feeling fresh. I think we can make us some good
time."

With Soren leading and setting their pace, it took almost
three hours, rather than two, before the two hikers rounded
a bend and caught their first glimpse of Clear Lake. The trail
was steep and switchbacked, and they stopped frequently while
Soren rubbed his hip, looked up the slope, and grumbled about
the crime of living into one's old age.

Making their way to the lake took another hour and a half.

The sun was low by the time they got to where they could see the bend of the eastern shore. Ty stopped, scratched his head and looked up and down the trail.

"I'm sorry I took so long," Soren said. "Should've camped back at Big Sandy, like you said. Now you're gonna have to put your tent up in the dark."

"Putting up the tent in the dark's not a problem," Ty muttered. "I just wish I knew exactly where this campsite was, so we can find our stuff."

Soren removed his hat and put it back on. "Well, it looks as if that young fella left us a blaze there just up the trail."

"A blaze?" Ty looked. "Where?"

"Right up there. That bit of red," Soren said, pointing.

Ty looked again and finally caught sight of a tiny speck of color on a branch to the side of the trail. "Wow, Soren. You've still got some eyes on you."

The old man chuckled. "Eyes ain't worth beans. But Edda's found us one crackerjack of an eye *doctor*. That fella can turn out eyeglasses that'll have you seein' fly spit at fifty yards."

They walked up the trail to where Ty retrieved the blaze, a torn strip of red bandanna. Off the side of the trail there, a fainter footpath led toward the lake, and now that they were on top of it, both men could see the impression of the pack string's hooves in the softer lakeshore soil.

Hanson hadn't been kidding—the campsite was well off the trail. They walked for twenty more minutes, finding and following four more strips of bandanna, before they finally turned off the footpath and mounted a rise, where Hanson had not only set up the gear but put up the tent as well.

"Well, bless his heart," Soren said.

"No kidding," Ty agreed.

A note was pinned to the mosquito netting on the front of the tent. Ty removed the note and read:

Boss,

Your food sack is hanging about 75 yards east of the camp. Wind here usually blows west to east, so that way, if a bear does catch a whiff of your provisions, you won't have him walking through the campsite following the smell. About 30 yards past the bear bag is a creek, and it don't cross no trail anywhere above here, so you can use the water without treating. It's good water too. I fished here last month. See you on Saturday and I sure hope you enjoy it.

—HW

"Tell you what." Ty opened his pack and pulled out a collapsible jug. "You go ahead and relax, and I'll go fetch us some grub and get some water."

Soren shook his head. "No supper for me. I'm done in. I just want to catch forty winks; we can have a good breakfast in the morning."

"You sure?"

"You go ahead and eat if you want, but I'm turnin' in."

"Well, in that case, I'll just check the bear bag and then get water for the morning."

Setting sun at his back, Ty walked into the pines, the shadows long and low around him, the light a deep honey gold. He was seventy paces in when he saw the bear bag—secured to a tree by a twenty-foot loop of line on one side and a single line, thrown pulley-style over a high limb, on the other. The bag itself was a good dozen feet from either of the pine trees, and its bottom hung a good sixteen or seventeen feet off the ground: essentially bear-proof, even for a full-size grizzly, and absolutely untouchable for a black bear.

Through the trees there was the sound of running water, and Ty followed it to the small creek, rushing over mossy boulders like yellow glass in the failing sunlight. He held the jug in the water, shaping and filling it, capped it and then beat his hands against his thighs to get the feeling back into them after submersion in the icy snowmelt.

When he got back to the campsite, Soren was pulling his ground pad out of the tent.

"Soren?" Ty set the jug down by the fire ring. "What're you doing?"

"I'm gonna sleep outside."

"There's plenty of room. It's a three-man tent."

"Ain't used a tent since before they gave me the hip. Besides, you don't want me in there with you. My age, I gotta get up four, five times a night."

"That won't bother me."

"Bothers Miss Edda, and I thought that woman was unbotherable. And really, I like sleepin' under the stars. Got me a system." He pointed to where he had a waterproof nylon ground cloth laid out on a slight slope to the side and front of the tent. "See, what you do is you wrap the tarp around your staff up here, on the uphill side, and then I put my mattress and my bag on the downhill, like so. Boots go in the middle, right next to me. And if'n it rains, I just grab my staff and pull it over the top of me. Snug as a bug in a rug."

"Sounds pretty stuffy, if you ask me."

"Stays dry as powder."

Ty pointed across the lake. "Lenticular clouds over the peak there, Soren. It'll probably rain tonight."

"Let it. I'm ready."

"Well, if you're sleeping out, I'm sleeping out too."

"Don't be silly. You packed a tent in. You use it."

Ty sat next to the fire ring. "Well, it wouldn't feel right, with you outside here."

"This way takes practice. You'll get wet."

"I think I can rig something like that."

Soren shrugged. "Suit yourself."

Ty got the spare ground cloth out of his pack and laid it out, flat on the ground. Using the last of the daylight, he found a long stick about the same length as Soren's staff, cleaned the bark off of it with his pocketknife, and rolled it two turns in the ground cloth on the uphill side. He surveyed the campsite; Soren was already in his sleeping bag.

Ty sat down, pulled off his boots, and then glanced at the tent. He got up, padded stocking-footed the ten feet to the tent, zipped open the screen and set his boots inside. Then he went back to his ground cloth, wiped off the bottoms of his socks, and got into his sleeping bag.

"Good night, Soren," he called across the shadows. "See you in the morning."

"G'night, boy. You're gonna get wet."

Ty lay there staring up at the vast gulf of space above him. He sat up in his bag and looked down the slope and across the broad bend of the upper part of the dark lake. Over some peaks to his left, the stars of Orion's belt and sword twinkled and shimmered in the exceptionally clear air. As he watched, the sword stars dimmed, brightened, and then dimmed and disappeared completely, hidden behind an unseen cloud. He heard the low echoing rumble of distant thunder.

Two minutes of quiet passed before the clouds behind the far peaks glowed blue-white with lightning.

"One thousand one, one thousand two, one thousand three . . ." Ty whispered. At "one thousand nine," the thunder rumbled again.

"Two miles," Ty mouthed. He glanced over at Soren. The old man was buried in his mummy bag, just a wisp of white hair showing in the dim light. Ty reached over for the ground cloth—wrapped stick and gave it a tentative tug. That whole side of the waterproof nylon square lifted easily.

Ty lay back down onto the folded shirt he was using as a pillow. Another puff of light from the clouds closing in. This time it was eight seconds before the thunder rumbled, and a bit louder.

The storm increased in tempo, rumbles grown to echoing crashes, the lightning now jagged bolts that danced along the ridgeline. In minutes, the light and the noise had become nearly continuous.

Across the campsite, Soren snored, unmoving.

One fat raindrop hit Ty on the cheek, another on the forehead.

"Okay . . ."

As Ty reached for the stick, the rain began to fall in earnest:

big splashy drops he could feel even through the thick fiber filling of the sleeping bag. He grabbed the stick and lifted the ground cloth, but then the wind caught it, unwrapping the one corner from around the stick and flapping it. Now he was covered except for his feet—the rain continued to beat on the bottom of the sleeping bag.

Ty rolled on the ground, trying to wrap the ground cloth around him. But if he scrunched down enough to keep his head out of the weather, the bottom of the sleeping bag would poke out of the rolled ground cloth like a hot dog sticking out of the bun. It was raining steadily now, the lightning and thunder almost constant. As his hair began to stick together from the wet, Ty made a sound halfway between a growl and a moan.

He sat up, wriggled out of the end of the sleeping bag without unzipping it, picked up the whole dripping mess—sleeping bag, pad, ground cloth and all—and sprinted in the rain for the tent, the stick falling out of the ground cloth as he ran. He got to the tent, pulled up the zipper on the mosquito netting, jammed it, forced it back down again, then lifted it more carefully this time, rain drumming on his T-shirted back. He shoved the sleeping bag and pad in through the opening, dropped the muddy ground cloth outside the entrance, and dived in after his bag.

Soren . . .

Ty peered out the screening of the tent. A few feet away, Soren lay with his tarp pulled snugly over him like a giant rectangular clam.

Working by the nylon-diffused light of the lightning flashes, Ty laid out his pad and his bag and pulled his wet jeans and T-shirt off, laying them on the tent floor next to him. He hung his socks on a laundry line that ran the length of the eave and then wriggled back into the bag.

"It's wet," he said to himself.

As quickly as it had begun, the rain stopped drumming on the tent. Soon only the occasional drop splattered against the rain fly over his head. Gritting his teeth as his feet contacted yet another wet patch, Ty closed his eyes and tried to mimic sleep.

FOURTEEN

Ty woke up sniffing.

Unzipping the flap in its broad upside-down U, he opened the entrance to the tent and peered out the screen. Deep blue sky and sunshine flooded back at him.

"Is that bacon I'm smelling?"

"Bacon, and eggs, and warm trail bread, if you're quick enough." Soren waved him a hello with the hand not holding a spatula.

Ty opened the screen and began pulling on his socks, then stuck his feet out the tent door and put on his boots. He stood in his T-shirt and skivvies, reached back into the tent to grab his sleeping bag and jeans. He turned both inside out and laid them atop the rain fly on the tent.

"Morning, Tiger," Soren said without looking up. "Get wet last night, did you?"

"No." Ty waved at his bare legs. "This is just the latest fashion back East."

"I can believe that." Soren turned the bacon and the eggs.

Ty pulled the rain cover off his pack and dug into the main compartment. He came out with a short-sleeved canvas shirt, which he put on. Reaching back in, he found a second pair of jeans, shed one boot, pulled that leg of the pants on and slipped the boot back on. Then he did the same with the other leg. He tied both boots and sat down on a boulder facing the fire ring.

"There's coffee I just brewed in that billy pot there," Soren said, nodding at a stainless steel pot with a lid on it. "You want to settle it?"

Ty smiled. "Sure thing."

Taking a spoon from the plates and utensils piled next to the one-burner camp stove, Ty lifted the billy pot by its bail and struck the side of it twice with the spoon. Then slowly, methodically, he began swinging the pot back and forth, back and forth, swinging it farther each time until finally he was making complete circuits, the pot upside down at the top of each arc, the hot liquid within it kept in place by centrifugal force. He wheeled the pot faster and faster and then began reversing the whole process, slowing down and going from full circles back to a swinging motion until finally the pot came to a rest. Next, he gave the pot two more strikes with the spoon before removing the lid.

"Didn't spill a drop." Soren was nodding his approval.

"Of course not. Coffee, m'lord?"

"You bet."

Pouring so the coffee ran over the hinge of the bail, Ty filled Soren's enameled steel mug and then his own Sierra cup, pouring slowly to keep the settled grounds in the bottom of the pot.

He handed the mug to Soren, who gave him a metal plate of eggs and bacon and sliced bread in return. Without a word, both men dug in.

"Wow." Ty shook his head. "Why is it that food tastes so much better up here?"

"Because it is."

Both men laughed at the familiar exchange. Later, as Ty was wiping his plate with his last slice of trail bread, he looked up. "Well, since you cooked, I'll clean. Leave everything where it is, and I'll get some water boiling and get the cookware squared away."

"Fair enough."

Ty set his plate aside. "And then what do you want to do?"

"Do?" Soren cocked his head.

"With the rest of the day."

Soren smiled and patted his rod case. "I'm goin' to start working on lunch and dinner."

The waders Ty had brought with him were not the heavy coated-canvas variety that one sees in sporting goods stores. His were a thin coated nylon that he had to pull on carefully over his stockinged feet, never stressing or pulling on the waterproof material, and adjusting the nylon-web suspenders so they held the waders up at his chest, yet did not strain them.

The bottoms of the waders were simple waterproof socks, and he pulled an old pair of woolen rag socks over those. He topped these with wading shoes—cheap K-Mart variety canvas sneakers with carpeting glued to their soles.

"That's a good idea." Soren nodded at Ty's footwear.

Ty laced and tightened the sneakers. "Well, regular wading shoes are pretty expensive, and they stay wet a good long time. I really didn't relish the idea of having them turn into a biology experiment in the back of my truck after this trip. These cost me eight bucks—ten if you add the carpet remnant. So when the trip's over, I can just pitch 'em."

"Like I said, it's a real good idea. Clever."

Ty looked at Soren's bib overalls. "Did you bring waders?"

"Me?" Soren shook his head in an exaggerated manner. "No. I'm not doing me any wading until them doctors get this hip overhauled and do it right this time. As it is, I'd take two steps and slip—and if I end up goin' swimmin', I don't want to do it with a double sackful of water on my legs."

Ty glanced at the lake. "The pines grow pretty close to the water here. Not many places where you can get in a decent back cast."

Soren smiled. "Don't you worry. I know me a way."

The two men walked to the water, threading thin, silky tippets through the rod guides as they went. When they got to the broad lake's edge, they stopped, each man looking silently at the surface, a section at a time, reading the water.

"What you going to fish?" Soren asked.

"Adams," Ty said, opening a soft, floatable fly box.

The old man raised an eyebrow. "A dry fly? There's nothing rising."

"I know. But I like fishing a dry fly. I like the way it picks up. The feel of the cast too. Besides, if I cast enough, I can make my own rise."

Soren chuckled and looked over the blue water. "That's a lot of work."

"It's what we came here for. So I take it you're fishing wet?"

Soren nodded. "Woolly bugger."

"Imagine you'll have a fish on long before me."

"True." Soren glanced Ty's way and grinned. "But until I do, it won't look near as pretty."

Soren walked west along the shore as Ty stepped into the water, planting his feet with care, feeling for stones and trying to move quietly so as not to knock rock against rock and in doing so, frighten the fish.

When he was knee-deep, he stopped to thread the tippet into the eye of the small fly. He wrapped the tippet end around itself, passed it back through the loop holding the eye, licked the loose knot and pulled it taut. Clipping off the tag end, Ty worked powder silica floatant into the Adams' ruff, and then, moving slowly and quietly, he walked out into the lake, not stopping until the water level had reached his waist.

After glancing over his shoulder to make sure he had room for a back cast, he pulled the tippet and about ten feet of fly line through the guides. He then stripped more line off the reel, allowing the extra line to float at his waist, and then flipped the line forward, picked it up off the water with the rod tip and let the back cast load the rod, bending it. As the rod began to rebound, he brought it forward and fed a little line into the forward cast.

Ty did this four or five times, and soon he had fifty feet of yellow floating fly line going forward and backward in long, sinuous loops. Then he found his aim point—a shadow behind an underwater boulder—pointed the rod tip at it and allowed the front cast to collapse, the tippet straightening and dropping to, but not slapping, the water. The trout fly lit directly over the underwater shadow, only the tiniest of ripples radiating from it.

Ty waited a moment before raising the rod, lifting the line from the water and working it back and forth three times, drying the fly. When he allowed the fly to settle to the water this time, it was a couple of feet to the right of his first cast. He repeated the process, this time placing the fly slightly to his left. Then he did it all again—center, right, left—letting himself fall into the rhythm of the casts, the yellow line bold against the rich, blue mountain sky and the gray of the granite walls bordering the lake.

One of his casts had just settled when he heard a splash and a whoop from farther up the lake.

Ty turned. Sure enough, Soren had a fish on. Ty watched as the old man—standing on a flat rock just a few feet out from the lakeshore—dipped and tilted the rod to guide the fish toward him, close enough for Soren to reach down and lift a brown trout from the water and hold it out so Ty could see it: the fish was longer than the old man's forearm.

Ty shook his head and, holding his fly rod under his arm, held his hands apart: *nope—too big for our frying pan.*

Soren chuckled, unhooked the big brown and stooped low with it, moving the fish back and forth in the lake water until it swam away. Then he stood, looked Ty's way again and shrugged.

Ty peered behind Soren. Tall pines were growing to within twenty feet of the shoreline.

"Old man," Ty whispered to himself, "how on earth can you make a cast with the trees that close?"

As if in answer, Soren raised his rod tip until it was pointed behind him at about a forty-five degree angle. He then brought the rod smartly forward, sending a large hoop of fly line rolling across the surface of the water.

Then, when the line was straight in front of him, Soren lifted it up off the water. But instead of casting it back over his shoulder, he shot the line straight up in the air, less than a few feet behind him, bringing it forward again when it was vertical and on the verge of collapsing. The old fisherman did this twice, letting a little more line out each time until he had the fly floating over where he wanted it—where he let the line settle.

"You sly old fox," Ty muttered to himself. "When did you learn how to do a steeple cast? I've never been able to . . ."

But before he could finish the sentence, Soren had another fish on, a brookie this time. But again the fish was too big for their pan. Ty made a *get out of here* gesture with his free hand and turned back to his fly line.

He false-cast the line five times, drying the fly, and let it settle into the sweet spot behind the rock again. He squinted; the fly was still riding high on the water, the floatant not worn off yet. So he lifted it, false-cast twice, and set it down again, in almost exactly the same spot.

He did this five times, never letting the tiny trout fly rest more than a second or two. Then, on the sixth cast, he let the fly linger and saw a shadow rise beneath it.

The shadow became a swell, the briefest possible glimpse of a speckled back under a crystal sheen of water, and then the fly was gone and only ripples remained where it was.

Even before the rod tip bent toward the water, Ty was taking in line, pulling out the slack and giving a tug to set the barbless hook. The rod bowed, and he fed line through his closed hand, keeping the strain of the fish's pull within the meager breaking strength of the gossamer-thin tippet. The fish was headed back toward the rocks, so Ty walked in deeper, the water creeping above the waist of his waders, pointing the bending rod tip lakeward.

The tactic worked; the fish turned and sounded for the lake bottom. But moments later, it was headed shoreward again, and Ty stepped even deeper—the water was now only a few inches from the top of his waders—to keep the trout from reaching the rocks and snapping the thin monofilament tipper.

Finally, on the trout's third run, it tired, the rod tip lifting somewhat as Ty began to pump the rod tip up slightly, then reel in as he lowered it. The trout became exhausted, no longer swimming but now just a brown oblong shape that Ty brought over to his side. Slowly so as not to spook the fish, Ty slid his left hand into the cold water, his right hand holding the rod skyward. He slipped his hand under the fish's belly, trapped his rod under his arm to free the other hand and lifted it.

The trout was at least twenty inches long, an ample swell of gasping sheen and color.

"Attaboy, Tiger!"

Ty turned and held the trout up so Soren could see it. The old man, standing on a distant rock, laughed and repeated Ty's earlier gesture—shaking his head and holding his hands far apart.

"I don't know," Ty called. "We might just have to wrap one of these hogs in tinfoil. That, or cut a fillet in two."

"Lunchtime ain't for a while yet," Soren called back. "Gotta be somethin' smaller here, somewhere. 'Sides—this is fun."

Ty nodded and slipped the chewed and matted fly from the big trout's mouth. He lowered the fish into the water, moving it back and forth slowly, running cold lake water through its gills. On the fourth pass it quivered, and on the sixth it bolted from his hands: a sleek brown torpedo headed for the deep.

Ty clipped the fly from the tippet and hooked it onto the lamb's wool drying patch on his vest. He selected the unmangled twin of the Adams from his fly box and, after stretching out the tippet and deciding that the end section was still serviceable, tied the fly on with the same practiced cinch knot. He treated the fly with floatant and began casting again.

The two men fished for another hour, each of them catching and then releasing one more trout too large for the pan, Ty coming back to shore once for five minutes to warm his wadered legs in the high mountain sun. He walked back and forth on the rocky verge next to the scrub grass and watched the old man cast, his fly line lifting skyward in the seemingly impossible mechanics of the steeple cast, and then rolling forward gracefully, a long, inscribed tan loop against the gray of the distant mountains. Then the line straightened and settled on the still, steel blue of the lake.

Moments later, Soren had another fish on. Ty shook his head and stepped back into the water. The old man's fish was too large again, and his laughter rang out across the water as Ty began to false-cast, paying out his line.

They continued to fish in silence. At one point, the distant, shrill call of a bird brought Ty's head up. He gazed at the sky for nearly a minute before seeing it—an eagle circling high above the lake, apparently calling to another, because soon a second eagle, which seemed to come out of nowhere, joined it, and the pair began soaring together.

"Do you see—" Ty began to say, but that was all he got out, because his line went taut just then, the rod tip pointing insistently toward the submerged rocks. After one final skyward glance, he cupped the reel with his left hand, lifted the rod tip and began to play the fish.

This one did not have as much fight as the others, and he saw why once he had swum the rainbow trout to his side: it was smaller, just over a foot long—pan size, if they filleted it. And when he lifted it from the water to show Soren, he saw that the old man had the twin of the trout in his hands, holding it up and calling, "Supper!"

Ty nodded, and as he unhooked his fish, the brown streak of a single golden eagle swooped down low over his head, its mate banking a hundred feet above Soren before both big raptors began climbing steadily, back up into the blue bowl of mountain sky.

The two men walked back to their camp, where Soren fired up the little backpacking stove—nothing more than a burner mounted on a fuel tank—while Ty got out his fillet knife and cleaned the fish.

"Edda sent us nothin' but this can-ee-ola oil," Soren was muttering, looking at a plastic squeeze bottle. "Thought I'd snuck in some Crisco, but looks as if she snuck it back out when my back was turned. Shoulda saved us some bacon grease—would've saved it if I'da known this."

He poured a little oil into the frying pan, then turned the fillets in cornmeal on waxed paper.

The sun was high and warm now. Ty sat down, pulled off his improvised wading shoes and, working slowly and taking care not to tear them, peeled off the packable waders. He pulled on his boots, leaving them unlaced for the time being, and draped the thin waders over the top of the tent where they could drip.

Sitting down by the fire ring, he poured some lemonade mix into a water bottle labeled *Flavored* in black Magic Marker, added water and shook it.

"I'm done," he told Soren. "You?"

The old man looked up and rolled his eyes.

But five minutes later he was done as well, and Ty smiled as he accepted a metal plate with two of the trout fillets, a slice of trail bread, and half an apple.

"All the food groups," Ty said.

"Not sure if an apple counts as a vegetable. And I think we're missing dairy."

Ty took a forkful of trout, closed his eyes, nodded and shook his head. "It doesn't matter. This is great, Soren."

"Woulda been better if I had Crisco. Eat it up afore it gets cold."

Despite Soren's admonition, the two men ate slowly, savoring the fresh-caught trout, neither one commenting on the obvious—that not even the finest restaurant in Paris or New York could do justice to a rainbow trout the way a man could if he had a fish fresh out of a cold mountain lake—because each one knew it, and knew the other one did as well.

Finally, when he'd sopped the last bits of cornmeal off his plate with the trail bread, Ty got some water boiling and did the dishes guide-style, not using soap but scouring everything shiny with sand from the verge of the lake and then plunging it all in boiling water to sterilize it.

When he'd finished, he looked up at Soren, who was leaning back against a pine, contemplating what appeared to be a completely empty patch of clear blue sky.

"Dishes are set," Ty said. "What do you want to do this afternoon?"

Soren stopped memorizing the sky and turned to his young friend. "Do?" he said, furrowing his brow. "I'm eighty-six years old. I'm gonna take me a nap. You?"

Ty laughed. "Maybe I'll take a walk around the lake." He glanced at his watch. "Want me to come back at any particular time and wake you?"

Soren shook his head, pointing a thumb to his empty lemonade bottle. "I finished that off. Oughta get me up in twenty minutes. Thirty, tops." The old man pulled his faded John Deere hat forward to shade his eyes.

"Okay," Ty told him. "I'll be back about then."

Leaving his rod and fishing vest in the tent, Ty walked down to the lake. The *ki-eee* of an eagle sounded in the distance, and he searched the sky for several seconds. The two big birds of prey were nothing more than commas in the sky, so high up that at the ends of their turns, they disappeared entirely, only to reappear when they came back level again.

"We're over a mile and a half high here already," he whispered. "Just how do you manage to get *up* there?"

He made his way along the shore, toward the rocks where Soren had been fishing. Then he looked at the sky again.

"Eagles mate how long? For life?" he said to himself.

He walked a few feet more and then touched his left hand— the place where Kathy had touched him on the porch two nights ago when she'd said, *"I didn't think I saw a ring earlier. But I can feel it: where one used to be."*

He touched the smooth band of skin. And then he stopped walking. Stepping out onto the rocks where Soren had been fishing, Ty checked his watch, lay back on the sun-warmed granite, stretched and moved, matching his body to the stone. Then he stared at the sky, looking for the eagles. He rubbed his finger again, feeling the smooth girdling indentation where his wedding ring had been.

CHAPTER
FIFTEEN

HALF AN HOUR LATER, WHEN TY SAT UP, A BIRD—A GRAY, BLACK-billed camp robber—was perched in one of the pines near the shore, scolding him for moving.

Ty looked up the hill at the campsite. Soren was no longer napping against the tree. He was, in fact, nowhere in the camp.

"Looks as if the Indian alarm clock worked," Ty told the bird. He got to his feet, crossed from stone to stone to get to shore and strolled up the hill.

Soren was just coming back out of the woods when he got there.

"Have a good nap?" Ty asked.

"A short one. They're all short ones these days. How about you?"

"I wasn't napping. I was looking at the clouds."

Soren glanced at the sky.

"No clouds," he said.

"I noticed that."

Both men laughed.

Soren pulled the rain cover back off of his pack, opened the top and pulled out his old black Vivitar and a Ziploc bag full of gray and black Kodak film canisters.

"Still using the same SLR?"

Soren nodded. He opened one of the canisters and, shielding the open camera from direct sunlight with his body, dropped in the film and laid the tag end on the take-up cogs. "Don't see no reason to change. Still works."

Ty shrugged. "I would've thought you'd have gone to digital by now."

Soren looked up at him.

"I took me a walk up here about four—no, maybe five years ago. Was with a fella from the *National Geographic*, and he had him one of those digital cameras. A Nikon, it was. And I swear this man never took the camera away from his face. Showed me this little card that went in it, and said it would hold as many pictures as ten rolls of film."

"Saves weight."

Soren closed the camera back and pushed the winder, advancing the film into the camera. "I'm sure it does. But I'm tellin' you, all this man did all day was click, click, click. I'd take me one picture of War Bonnet, and he'd take fifty. And I asked him how many of them he was plannin' on usin', and he said maybe one. But I don't think this fella ever even saw anything that we looked at that day. If he wasn't lookin' through the camera, he was holdin' his hand over the back and starin' at that little screen there, talkin' to himself. And I think that stinkin' camera cost plenty close to what I gave for my last pickup, A-C and all."

Ty smiled. "You'd save a lot on developing, though."

"Won't live long enough to save that much up. 'Sides, remember how I taught you how to shoot pictures up here in the mountains?"

Ty thought for a moment. "You shoot Kodachrome 64, but you set the camera at ASA 80. That way, everything's just a little underexposed, and you get better colors."

Soren nodded once. "Exactly right. But this fella said if you do that with one of them digitals, it all goes catawhompus on you. He says you gotta go the other way. Overexpose it. So now I'm supposed to take something I spent fifty, sixty years learning to do right, and throw it out the window and relearn it?" He unscrewed the filter from the camera, breathed on it, polished the filter with the flannel of his shirtsleeve and replaced it. "Nope, Tiger. I don't think so." He looked up again. "If that fella was any example of what shootin' digital is like, I don't think I need to go spend me a boatload of money on some machine that's gonna make me act like an idiot."

Ty laughed. "Okay. So, want to go shoot some film?"

Soren squinted. "Well, if I see me anything that's worth the shootin', then sure."

The two men set out walking, Soren using just a single staff—the long, old burl-topped wooden one—while explaining that the sun was still too high for landscape work. "You want you some long shadows for that sort of stuff. Better still, wait until the sunlight turns golden. *That's* a picture."

He was looking instead, he said, for wildlife. So Ty told him about the camp robber in the pine by the lake, and they headed down there.

The bird was still in the tree, up near the top, and was making a *cu-ah, cu-ah* sound, almost like the cluck of a chicken or the gobble of a turkey.

"He don't mind that we're here," Soren said. "If he did, he'd be sayin' *jay*."

The old man looked around on the ground and found a pinecone that was still tightly closed. Taking out an old Buck pocketknife, he began prying the scales back, extracting one or two tiny pieces of what appeared to be bark from beneath each scale.

"Pine nuts," Soren said. He offered one to Ty, who chewed it and nodded.

"This here's bristlecone pine—not really worth much for chewin', seein' as the pine nuts are so puny. Europe and Asia have the pines that are really worth harvesting, although some of the tribes here in the Rockies'll still harvest pinyon pines." He nodded at the bird, which was still calling, as he kept on opening the cone. "But this little fella probably don't care about size, long as it's free."

Soren walked around, found a half-buried boulder with a fairly flat top, and dumped half a handful of tiny nuts on the rock. He stooped down to take a closer look, then backed up to another pair of boulders.

"Have a seat," he told Ty.

They sat. The breeze stroked the tops of the pines and the bird stayed where it was, still calling.

"When I was little," Ty said, "you told me that some of these birds can live nearly twenty years."

"That's right. Surprised you can still remember that."

"I couldn't forget. I think I was about nine at the time. It made me mad that a bird could be twice as old as me."

"Betcha ain't mad now."

"Betcha not."

The bird hopped to a lower branch, then hopped back up again. Ty watched it.

"My mother used to call them whiskey jacks. What do they do, drink whiskey?"

Soren shook his head. "Naw. That's just white folks messin' up the Indian language. The Cree call these little guys *wiska-chahn*. Not sure what it means; I don't speak Cree. But settlers heard it and decided the Indians were saying whiskey jack. Don't even sound similar, if you ask me."

Ty looked up. The bird was cocking its head, looking back at them.

"I heard a story once," Ty said, "that one of the first English explorers in Australia was asking some of the aborigines what they called this one animal, and the aborigines replied, 'Kangaroo.' Which is why they're called that now. Except it's not what an aborigine calls it. Turns out, seeing as English was a foreign language to them at the time, the aborigines were telling this explorer, 'I can't understand you.' Which is what *kangaroo* means in aborigine."

Soren chuckled. "I like that. I think I'll remember that one. Is it true?"

Ty shrugged. "Beats me. You don't speak Cree, and I don't speak aborigine."

They both watched the bird for a minute.

"I don't think he's coming down, Soren."

"Give him time."

Soren leaned down low and aimed his camera at the boulder with the pine nuts. He peered through the viewfinder, pressed a button next to the lens, turned a ring that encircled the lens, looked through the viewfinder and pressed the button again.

"What are you doing?"

"Checkin' depth of field." He pronounced it *deptha field*.

Ty gave him a blank look.

Soren held the camera up. "The lens has got an iris, same as your eye. Ever notice how, when you're up in the mountains, up on the glacier and the sun's high, everything looks razor-sharp and crisp?"

Ty nodded.

"That's because in bright sun your pupil—the iris in your eye—contracts. It gets real tiny. And a tiny iris has a long depth of field—everything looks sharp, both near and far. You don't have to refocus to go from one to the other."

"Why is that?"

"Don't know. Just the way it is. Has to do with the rays spreading out or somethin'. But when your pupil opens wider, like the iris opening on this camera—" Soren worked the ring on the camera, and the iris spiraled wider behind the glass of the lens— "then the depth of field gets shallow. Only what you're focused on is sharp, and things in front of it or behind it go soft. See how the lake and the sky and that cliff are behind the rock?"

Ty leaned down, looked and nodded.

"Well, that's a nice background, but if it's in focus, it'll take our attention away from the bird."

"Who's still up in the tree."

"Give him time. Anyhow, I want the bird in focus, but it's also important to have *all* the bird in focus. If I open the lens all the way, up to *f* 2.8, I'll probably have his eye nice and sharp, but the feathers'll be blurry, and that'll ruin the shot. So what I'm doin' is making sure that on top of that rock I got me several inches where the crystals in that granite are good and sharp, yet the background still goes soft. Do that, and if the bird's in the middle, he'll be good and sharp too." He offered the camera to Ty, who looked through it as Soren pressed the preview button.

"I see." Ty handed the camera back. "Learn something every day."

"I hope so," Soren said. "Otherwise I'm just wastin' my time, bringin' you all the way up here." He smiled and both men laughed.

When Ty checked the tree again, the camp robber had descended halfway down the tree and changed its call to a whistle—a clipped *whee-ooh, whee-ooh, whee-ooh.*

"Looks like he's warmin' up," Soren whispered.

"A watched pot never boils."

"Somethin' like that."

Ty gazed out at the lake, then at the sky. The eagles were either so high as to be invisible or they were gone. The air over the lake was one vast inverted bowl of blue. When he looked back at the boulder, the jay was on it, eyeing the pine nuts.

Ty nudged Soren.

"Yeah," Soren whispered. "I see him."

"Well . . ." His voice low, Ty didn't move his lips as he spoke. "Aren't you going to shoot him?"

"Not yet."

"Why?"

"This ain't the picture. He ain't facing right."

Ty looked back at the bird. "But what if he doesn't turn around?"

"Then he gets himself a free lunch."

The gray and black bird pecked at the nuts and then raised one in its beak, breaking it. It hopped to the side of the boulder and cocked its head again. Then it bent low and shook, scattering nuts left and right.

Soren raised the camera to his eye.

"Shoot," Ty whispered.

"Not yet."

The bird pecked, ate a nut and shook its head again, scraps of pine nut flying off. Soren bent lower, his left hand cupping the camera lens, turning the focus ring ever so slightly.

The bird ate the last nut. Then it straightened up and looked directly at the two men, its eyes clear and bright as if mentally conveying some profound nugget of interspecies communication.

Ty sucked in his breath. Just then Soren's camera clicked— a single, rusking *click*. Two seconds later the camp robber flew away.

"*Digital* photography." Soren spat out the words as if they were something filthy. He wound his camera and snapped the lens cap on. "Right. Let's go catch us some fish."

Ty had told Soren that he could run up to the campsite and get both of their rods, after which Soren had pulled off his John Deere hat, scratched his white hair and said, "Well, I suppose you got a lot more steps left in you than I got left in me, so sure. Go ahead."

It took Ty a few minutes—he stopped to put on his waders and wading shoes—and when he got back to the water, Soren was standing there studying the lake. All over the surface, tiny ripples were radiating and colliding with one another.

"Somebody up there likes you," Soren said as he accepted his rod. "There's somethin' risin'. Dry-fly water."

"I would've fished dry anyhow."

Soren bent lower to get a better look at one of the rings near shore. "I don't suppose you want to find out what's hatching, and try to match it?"

Ty shook his head. "No. I'll just fish an Adams."

Soren looked at him, one eyebrow quirked. "You even bring anything else in that fly box of yours?"

"Bring? Sure. Use? No. I figure if I can eat a cheeseburger for lunch five days a week, a trout probably won't pass up something that looks like a mosquito. There's always mosquitoes up here."

Ty slapped his neck as if to prove his point.

Soren laughed. "Man. Who taught you to fish?"

"You did."

"Oh. That's right." Soren unhooked the woolly bugger fly from the cork handle of his rod and clipped it off of his tippet. He opened his aluminum fly box, put the wet fly away, reached for an Adams, hesitated, then selected a Royal Wulff instead, a black-bodied fly with a bit of scarlet wrapped around its thorax. Tying it on, he said, "Well, we might as well get at it."

Ty worked a little to the left of where he had been fishing that morning. Soren found a place along the shore where the light breeze would allow him to sneak a back cast into a gap in the pines behind him. Both men fell into an easy pattern, casting smoothly, working the mends into their lines to reach farther, using the breeze across the lake to lay their tippets on the water with hardly a ripple.

The trout were active, and both Ty and Soren had fish on in a matter of minutes. Soren landed his first, and held it up: "A brownie, and it's eatin' size. I'll keep him."

Ty nodded and then, just as Soren had made another cast, Ty landed a brown trout as well, about the same size as Soren's.

"Well, that was easy." Soren was grinning as Ty waded ashore. "Let me just reel in and we'll go cook supper . . . oops."

The old man had made only two cranks of the reel when his rod bowed, the tan line pulling straight to a quivering ripple on the surface of the lake.

"Never rains but it pours," Soren said as he reeled. "Just let me get this one in and unhook him. We'll put him back and catch him again in the mornin' for breakfast."

Ty watched his old friend land the fish and then glanced up the hill at the campsite.

"Hello," he said. "We've got company."

Trout in his hand, Soren followed Ty's gaze. There was a man standing next to their fire ring, dressed in green, a pack on his back. And he was waving at them. Soren peered through the upper half of his glasses.

"Well now!" He trapped his rod under his arm and waved back. "It's that young fella from breakfast at the lodge. That Bridger boy."

"Oh . . . yeah." Ty made a halfhearted wave. "Kathy's fiancé."

CHAPTER
SIXTEEN

"Boy, your timin' couldn't be any better," Soren called up as they walked to the campsite. "Shuck that pack'a yours. We're just about to cook us some supper."

"Oh no. I couldn't do that. I don't want to go eating your fish."

Soren cocked his head at the ranger and held up the stringer. "Only kept the third one 'cause we saw you. Besides, they ain't our fish. This here is Forest Service land, is it not?"

The ranger nodded. "Yes, sir. It is."

"Well then, the way I see it, you're the only Forest Service person of the three of us, so these here are *your* fish. Tiger and I are just helpin' ourselves to 'em. Now, you got a mess kit in that pack'a yours, don't you?"

The ranger grinned. "Yes, sir."

"Well, break it out and take a load off. Won't take us but a minute to fry these up."

This time Soren did the filleting while Ty handled the stove.

He got a billy of water boiling first and started some pasta in it, setting the pot aside to cook on stored heat and warming up the frying pan once Soren had begun breading the fillets.

"Can-ee-ola oil," Soren muttered.

"It's good for the heart," the ranger said.

"Hear that?" Soren said to Ty. "This boy's in league with Edda!" Soren wagged a finger at the ranger. "No more talk like that or I'm takin' back the supper invitation."

Bridger laughed.

Soren glanced at Ty. "The boy thinks I'm joking."

Ty fried the first trout and held out his hand for the ranger's mess plate.

"No—please, serve Soren first."

The old man shook his head. "Camp hospitality, boy. You're our guest. Eat up."

The ranger passed his plate to Ty, who filled it with buttered pasta and trout. Soren mixed up some cherry drink and filled the man's mug. Within a few minutes all three men were sitting back and having dinner.

"Appreciate this," Bridger said. "I was ready to make do with jerky and trail mix tonight."

"If you're still hungry, I can head down to the lake and pull another one out," Soren offered.

"No, sir. This is great." Bridger forked up the last of his pasta.

"Well . . ." Soren shrugged. "You're welcome to throw down your bedroll anyplace you want."

"Room in the tent," Ty added. "Soren's on a fresh-air kick."

"No, thanks. I'm hiking all the way out to the lodge tonight."

"In the dark?" Soren asked.

"Not the first time. Actually, I planned it this way—been hearing about a young black bear bothering campers over at Big Sandy."

"A last year's cub?" Soren asked.

"I think that's exactly what it is. And there's a couple of newer folks there. Honeymooners. I want to make sure he's not coming around and troubling them. Maybe move him off if he is. That, and make sure they're bear-baggin'."

"What time'll you get to the lodge?" Ty asked.

"About ten. Kathy's saving a room for me. And tomorrow's a day off for both of us. Figured we'd drive up to Jackson Hole for lunch. She likes the galleries there."

"That sounds nice," said Soren.

Ty stayed quiet.

The ranger turned to him. "Kathy said you two went to school together?"

"Yeah." Ty nodded. "She was a year behind me."

"So, you still live around here?"

Ty shook his head. "Virginia. Finished my hitch with the Marine Corps couple years ago and then just stayed in Quantico."

"Family back there?"

"Wife."

"Oh. You're married?" The ranger seemed to straighten up an inch or two.

"Five years, come December. Tied the knot right after recruit camp."

"Well . . . congratulations."

Ty nodded, took the ranger's plate, mug and utensils, and washed them with the rest of the mess gear.

Ten minutes later, Bridger had his pack on his back.

"Gentlemen, I appreciate the hospitality," he said.

"Any time," Soren told him. "You give our best to that young lady'a yours."

"I sure will, sir." The ranger turned to Ty. "See you 'round."

Ty nodded.

The two campers watched as the ranger set off down the path toward the main trail in the waning dusk. Soon he was out of sight.

"Nice fella," Soren said.

"Uh-huh."

"Mind if I build us a fire?"

"Good idea—keep the bugs away. I'll help."

The two men used branches to rake a level spot in the fire pit. Then Soren took out his pocketknife and shaved tinder off several sticks. He made a tepee out of the sticks and placed the shavings around the tepee, and then finally added larger bits of wood. While Ty gathered more fuel, Soren fished a butane lighter out of his pack and lit the tinder. In less than a minute, long yellow flames were licking at the larger pieces of wood.

Ty came back and dumped an armload of branches next to the fire ring.

"Hung the food bag too," he said. He nodded at the branches he'd brought. "Not much big here."

"Big enough. Won't need to split this. And this way, we can let it burn low afore we bed down."

Ty brushed bits of bark off his arms and sat on a halved log facing the fire ring.

"So . . ." Soren leaned forward and prodded the fire with a stick, sending up a stream of sparks, not looking Ty's way. "Glad to hear you're still married."

"Why wouldn't I be?"

Soren poked the fire again. "Well, you ain't mentioned her since you got here."

"Here, camp? Or here, Wyoming?"

"Either. Both."

"Thought I had."

Soren glanced his way, shook his head. "Huh-uh."

"Maybe it was Edda I mentioned her to."

Soren looked at Ty over the tops of his glasses. "Maybe."

Somewhere deep in the woods behind them, an owl hooted.

"Or maybe not." Ty leaned forward and added some wood to the fire.

"Don't bank 'er too much, boy. I'll be turnin' in before long."

Ty sat back.

"That young lady up at the lodge . . ."

"Kathy."

"Ayup. Seemed pretty upset when you two was out on the porch, other night."

Ty leaned forward, hands clasped. "Yeah. I suppose she was."

"And this young fella, this Bridger—he seemed awfully happy when he found out you was already took."

"Did he?"

Soren looked at Ty, but did not answer. The campfire flickered, the orange flames reflected in the old man's eyeglasses.

"Soren, I didn't even know Kathy was up at the lodge."

"That so?"

This time it was Ty who stayed quiet.

"Tiger . . ." Soren took his glasses off, breathed on them, polished them with a bandanna from his hip pocket and settled the glasses back on his nose. "How come is it that I get the feeling that takin' some old geezer fishin' is not the only reason you come out to Wyoming?"

"Soren, I didn't come to see—"

"I ain't sayin' you come to see anybody. I *am* sayin' that maybe you come to get *away* from somethin'."

Ty said nothing.

"And I'm suspectin'," Soren added, "that runnin' into an old flame—maybe that complicates things?"

"Soren . . ."

"I ain't faultin' you, Tiger. It's just human nature. Your life gets complicated, you run into someone from a time when life was simpler, and you get a yen—"

"Soren . . ."

"Not for another woman, Tiger. For the other thing: that simpler life."

Ty gazed into the fire.

"Tell me I'm all wet and I'll shut up about this."

Ty looked his way. "No. You're not all wet."

Soren nodded slowly. "That little wife'a yours . . ."

"Angie."

"Sure—Angie. You know, Miss Edda and I was gonna come out for the weddin', but then I broke my hip that first time."

"I know, Soren. And you sent us the mirror. Angie loves that mirror."

"Yeah. But I regret not ever meetin' her. All these years, to Edda and me, well, you been like blood to us, Tiger. I know school and the war took you away, but that don't change nothin'. And if you're blood to us, then your Angie is also blood."

Ty looked the old man in the eye and blinked. "I appreciate that."

"Just the truth." Soren put his left hand to his chin, took his hand away. "So what is it, Tiger? What come between you two?"

The owl hooted again, and Ty sat forward, his fingers knitted together, still looking into the fire.

"I did," he finally said. "It's not Angie. It's . . ."

He fell silent again.

Soren bowed his head. "I don't want to be pushin' in where I'm not welcome."

"No. No—you're right. I'm out here with you partly because . . ." Ty brushed his hair back. "I think maybe I should tell you. If nothing else, because I don't want you thinking ill of Angie."

"Wouldn't do nothing of the sort."

"I know. But still . . ." He shook his head. "No. You don't need to be burdened with—"

"Tiger!" Soren interrupted. "Ain't I ever told you that I don't have to do nothin' but die and pay taxes?"

Ty paused for a moment. "You used to say, 'Die and pay taxes, and if Jesus comes, then all you'll owe is the taxes.' "

Soren thought about that. "Yep. Guess that's true." He pushed his glasses back on his nose. "But my point is, there's things I gotta do and things I wanna do, and if there's something wearin' on you, boy, I want to hear about it. It ain't no burden. It's what a body does for those he cares about."

Ty began to speak, stopped, and drew in a long breath.

"If you don't mind talkin' about it, that is," he added.

"No. I don't mind. And I suppose it's time."

"All right." Soren leaned forward. "I'm all ears."

"Okay." Ty stood. "But if we're going there, I'd better bank up this fire."

CHAPTER
SEVENTEEN

THE OLD MAN MUST HAVE GOTTEN UP WITH, OR POSSIBLY BEFORE, the sun the next morning. His hat was pushed back on his head, and he was bent over the cookstove with his flannel sleeves rolled up, the Dickies tag a red rectangle where the blue straps of his bib overalls intersected. Ty peered out the tent door at the startling brightness of shimmering treetops and lake water and sun-whitened cliff and blue sky, a mountain vista that made him blink, even though it was mollified somewhat by the mosquito netting.

He dressed, all except for his boots. Then he unzipped the netting, stuck his feet out the door and pulled his boots on as well.

"Hey," the old man said without turning. "You're just in time to swing the coffee."

Ty took the billy and walked off a safe distance, whirled it in a circle and turned himself into a human centrifuge, just like the day before. Then he brought the coffee back and poured it: a mug for Soren and a Sierra cup for him.

"Flapjacks this morning," Soren said, handing him a plate. "Ain't no more bacon, but I got butter and real maple syrup—none'a that corn syrup with food coloring."

"Thank you," Ty said, breaking his silence.

The two men ate quietly, cleaning up the mess gear without needing conversation to do so, Ty carrying the food supply back to the bear hang while Soren shuffled off into the woods for his constitutional.

After that, they fished again. The trout they caught this time were mostly pan size, but they released the early ones anyhow, lunchtime still being several hours away. So it wasn't until the sun was high, and Ty had twice left the water to let the sun bake on his waders and coax feeling back into his legs, that the two fishermen finally left the lake carrying a single trout apiece, a brookie and a brown, and walked back up to their campsite.

Ty began to sharpen the fillet knife, pulling it through the carbide rods set at an angle into a slot in the knife's plastic scabbard. Soren put his thumb over the air hole and began pumping up the stove, building pressure in the fuel reservoir. He opened the gas orifice and turned the little striker in the burner bowl. Yellow flames danced up and Soren adjusted the burner, bringing it down to a ring of small blue flames. In seconds the stove began to hiss as the heat of the burner warmed the generator tube.

Soren placed the frying pan on the stove and began heating some cooking oil.

"You know, Tiger," the old man said as he sprinkled cornmeal and flour on a sheet of waxed paper, "I meant what I said last night."

The younger man said nothing as he placed the first fillet on the waxed paper. Soren turned it, coating it with cornmeal and flour, and then placed it in the skillet. The fish sizzled as it touched the hot pan.

"You know that old fella you was tellin' me about?" Soren kept looking at the skillet as if he were talking to the fish. "Well, it's a shame how he tricked you, but you were at war, son, and you did your duty. Nothing to be ashamed of there."

Ty laid the other fish, filleted in two halves, on the dusted waxed paper.

"Thank ya, Tiger." Soren turned the fillets in the flour and cornmeal. He grabbed the turner and flipped the trout that was in the pan as well. "And as far as the fellas in your unit . . ." Soren looked up. "Did I ever tell you about the time I went to join the Army?"

Ty sat up a little. "You never told me you were in the service."

"Never was. But I tried to be. It was a little over a week after Pearl Harbor. Everybody in the country was feeling about how I imagine you all felt right after that nine-eleven. And Miss Edda and I had sat down and we'd gone through what we had saved up and figured out a plan that would keep her comfortable while I was away. We were living down in Green River at the time.

"Not that she wanted me to go, mind you. Begged me not to, but I told her it was my duty. So I took me a bus all the way to Salt Lake City, figurin' that was it, you know? I didn't think I'd see Miss Edda for months and months. But when I got to the induction station they'd set up, and it came to the physical, the doctor said I had flat feet. Told me I couldn't march all day and carry a pack."

Ty laughed.

"I know," Soren agreed. "Seems funny now, seeing as I've done enough hiking with a pack on to cross the country three times. But it weren't funny back then. No sir. I told that doctor my feet was just fine, and he said, 'What are you raising a ruckus for, son? I'm keeping you out of the fighting.' And I told him that if he'd care to step outside, I'd fix him up so he didn't have to worry about going off to no war, either.'"

"Oh, boy," Ty said. "I'll bet that went over well."

Soren looked up, at the blue sky. "Yeah. That about fixed it. They had a couple of big, husky fellas see me out. I tried the Navy next, but they'd already heard about me; I never got past the part where you fill in the papers. I went home the next morning; Miss Edda was happy—said it was the Lord's work—but I was too worked up to spit for about the next month and a half."

"Flat feet." Ty laughed again.

Soren nodded. Then the smile fell away from his face.

"I never lost friends the way you lost yours over in that Iraq, Tiger . . . never saw nobody die in combat. But I've lost friends over the years, nonetheless. Lost some of them all of a sudden, too: logging accidents, fightin' forest fires. Good friends. And I'll tell you something: I don't think there's a one of those fellas that believed it would have made things any better if I'd gone ahead and died along with them. I imagine your buddies felt pretty much the same way."

Soren scooped the first trout up with the turner and set it

on an aluminum plate. He handed it to Ty, who set it on the halved log next to them.

"Soren," Ty said, looking out at the lake, "I told you last night; it's not the same thing."

Soren began frying the second trout.

"You're sayin' that because you think your friend died in your place." He glanced up from the skillet as he said it.

Ty nodded, blinked. "He took my squad out, Soren. I was hung over, and he took them out. He was where I was supposed to be."

Soren moved the fish with the turner to keep it from sticking to the pan. "Let me get this straight. Whose idea was it to take you out drinkin'?"

Ty sighed. "The gunny's."

"And who made the decision to leave you at the base that morning? You?"

"No. The gunny."

Soren used the turner to flip the fish. "This gunny. He was a good man? A good marine?"

"The best."

"Capable of leading that squad?"

"Sure."

Soren moved the fish again. "Well, you ain't sayin' that he made some sort'a mistake that got hisself and those other fellas killed, are you?"

Ty scowled. "Of course not."

"Or that if you'd a been there, none'a that woulda happened?"

Ty straightened up. "No, Soren. I'm not saying that. But I

am saying that he'd be alive today, and I'd be the one who got killed with the squad."

"Maybe. Maybe not. But what I'm tellin' you, Tiger, is that your friend the gunny knew what he was doin'. He knew the risks. And he's the one who decided to fix things so you couldn't go out that day. You said yourself that he said he'd talked to your commander the day before—he planned it the way it went. He fixed it so you couldn't go."

Ty said nothing.

Soren shrugged. "I don't blame you for mourning your friends, Tiger. I don't blame you for grieving over losin' that gunny. But as far as beatin' yourself up over it, there just ain't no substance to it. It weren't your doin', you need to move on. You sure don't need to be ignorin' that pretty little wife'a yours. You gotta get over this thing."

Ty looked at Soren, his head cocked.

"That's all I got, Tiger," Soren told him. He looked down at his plate. "Hope it's enough. Now eat your fish afore it gets cold."

CHAPTER

EIGHTEEN

AFTER LUNCH, SOREN AGAIN CLAIMED THE PRIVILEGE OF AGE, electing to take a nap. But before settling down, he told Ty, "No need to feel you have to wake me up. Won't take but a little fishin' to catch us dinner. And I like the sound of the pines in the breeze. Think I'll take five and listen for a while."

With that, he pulled the bill of his cap down low, shielding his eyes from the sun. Less than two minutes later, he was snoring.

Ty napped for a while as well, re-finding his place on the sun-warmed rock by the lake. Half an hour later, when he awoke, blinking at the cloudless blue sky, he glanced back at the camp; Soren was still under his tree, asleep. So Ty splashed lake water on his face and then went for a walk, heading around the near end of Clear Lake and then up a draw in the cliffs on the far side. By the time he neared the top, he was climbing, using his hands as well as his feet to make progress. But once he'd made it to the top, he had a view of snowcapped peaks to the north and to the east. He sat on a granite outcropping for several minutes, taking it all in.

Ty clasped his hands. The tip of his right-hand ring finger touched the base of the ring finger of his left, rubbed it once. He unclasped his hands.

He turned at a sound from behind—something halfway between a squeak and a bleat. Its owner was perched on a rock about ten feet away. It was a pika—a little gray-brown animal that looked like a small rabbit with mouse ears.

"Hey," Ty said, his voice low.

The animal squeak-bleated again.

"Aren't you supposed to be down on the scree field, gathering leaves or something?"

The pika sat up a little higher, looking at him.

"You look to be a little out of your element."

The little animal squeaked.

"Okay. You're right; so do I."

He stood and the pika hopped away.

Ty glanced down the draw he'd used to get to the top, looked left and then right, then walked off to his right, stopping every few feet to peer over the edge. After a couple of minutes he came to an opening in the cliff top that merited more than a cursory inspection. Finally, he began making his way back down.

Which soon turned into hands-and-feet downclimbing as well. But Ty moved easily, finding the holds without trouble, looking out at the lake as he made his way down. In fewer than five minutes he was on the edge of the lake and walking back to camp.

Soren was awake and knotting a wet fly onto his tippet when Ty cleared the rise to the camp.

"Heading down?" Ty asked him.

"Only long enough to pull out a couple of trout for supper."

"I'll get my stuff."

"No need." Soren looked up. "That is, unless you want to. I was just thinking that you could get some water going on the stove, maybe make some rice. And Miss Edda sent some snow peas in with us—tonight's probably the last night they'll be any good. Got any ideas on how to cook those up?"

"Sure."

"That is, unless you wanted to fish."

"No. No—I'm fine, but . . ." Ty checked his watch. "Sun's not going down for a few hours. Sure you want to eat this early?"

Soren clipped the excess off the knot and nodded. "I'd like to turn in early tonight. Get an early start on the morning."

Ty cocked his head. "Did you get your nap?"

Soren nodded.

Ty leaned down. "You feeling okay?"

" 'Course I am." Soren looked up at him and scowled. "Don'tcha know nothin'? Old men are like old dogs, Tiger. The more years we got on us, the more we like to sleep. Comes with the territory."

Ty looked him in the eye and smiled. "Okay. I'll get the sides going. You go catch the main course, and we'll turn in early tonight."

"Now you're talkin'."

Ty got the provisions down from the bear hang and fetched a fresh jug of water from the stream.

The first thing he did back at camp was to fill the billy pot halfway up with water, start the stove and set the pot on the burner. Then he opened the food bag.

"Snow peas . . ." Ty leafed through the bags of food and found a Ziploc filled with what looked like brighter, flattened green beans. He opened it and bit into one. It snapped crisply, and he wiped his cheek with the back of his hand.

Next, he found the rice, in a larger gallon-size bag. He glanced into the pot; small bubbles were already rising to the surface of the water.

Pouring some of the rice into the billy pot, he found a smaller sandwich-size bag. In it was a smaller bag containing rust-colored powder, a Post-it note attached to the outside. Ty took the little bag out and read the note:

T—
> *Remembered how much you enjoyed the rice at Pad Prik. This is saffron powder—just a pinch in each pot. Probably won't be quite the same with Minute Rice, but it'll be close.*
>
> Love,
> Angie

Ty read it again and rubbed the edge of the note with his thumb. Then he put a pinch of the powder in with the rice, covered it and returned the rest of the rice to the bag of provisions.

He took out his Swiss army knife, opened the short blade and inspected it. Deciding it was clean enough for the task at hand, he began making small cuts at the ends of the snow peas and pulling off the string of fiber that ran the pea's length. After two or three peas, he tried pulling the string without making the cut with the knife. That worked, so he wiped the blade on his jeans, closed it, returned the knife to his pocket and continued to work his way through the rest of the peas by hand, stopping once to turn the rice with a spoon.

By the time the peas were all clean, the rice was close to done, fluffy and yellow with the color of the saffron. Ty took the billy off the stove and put the covered pot aside to continue to cook on stored heat. He put the skillet on the burner, turned the flame up just a touch and poured a little cooking oil into the pan, smiling as he muttered, "Can-ee-ola oil."

After a few minutes he wet his finger and shook a single drop of water into the hot oil, nodding when it sizzled. Then he added the snow peas, steam rising as he did so. Keeping the peas moving with a small flipping motion of the pan, he dug a little squeeze bottle of soy sauce out of the provisions and gave a long, dark squirt to the skillet.

Soren was just walking up from the lake, two trout on the stringer, when Ty was taking the skillet off the stove and setting it on one of the fire ring's flat rocks, covering the still-sizzling pan to finish its cooking off the flame.

"That was quick," he said as Soren came nearer.

"Rainbows," Soren said, holding the stringer up. "Ain't got no brains—you could catch 'em on a safety pin. Now, if there was nothin' but cutthroats or browns in that lake, I'd a had me a chore."

"Nothing wrong with how they'll taste, though."

"Ayup. That's the good part."

Soren got out the fillet knife and began to clean the fish as Ty spooned the snow peas off onto a spare plate.

"What's wrong with the peas?" Soren asked.

"Wrong?"

"The brown stuff. And they look shiny."

"That's soy sauce," Ty said, covering the first plate with a second one upside down, to hold in the heat. "I stir-fried 'em."

"Soy sauce? Ain't never had that but once. Trip to Salt Lake: Edda talked me into tryin' chop suey. Vegetables and gravy on rice. Didn't like it."

"You'll like this."

"If you say so." Soren handed Ty the first two fillets, and he began frying them in the oil and soy sauce left over from the peas.

In a few minutes the first trout was done. Ty put a fillet on each of their plates, divided the snow peas between the two and added a heaping scoop of rice to each one.

"Rice is yella." Soren held the plate up to eye level and inspected it.

"That's saffron."

"What's that?"

"Stuff that makes the rice taste good."

Soren raised a single eyebrow.

"Angie sent it," Ty added.

"Oh. Shoulda said so. She send along the soy sauce, too?"

"Nope. That's my doing."

Soren sniffed the plate and shrugged. "I'll give it a try anyhow."

He took a tiny forkful of the trout. Then he took another one—larger. Then he tried the rice. And tried the rice again.

"You approve?" Ty asked, laughing.

"You better get eatin' on yours, boy. Good now; won't be if it gets cold."

The sun was still well above the western horizon when they finished cleaning up the cookware and returned the provisions to the hang. Soren picked up his fly rod when they got back, and Ty glanced at the lake, but when he looked back, the old man was clipping the fly off his tippet.

Soren wound the line and tippet back onto his reel, removed the reel from the handle, broke the rod down and then packed it away in its aluminum tube. Then the old man shook out his sleeping bag, fluffing more loft into it, settled the bag onto his ground pad and sat down on it, taking off his boots.

"You really want to turn in this early?" Ty asked.

"Yep. I want to get an early start tomorrow. Gonna take me a walk. You're welcome to come along, if you want."

"Sure. You want to hit the other end of the lake?"

Soren shook his head. "No. I thought I'd take me a walk up to Cirque."

Ty turned to Soren, giving him his full attention.

"Cirque Lake?"

Soren nodded.

Ty sat down on one of the halved logs near the fire ring.

"Soren, Cirque Lake is better than four miles from here."

"Near five, 'cording to my trail notes."

Ty glanced north. "And it's mostly uphill."

"Just means it'll be downhill comin' back."

Ty sighed. The breeze ruffled the tops of the pines behind them.

"Soren, I'm not sure we're up to that."

"Why not? Feet troublin' you?"

He didn't answer.

Soren chuckled. "Tiger, I know I took my own sweet time gettin' up here from Big Sandy. That was just my hip—saddle sore. Don't worry; I can make it fine. Sure, it'll take longer than it used to; that's why I'm gettin' an early start."

Ty clasped his hands atop his head. "Listen, I know that they're naming the lake after you. . . ."

"Edda spill the beans on that?"

Ty shook his head. "Kathy—at the lodge."

"Figured that somebody would. . . . I need to see it again, Tiger. I need to go there. Before they have that ceremony or whatever. I need to go there."

Ty dropped his hands in his lap. "Soren, you've been to Cirque Lake."

The old man nodded. "Sure. Lots of times."

"Well, I don't think it's changed much since the last time you were there."

"I don't think Miss Edda has changed much since the last time I saw *her*, but I'm plannin' on seein' her again. Hopin' to, at least."

Soren took his socks off, revealing a pair of very nearly alabaster white feet. He flexed his toes, set the socks on his boots and put the boots on his ground cloth, on the uphill side of his sleeping bag. Then he looked up again at Ty.

"Tiger, I don't think Cirque Lake has changed one little bit since I was there last. But that's why I have to go there again."

Ty raised his eyebrows.

Soren leaned first to his right, then to his left, found the zipper to the sleeping bag and opened it up.

"I'm eighty-six years old. I don't know if I'll ever be back up here again. This might be my last chance."

"Soren . . ."

The old man waved a hand. "You don't have to go up there with me. I found Cirque plenty'a times by myself. I can do it again."

Ty lifted his hands, dropped them. "Soren, I'm not going to let you go up there by yourself."

"Well, I'm goin'."

Ty's shoulders sagged. "Then I'll go with you."

"If you want." The old man swung his legs into the sleeping bag, going to bed with his overalls on. "But if you're comin', you'd best turn in. I'm fixin' to get outta here early."

CHAPTER
NINETEEN

Ty woke to the sound of thunder. He rubbed his eyes, found his jeans and fished in its pockets for his wristwatch. The glowing green tritium hands showed just a few minutes after midnight.

A dim fog of blue-white light illuminated the inside of the tent, flickered, brightened and then died away completely. Ty rolled over on his stomach and peered out the mosquito netting at the inky night. Thunder rumbled again. A cloud to the west lit up from the inside with lightning, followed by a bright white bolt shot from the heavens to the cliff tops on the far side of lake. Less than two seconds later the valley shook with thunder, the sound of it echoing and reverberating. Soon the first drops of rain began their wet staccato on the rain fly over his head.

Blinking, Ty opened the mosquito netting and stuck his head out. Another thunderbolt ripped the sky, the sound nearly simultaneous with the flash. Over on the ground, Soren reached for his tarp-wrapped hiking staff and did his world-famous imitation of a giant clam, just as the rain started pouring down in earnest.

"Soren? You okay?"

As the lightning flashed, the old man raised the tarp enough to wave, then quickly closed it up again.

"Okay." Ty zipped shut the mosquito netting, unrolling and zipping up the tent flap as well.

"Well," he muttered as he settled back into his sleeping bag, the rain a constant noise now on the fly, "I guess this'll do it for our early morning start."

The rain had stopped when Ty next awoke. So had the thunder. He blinked in the near total darkness of the tent and half sat up, listening.

There was the rattle of metal from the direction of the fire ring.

"Oh, man . . ." Ty unzipped his bag and swung his feet out, fumbling for and then finding the zipper on the tent flap. He was halfway through the mosquito netting when the beam of a flashlight panned his way.

"Soren?"

"Hey, boy." Soren reached up and flipped off the switch on the headlamp elastic-strapped over his John Deere cap. " 'Bout time you got up. Gonna be daylight before you know it."

Ty looked up at the luminous fog of the Milky Way and hundreds of icy white stars. He reached back into the tent to get his watch from the front pocket of his jeans. "Man, Soren, it's the middle of the . . ." He squinted at the luminous dial. "It's not even three in the morning!"

Soren nodded, switched his light back on and returned to the billy pot on the camp stove.

"Figured it was about that time," he said. "Got us some oatmeal cookin' here. Be done in just a minute."

Ty rubbed his hair. "Don't you want to wait until we have a little more light?"

Soren pointed to the rig on his head. "Got light right here. You'd best get some britches on. It's a bit brisk."

Ty flapped his jeans out and pulled them on. "I thought you were a raccoon getting into . . . I don't know, the packs or something."

"Raccoon, huh?" Soren chuckled and handed Ty a metal bowl and a spoon. "Powdered milk don't taste much like milk, but it's what we got. Put a lotta sugar on the oatmeal; it'll cover it up."

"Thanks." Ty stirred the oatmeal absently with his spoon. He looked again at the starry sky. "Man, Soren. Last time I got out of a sleeping bag this early, I was trying to get across an ice field before the sun hit it. You come up with some new way to get up to Cirque that I don't know about?"

Soren shook his head, the beam of the light playing left, right, left, right as he moved. "Ain't but the one trail up there—unless you want to go cross-country. But I figured we might need some extra time to get there."

Ty yawned. "I guess we'll have that."

"Eat your oatmeal, Tiger. That'll stick to your ribs."

Breakfast took all of five minutes. Soren already had coffee brewed as well. Afterward, the two men fell wordlessly into the task of cleaning up the cookware, Soren working by the headlamp shining from the bill of his cap, Ty holding a penlight in his teeth.

"Reckon we oughta take the plates and fry pan and this stove along with us," Soren said, touching the burner once quickly, and then a second time, letting his hand linger to make sure it was cool.

"I'll empty out my pack." Ty looked in the direction of the tent for a moment.

"What?"

"Well . . ." Ty disconnected the little stove from its fuel cylinder and glanced over at Soren's ground pad. "I was just thinking that, as long as I'm carrying my pack up there anyhow, we might as well take along a couple of ground cloths and our sleeping bags."

Soren looked at him, the single light on his cap glaring like a bright off-center eye. "Whatcha plannin' on doin'—camping up there?"

"Not planning on it. But that way we would have 'em with, just in case."

"In case we need to bivouac, you mean."

"Well, yeah."

Soren shook his head, the little light panning back and forth again. "Boy, what'd I teach you about carryin' gear for a bivouac?"

Ty grinned in the dark. "That if you start a day hike prepared to bivouac, you *will* end up bivouacking."

"There you go. Seen it happen time and again. Ain't no use carryin' extra if you don't have a plan to use it."

Ty looked at Soren: the old man was busy packing up the

mess kit. The headlamp and the bill of his cap hid all details of his face. "Okay . . . You're that sure you're up for a walk to Cirque and back again today?"

The light bobbed. "Wouldn't be suggestin' it if I wasn't sure."

The two men fell silent, readying their gear. A moment later, Soren slapped his thigh and said, "We'd best get a move on, boy. We're burnin' daylight."

Ty looked up. The sky was strewn with thousands of glittering stars and the ethereal fog of the Milky Way.

"Best if we make a little noise as we go," Soren said as they turned away from the lake and made their way uphill, toward the main trail.

"I'll have to unlearn a couple of Marine Corps habits to do that." Ty rolled his shoulders and resettled his pack straps. He peered ahead in the darkness. Even in the starlight, it was possible to see Soren's flannel sleeves keeping cadence with his staves as he walked—the lightweight hiking pole in his left hand, and the old burl-topped oaken staff in his right.

"In the Marines, you needed the element of surprise." The beam of light coming from Soren's headlamp played on the foliage at the side of the trail when he turned to answer Ty. "Up here, we don't want none'a that. We come up on some momma bear takin' her little one out to do some early mornin' fishin', the last thing we want is to surprise the old girl."

"You've got a point there." Ty reached back, got his metal Sierra Club cup out of the side pocket of his pack and slipped the metal handle under one of the web straps securing his fly-rod tube to the backpack. The cup began to tap a rhythmic *tink tink tink* against the aluminum tube as he walked along.

"That'll do it," Soren said. "Know some folks who tie them little silver Christmas bells to their shoelaces in bear country."

"Must make the bears think Santa's coming."

"That, or the Salvation Army."

The two men laughed. Then they walked on in the starlight, the only sound the dull, regular tapping of Ty's metal cup.

They'd been hiking steadily for an hour when the first sliver of gray, a thin bar on the horizon, became visible through the passes to the east. The mountaintops took form as blacker shadows against the still-dark sky. Off in the trees, a night bird called sleepily. Soren switched off his light, pulling it from his cap and depositing it in a screwdriver pocket on the leg of his overalls.

"Up for a break?" Ty asked.

"Suspect so. You?"

"Anytime you want."

"Well, let's wait till we top this rise. Trail levels out pretty much for a while after that."

So they continued walking uphill for another ten minutes. Even after the trail had leveled off, Soren kept moving forward without so much as a glance back, but Ty kept silent. Finally, they rounded a bend and the ground fell away for hundreds of feet on the right side of the trail, a soft, cloudy layer of ground fog barely visible in the valley below.

Soren nodded at a flat-topped collection of boulders on the inside of the trail. "These do for you?"

"Perfect." Ty backed up to the boulders and easily shrugged

the light backpack off. He opened the tall side pockets and took out two plastic water bottles, handing the first one to Soren before unscrewing the cap on the second.

"Good place to stop," he said. "Bet it's something else when the sun rises."

"You'd think so," Soren said, "but it's better before. 'Specially when this valley's full of cloud, like today. Looks like a little bit'a heaven. But when the sun comes up, it throws the valley into shadow most'a the mornin'. And by the time the shadow's off, it just looks like anyplace else."

Soren wasn't sitting yet, so Ty asked him, "You want to wait and watch it for a while?"

"Nope." The old man opened his water bottle and sipped it slowly, as if it were hot. His back was turned to the valley below. "I seen it before; I remember it." He lowered the bottle and looked at Ty. "I'm sorry I move so slow, boy."

"You don't move so slow."

Soren shrugged. "If you was by yourself, you'd be up at Cirque by now."

"Fishing in the dark?"

"You know what I mean."

Ty rolled his lips and exhaled. "Soren, if I was by myself, I probably wouldn't even be heading to Cirque right now. I might not even be in the Winds this week. And I'm glad I am. This is a good trip. I owe you."

Soren chuckled and handed the water bottle back. "Tiger, you don't owe me a thing."

"We'll agree to disagree. You don't want any more water than that?"

"Naw. If I drink too much, I'll just have to stop and pee. We'd best get a move on afore this hip'a mine starts to stiffen up."

"You haven't even sat down. Take a load off for a few minutes."

"I'm okay. I'm fine. Let's go."

As it turned out, Soren's self-imposed water rationing didn't have all that much of an effect. After twenty minutes of hiking, just before the trail began to switchback and climb again, he turned and told Ty, "Hate to do it at the bottom of a hill, Tiger, but I've got to go see a man about a horse. Mind if we stop here for a minute?"

Ty grinned. "Make sure you get a good deal on that horse."

Soren glanced uphill and then down before stepping off into a stand of spruce below the path.

Ty lifted his pack higher on his shoulders and pulled the waist belt and shoulder straps snug. The Milky Way had faded entirely from the graying sky so that now only a few bright stars still burned in the west. To the east, over the shadowed peaks, Venus was the sole spark of light, and even it shone with less intensity than during their last rest stop.

The occasional weary calls of night birds were giving way to a wakening chorus of chirps and rasps—the birds of the day getting off to an early start. Small rustles betrayed ground squirrels stirring in the brush.

Up the trail, the tawny brown of its coat barely visible in the faint light, a white-tailed deer stepped onto the dark streak of the trail to nibble at something growing near the base of a pine. Then it looked up at Ty, its tail rising, hindquarters tensing, ready to flee.

Ty made a sound halfway between a cough and the *caw* of a crow, and the animal froze. Then Ty laughed and the deer turned and bounded away, the white flame of its tail bouncing twice before disappearing in the trees. The crashing of its retreat had barely faded when Soren reappeared noiselessly on the trail, a hiking staff in either hand.

"I coulda sworn I heard me a she-deer," he said.

"That was me, freezing a little buck."

"Was it?" Even in the predawn light, the old man's eyes twinkled. "Works good, don't it?"

"Worked great, until I started laughing."

"Yep. It's a good trick."

"Want some water?"

Now it was Soren's turn to laugh. "May as well. Can't see as it makes any difference."

Slowly, as the two men walked, the sky began to brighten. Only the dim spark of Venus testified to the fact that it was a perfectly cloudless sky.

At one point Soren paused and, with both poles in one hand, knelt down and with his free hand felt the pine needles and leaves along the trail. "This brush is dry," he said over his shoulder.

"Got rain just last night," Ty said.

"Where we were. But even then, not near enough. These mountains are due for a good soakin'. Otherwise, all this lightning we've been gettin' after midnight? That could touch her off for sure."

"That wouldn't be good."

"Not for us, maybe." Soren stood, looked ahead and pointed with his pole, the longer oak one. "See them trees down there, on that slope? Them's lodgepole pines, same as what we have growin' up above our camp at Clear Lake. A lodgepole's got itself an itty-bitty cone—ain't any bigger than a walnut—and it stays closed up real tight until a fire comes through. A warm day ain't enough to open it. Fact, you might have trouble to get one to open stickin' it in the oven. But you get a forest fire—one hot enough to burn the tree? That lodgepole cone'll open and send out a whole bunch'a pine-nut seeds. That entire stand of pines might burn up and die, but the stand that grows up after it will be bigger, because each tree'll shed hundreds, maybe thousands of seeds as it burns."

Walking again, Soren came to a step in the trail, a granite shelf about a foot high. He used the walking sticks to keep his balance as he mounted it. It took him two tries, but he made it without stumbling.

"And them trees up ahead of us?" Soren continued. "Them's ponderosa pines. A ponderosa's got itself this thick, loose bark. You get a brush fire going around a ponderosa, its bark might catch fire, but it'll pop off the tree afore the thinner bark underneath it gets hurt. That way, you get yourself a fire in an area that's got just a little brush, them trees don't get hurt at all."

He said "at all" so it sounded like *a-tall*.

"But if man comes along and stops the forest from burnin', the brush'll grow too thick and the fire'll burn too hot. The tree loses its defense against the fire. Or it still has it, but it ain't enough, 'cause now the fire's too hot."

"Like we're messing with a design put together by somebody who knows a lot better than us," Ty said.

Soren mounted another shelf of rock but did not reply.

Ty tried again. "Because that's what you see when you look close at things like that, isn't it? That they aren't accidents? That all these things were designed for the places where they live?"

Soren picked his way through some loose rock on the trail with his hiking poles. Still he said nothing.

"Soren?" Ty said. "You okay?"

"I'm all right," the old man finally said, continuing on with the two poles gripped tightly in his hands. "But this trail's gonna start to steepen up from here on out, boy. We'd best save our breath for the breathin'."

Soren was right; the trail did indeed begin to steepen, and abruptly. Not only that, but the mountains began to rise even more steeply on all sides. Twice, the trail ran through draws so vertical that Soren had to leave his hiking poles with Ty while he clambered up using his hands and his feet. Both times he pulled deerskin gloves out of his overall pockets and cinched them on at the wrists, tugging on the threaded red beads on the backs of the gloves.

"My skin's gone all thin on me in my old age," he'd told Ty the first time he put the gloves on. "Back home, Miss Edda gives me a jar to open? Five times out of ten, I'll scrape a finger or cut the palm of my hand doin' it—get bleedin' so bad I have to put a Band-Aid on. Don't get old, Tiger. You wouldn't enjoy it."

On the second draw, one part was so steep that even Ty had to use his one free hand to steady himself as he made his way up carrying the backpack with their fishing gear and Soren's two poles.

But it was the third draw that gave Ty pause. This one was higher than the other two put together, and for ten or twelve feet in the center it looked more like a rock climb than a hiking trail.

By now, the sky over the cliffs was a clear robin's-egg blue, and a raptor—a hawk or an eagle, it was too far up to make out which—was circling above them, the brown of its feathers flashing golden when it drifted near a high pass and the sunlight caught it. The treetops and trail behind Soren and Ty were all still in deep shadow, but the sun had obviously been up for a while, the light coming through the pass pure and white.

Ty turned back to the draw.

"Soren, I don't know about this."

The old man was sweating, his breathing heavy.

"Don't see what there is to know about it. The trail goes up there. We're following the trail."

"You know what I mean."

Soren pulled a bandanna from his hip pocket, took off his John Deere cap and mopped his brow, not disguising his discomfort.

"You're a good man, Tiger. You truly are. But sometimes you worry more than two women. I been up this draw once, I been up it a hundred times."

"I believe that." Ty looked up the draw. "Then again, you've never been up it when you're as old as you are now."

Soren stared up at the bird and said, "True. Then again, neither has anyone else."

"How's that?"

The old man looked at Ty. "Been up this draw when they're as old as they are now. Son, I do believe that might be just about the most stupid thing you ever said to me. I don't mean to offend, Tiger, but really . . . just listen to yourself!"

Ty laughed. "Okay. We can go up. But I'm going right behind you."

Soren lifted an eyebrow, the John Deere hat riding up on that side along with it. "Oh. I see. If I slip goin' up the draw, you're gonna be Superman and catch me. Is that it?"

"Well . . ."

"More likely, we'll *both* fall down here and bust all four legs we got between us, and some idiot from Casper'll find what's left'a us both next spring when he comes up here to fish after the thaw."

"That's what I've always liked about you, Soren: your optimism."

The old man laughed and handed his hiking poles to Ty. "Up we go."

The draw would have been five minutes' work for a hiker in the prime of life. Soren took forty-five, but he never stopped moving for more than a few seconds at a time, and sweating as he was, he moved entirely silently and never missed a step. Indeed, the only time he spoke was when Ty's boot slipped on a dew-wet rock and the younger man had to steady himself with a hand on a ledge. When that happened, Soren glanced down and said, "Guess it's good we didn't have you go first."

Soren stopped near the top of the rubble-filled cleft, standing on a shelf in the dihedral, where two faces of granite came together. But he wasn't stopping because he was winded—even though he was. He was smiling, one hand out, pointing toward a corner in the cleft, a way through, indicating that Ty should go first.

"Okay." Ty edged past his friend and stepped around a large boulder. Sunlight fell on his face for the first time that morning, and he blinked. Then he looked at what lay beyond the draw, and his mouth fell open.

"Oh, Soren," he said, not turning, not turning away for one second from what he was looking at. "This is amazing."

CHAPTER
TWENTY

THE CIRQUE WAS A GREAT OVAL VALLEY, THE REMNANT OF A glacier that had retreated over the millennia until it was nothing more than an icefall at the far end of the mile-long lake.

But in its place, the glacier had left a majestic, roofless cathedral, the lake surrounded on three sides by mountains that rose steeply like rough gray granite ramparts, the tops of the tallest ones dusted white with snow. Scree fields angled down on two sides of the lake, while the dark pinnacled peak at its far end dropped directly into the water. And at the other end of the lake, a green meadow climbed to a U-shaped pass.

Soren joined Ty at the top of the draw, and as they watched, a bald eagle arced down to the center of the lake. The big bird reached forward, broke the glassy surface of the water and rocked its legs back, a wriggling fish grasped in its talons. The eagle sculled its wings heavily, offsetting the added weight, and slowly rose back into the air, banking to return the way it had come, beating its way back to the nest.

"Never been here before?" Soren asked.

Ty shook his head. "If I had, I'd remember."

"Always had a mind to bring you up here," the old man said. "But back when you was a little shaver, I always thought that last draw might be too much for you, 'specially on the return trip."

Ty glanced his way.

"Yeah," Soren said. "I know. What is it they say? 'What goes around comes around'?" He shrugged and pointed at the lake with the shorter of his two hiking staves. "Fishin's down there. Guess we may as well get a move on."

The lake looked bigger up close. As they walked along the verge of it, Ty pointed to a couloir at the end, the source of a small waterfall.

"Water's coming in up there," he said. "Where does it go out?"

"Rapids—little canyon at the far end, next to that pass," Soren told him, aiming his smaller hiking staff at a saddle on the far end of the cirque. "Ain't no trail there; the walls are too steep. 'Less a body wants to climb, the only way in or out of here is the way we came, or up over that saddle—that's the way the game gets in here."

Soren fell silent, and the two of them walked that way for a few minutes, the stones beneath their feet and a distant whistle of wind the only sounds. Soren looked around as they walked, not just taking in the view but really looking, as if he were memorizing the place.

Ty stopped when a shadow moved under the water, just

offshore. "Thought I saw . . ." He turned to Soren. "There's cutthroat in here?"

Soren nodded. "Ain't nothin' *but* cutthroats in Cirque Lake. Back in the sixties, the Forest Service was fixin' to stock cutthroats in some of these waters, but the temperature and the hatches have to be just right or they won't thrive. So they sent men up to study all these lakes, and they found one about four miles over that they figured would be just perfect, so they loaded up a bunch'a fry in a plane 'cause they planned to drop 'em in from the air. 'Cept the pilot was a fella from down Colorado way, Forest Service pilot, and he didn't know the Winds. Got confused with his maps and dropped the fry here instead of the lake they'd all picked out. Been cutthroat here ever since. Bigguns too—don't get fished all that much, and if the fish live long enough to get too big for the eagles, there ain't all that much to bother 'em."

Ty chuckled, studying the water. "They ever stock the right lake?"

"Yep." Soren nodded emphatically. "Got some more fry and flew 'em in the next month."

"They take?"

The old man shook his head. "They died out. Every single one of them." He looked at Ty and grinned. "So much for science, huh?"

There wasn't anything you could really call a trail along the lake—no visible way worn through the thick scatter of stones and scree. But the gravel underfoot was well settled after centuries of winter snow and summer storms, and the walking was easy, like strolling down a garden path.

At the fifth trolling shadow under the lake's rippled surface, Ty stopped and glanced at the stone beach behind him; the area was reasonably flat, the scree field a good thirty yards from the water's edge.

"Lots of room for a back cast here," he said. "And the sun's in front of us: no shadows on the water. What do you think? Fish here?"

Soren shrugged, his weight on the wooden staff. "Good as any. May's well give it a try."

Ty shifted the pack to one shoulder and lowered it to the ground, the back of his shirt damp where the pack had been resting against it. He put his arms over his head, stretching, and then unstrapped the two anodized aluminum rod tubes, opened the pack and got out his fishing vest and the two lamb's wool–padded reel cases, his old CFO reel in one of them and Soren's newer Battenkill in the other.

"Not even using your old reel, huh?" Ty asked as he handed it to Soren.

"Savin' it for a fella, along with the rod. 'Sides, this one came with that newfangled rod they sent me. Had the backing on it and everything. Only thing I changed was the fly line. It come with a dual taper; I like it level. You can turn it around when it starts to wear out, get another season out of it."

Ty laughed. "Soren, you can do exactly the same thing with a dual taper."

"Suppose so." Soren pursed his lips. "But I learned to fish

with the old stuff. Still works fine. Trout don't seem to mind, that's for sure."

Ty quickly assembled his rod and reel and ran the tippet and leader up through the guides. The old man had a battered Wheatley aluminum fly box open, but he wasn't studying the water; he was looking at the rocks and cliffs on the far end of the lake, down near the grassy, spruce-dotted saddle that ran up to the pass.

Ty selected a fly, a small Adams. "What are you looking at, Soren?"

The old man startled. "Me? Just gawkin', I suppose."

"Don't blame you—beautiful place."

Ty stripped out some line and began to cast, not wearing waders but just standing on the lakeshore, a little ways back from the water, where he wouldn't be visible to the big trout cruising slowly in the shallows. Soren put his rod together and began to walk slowly down the shore toward the saddle at the far end, using just the one hiking staff this time—the long one with the burl at its top. Ty watched him go, then he twitched the rod tip up, making the dry fly quiver on the surface of the water. After a moment, he moved it again, then lifted the rod tip back and began a series of false casts, drying the fly, before he set it down again just a few feet to the right of where it had been.

He went on that way for half an hour, presenting the fly, moving it, and then casting again. But while he could see the big cutthroats less than a foot beneath the water's surface, they didn't seem to notice the trout fly just above them, or if they did, they were not interested.

Lips thin, huffing once through his nose, Ty reeled in,

stripping the water from the line with his thumb and forefinger. He clipped the dry fly from the tippet and put it on his vest to dry. Then he opened the plastic fly box and glanced up and down the lake.

Soren still hadn't put a line on the water. For that matter, he wasn't even looking at the lake; he'd leaned his rod against a log down near the water, and he was walking the scree fields up near the cliff bottoms just shy of the saddle, looking at the rock.

Ty watched the old man. Then he shrugged, got his old Wiley X sunglasses out of a billows pocket on his vest, and studied the lake, the polarized lenses of the glasses cutting through the glare of the heightening sun. The big trout were still there. Closing that fly box, Ty got out another and selected a nymph, a Hare's Ear pattern tied on a fairly small number-18 hook. He studied the tippet end for a moment and then wet it with his tongue before tying on the trout fly, forming the clinch knot by feel as he looked down the lake again. Soren was still on the scree, right up at the very top of it, near the cliff base, reaching out every once in a while and patting the granite. Ty looked back at the fly and clipped off the tag end of the finished knot.

The nymph was marginally heavier than the dry Adams, heavier and without the wing of hackle tips to provide resistance to the cast, so Ty made his casts a little slower now, pausing at either end of the false casts to make sure he didn't snap the fly off the gossamer-thin tippet. Finally, when he had enough line out, he let the little fly drop to the water with the tiniest of ripples.

For six casts, nothing happened. On the seventh, he saw a shape move beneath the gray-brown body of the nymph and bump it, but the fly never vanished from the surface of the lake.

Ty waited for a moment, cast again just to the side of where the fly had been, and this time the trout attacked it, the slash on its gill plate a bright red-pink in the sun as it rolled, the water of the lake sheeting on the long fleet curve of its body.

Ty set the hook with just the slightest lift of the rod tip and then let the big trout run, the drag singing out in a shrill, prolonged buzz as the fish dove for the familiar sanctuary of deeper water. When the reel had spun down to just the braided Dacron backing line, the fish stopped, and Ty began stripping line in, letting it pool at his feet, not bothering to reel and maintaining just enough tension on the fly line to keep the barbless hook firmly in the big trout's jaw.

When the trout got near enough to the shore to glimpse Ty, it spooked and ran again, and he gave it line, letting the yellow fly line run between his fingers, cold lake water stripping off of it and trickling over the back of his left hand. Three times they repeated the dance until the big fish tired. Ty began reeling rather than pulling in line. Taking the cherrywood landing net from the magnetic holder on his vest, he stepped boot-sole deep into the clear water of the lake, leaned forward and used the tension of the fly rod to guide the trout into the mesh pocket of the net.

Holding the rod up with a Velcro keeper, Ty slid his hand down the length of the trout's cold, wriggling body and took it from the net, quickly removing the small hook. The fish was huge—longer than his forearm from elbow to outstretched fingertip, and bigger around.

Ty looked at the gasping fish, the staring eyes, the colors still bright and glistening from its fight. Then he looked at the lake,

and finally at the watch on his wrist. It was after ten, still well
shy of noon, but better than seven hours since he and Soren had
eaten breakfast. He held the fish up again, gauging the length
of it.

Threading a stringer through its gill so it wouldn't get away,
Ty set the fish down in the water, rinsed his hands in the lake,
and cupped them to his mouth.

"Soren!"

The old man was still up near the base of the far cliffs,
wandering on the scree. He turned Ty's way and waved, hand
high over his head.

"Lunch!" Ty called. "Come on back."

In the distance, the old man waved again and began to pick
his way down the scree field, probing ahead of himself with the
hiking staff for support.

With the camp stove set up in the lee of two low boulders,
Ty had half the trout fried by the time Soren got there.

"Got yourself a monster, huh?" Soren said, accepting a plate.
He sat heavily on one of the boulders and forked off a bite of
the fish.

"Not quite the size to be called Nessie, but big enough." Ty
began frying the rest of the trout. "The cutthroat in this lake
are something else."

"Told ya." Soren bobbed his fork as he ate.

"So why haven't you been fishing? What were you doing
up there?"

Soren shrugged. "Lookin' around. While's passed since I
been here."

Ty used a fork to turn the trout in the pan. "You going to fish after lunch?"

"Oh, I might wet a line."

Ty glanced up, but the old man was looking away, the cliffs down the lake curved and distorted in the thick, clear lenses of his bifocals.

By the time Ty had finished his lunch, Soren was asleep where he sat. Slumped a little forward on his low granite seat, he looked considerably less than comfortable, but he was snoring as loudly and steadily as if he were home in bed.

Moving quietly, Ty took the metal plate and fork from where the old man had left it, next to him on the rock, and set about the chore of cleaning up the lunch things. It was a simple task: cooking for two, and a meal of fish only, didn't leave that much of a mess. Then he broke the stove down and repacked everything into kit bags, ready for the hike back to camp in the afternoon.

Finally, when everything was squared away, he stood, picked up his fly rod, and looked down at the sleeping old man.

"Soren?" He kept his voice low.

"Wha . . . ?" The old man startled awake, knocking his glasses askew with his left hand and then resettling them with his right. "Well, I dozed right off there, didn't I?" He looked around. "And I left you the cleanup, didn't I? Call me a blister."

"How's that?"

"A blister." Soren grinned. "Somethin' that don't show up until after the work's done."

"Oh, you were just getting a nap. I was the one who got to sleep in this morning."

"Till three!" Soren slapped his knee. He looked at the younger man's fly rod. "You fixin' to fish?"

Ty hefted the light rod. "Thought I might. Just catch and release. Took me quite a while to get the one we ate for lunch. Thought I'd try again and see if they're all as smart as he was."

"Wager you'll find they're smarter. If I was a wagering man. Which I'm not."

"One way to find out. You coming?"

"May's well." The old man got to his feet, and the two of them walked a few steps.

Then Ty stopped. "Forgot your rod, Soren."

"Rod? Oh, leave it. We ain't meat fishin' anyhow. I'll just watch you."

"But you haven't even fished yet."

"Not today. But I pulled me a ton'a cutthroats out of Cirque over the years. Don't worry; I fished my share. 'Sides, I like to watch you fish. You always been good with a fly rod, even back when you was a shaver."

"I wouldn't say that."

"Don't have to. I just did." Soren started walking down toward the water. Shaking his head, Ty laughed. Then he followed him.

When they got to the water, Ty looked around, then opened a bellows pocket on his fishing vest, took out one of his fly boxes and selected a dry fly, an Adams. He looked at Soren.

"Son, there ain't nothing rising here but your hopes."

"Bet it works."

"I wouldn't take your money. You know I never bet."

"Well, watch and weep." Ty bowed the rod forward and back, false-casting and feeding line until he had a good sixty feet, plus the leader and tippet, working for him. Then he let the line settle to the water, the leader and tippet lying straight out after it, the fly touching down last of all with barely a ripple.

"Nice cast. Too bad it's all for naught."

Ty said nothing, watching the fly. After a minute, he twitched the rod tip upward, making the fly appear to skitter on the water. A minute later, he did it again.

"I ain't weepin' yet, boy."

"Give it time." Ty lifted the rod up, the line, leader, tippet and fly coming with it. He worked the line back and forth in lazy, graceful, curling arcs, the yellow line bright against the blue mountain sky. Then he presented the fly again in exactly the same spot, repeated the trick of making it twitch on the water.

"Tiger, my eyes are dryer'n last year's leaves."

Ty didn't bother to respond. He kept casting. Finally, on the eighth or ninth cast, he patted the vest pocket where he kept the fly box.

"Try me a Muddler minnow if I was you. That, or maybe a woolly bear."

"Hate fishing wet unless I have to. Not as fun. Doesn't look as good."

"Lookin' good's for Natalie Wood."

"Natalie who?"

"Kids." Soren rolled his eyes. "Never mind. Before your time, Tiger. Way before your time."

After another cast, Ty reeled in. He clipped the dry fly from his tippet and hooked it onto the lamb's-wool patch on his vest. Then he opened his wet-fly box. Thumbing through the few flies there, he worked a woolly-bugger pattern out of its holder and held it up for inspection, smiling.

When Soren didn't say anything, Ty looked his way. The old man had turned and was looking off at the cliffs again.

"What'd you do, Soren? Lose something up there?"

"Lose?" Soren turned, his face pale, eyes wide behind his glasses. He looked like a man who had just come awake in surroundings he did not recognize. For a moment he just stood there, his color coming back. Then he smiled. "Ain't lost nothin'. Just takin' it all in. I figure that if they're naming the place after me, I'd best recognize it if somebody shows me a picture."

Ty lifted his head. "You sure that's all there is?"

This time Soren reddened. Then he waved his hand, palm down. "I'm just tired, Tiger. That walk up here this mornin' tuckered me out more than I'd thought it would."

"Well, no wonder. You've been on your feet practically since we got here."

"I may not get up here again. Gotta make it count, you know?"

"Well, why don't you sit down and rest awhile? I can pack the fishing gear and everything else back up, and we can start heading back to camp. Get there while the sun's still high. You can grab some Zs while I cook dinner, once we get there. And then we can turn in early again tonight."

"You can go. I was figuring on stayin' up here till morning."

Ty leaned back a bit. "What?"

"That old hip them doctors give me's actin' up. Don't think I could hike worth beans for the rest of the day. So you go on back. I'll stay up here, and I'll see you back at Clear, come mornin'."

Ty opened his mouth, closed it, blinked. "Soren, we don't have sleeping bags. We don't have ground cloths. I'm not even sure you have a decent jacket in my bag."

"Ain't askin' you to stay, Tiger. Seriously. Got my Case knife in my pocket. I'll just cut me some branches off them spruce, up there on the rise, make me a bed out of them. Be snug as a tick. Nothin' to it. Done it before—many times."

"Soren, I'm not leaving you up here all night by yourself."

The old man's face reddened again, but it was stern this time. "Don't you baby me, Tyler. Don't you dare. I'm a grown man."

"I'm not . . ." Ty looked skyward, then back at Soren. "All right. How about I do this—how about I run back to camp, get what we need for a bivouac, bring it back?"

The corners of the old man's mouth twitched up, then down again. "You was gonna do that afore we left this mornin', and I talked you out of it. Don't make no sense now, you got to hike nine, ten miles, on account of I'm pigheaded."

Ty closed his eyes, laughed, opened them. "Soren, if that was the only thing in my life that didn't make sense right now, I'd be the happiest man alive."

The old man's eyes moistened. "You're a good fella, Tiger. Real good. You always have been."

CHAPTER
TWENTY-ONE

THE EMPTY PACK RIDING HIGH ON HIS BACK, TY WALKED STEADILY up the steep, sloping talus, like a man making his way up a slate roof. When he got to the flat ground at the notch in the cliff, he turned, taking in the long expanse of the lake, the rough-toothed ramparts of mountain around it: different now in the afternoon, darker and less majestic.

He looked along the lakeshore and found the blue block of bib overalls and the green dot of Soren's John Deere ball cap. The old man was walking along the water and he stopped and waved.

Ty waved back. Then he stepped around the corner and into the early afternoon sunlight at the top of the draw. Blinking, he gave himself a moment to adjust to the change in the light. Then he made his way down to the trail.

Ty walked with his head up, eyes scanning the trail ahead— left, then right, then center. He moved with the gait and economy of a man who had been marching for years—a steady pace allowing him the breath to hum as he walked, yet covered the ground quickly.

The way back was mostly downhill, but he did not trot or hurry, did not make the sort of novice mistake that could turn an ankle and leave him injured and stranded miles from the nearest assistance. Instead, he planted each foot heel first, going then to the flat of his sole, and finally to the ball of his foot, where he pushed off, one stride taking him into the next.

Forty-five minutes after leaving the draw, he was not winded, did not show the slightest sign of fatigue, but he stopped just after the peak of a rise in the trail, shed the light pack and took out his water bottle, drinking in small, controlled sips. He did not sit, but leaned against the smooth water-worn granite of a half-buried boulder at the side of the trail. It was quiet when he stopped, but after a minute, perhaps two, birds began to call again from the pines in the forest below, the sound of them distinct, startlingly so, in the cool, still air.

A rustling sounded from ground level off to the side, and Ty turned that way.

A golden mantled ground squirrel—like a chipmunk, only slightly larger—scurried among the bases of the pines. As it came to a trunk, it would stop, dig frantically in the pine needles for several seconds, sit up, look around and then run on to the next tree, where it repeated the ritual.

Ty chuckled. "You lose something, fella?"

The ground squirrel ran off into the underbrush.

Ty grinned. Then he looked up for a moment, and after that,

he glanced back in the direction of Cirque Lake. Bit by bit, the grin faded from his face.

It took him just forty minutes more of steady walking to get to the turnoff to Clear Lake. Ten minutes later he was at the campsite, shucking his pack next to the fire ring.

Both his and Soren's Vibram boot prints were visible in the coarse sand around the ring. The only prints that overlay those were two different sizes of cloven hoof prints—a white-tailed doe and her fawn. The prints were fairly close together, indicating the deer had been walking slowly, not alarmed in the least by anything nearby.

Nodding to himself, Ty straightened up and glanced around. Soren's bag was lying on its ground cloth, so he started there, finding the sleeping bag's stuff sack under its foot, and stuffing the down-filled bag into the sack, the bag compressing and disappearing into the smaller sack like some Las Vegas magic trick.

He put the sleeping bag into his pack, lifted the ground cloth by the edge and shook it, scattering pine needles and dried earth, and then folded and rolled the ground cloth, clean side out, setting it aside for the moment.

Next he turned his attention to the tent, unzipping first the rain fly and then the mosquito netting, followed by the inner door. He packed his own sleeping bag and retrieved a ground cloth from the corner, leaving his thin foam sleeping pad where it was.

Ty glanced at his watch and then left the tent, walking off into the clearing in the woods where the bear bag hung, and getting it down so he could take out a minimal amount of provisions—granola, freeze-dried beef stroganoff, powdered eggs, plus Ziploc bags of coffee, sugar and powdered milk. Then he rehung the bag and walked back to camp with his possibles.

He put the food in the top of the main pocket of the pack, looked around the camp, then ducked into the tent one more time. There was a small pile of things he had emptied from his pack before they'd left for Cirque that morning, and from those he selected a pair of clean socks, a grommeted poncho that could double as a makeshift shelter, parachute cord and a candle lantern. Then, as he was gathering those into a pile, his hand brushed a small black book.

Scowling, he picked it up. Then his scowl went away; it was a pocket Bible, the one Edda had given him for Soren before they'd left the house in Pinedale. Tapping its cover twice, Ty tucked the Bible into his shirt pocket, gathered up the rest of the things, secured the tent, put the belongs into his pack, tied the ground cloths on top where they couldn't shed dirt on anything else and hefted the pack onto his shoulders for the return trip to Cirque Lake.

The sun was low by the time Ty got near the cirque, his shadow long and thin before him, touching the rock at the base of the draw several seconds before he got to it. His pack was a little heavier now than it had been in the morning, and he went up the draw carefully, using his hands to steady himself on one part.

When he stepped through the notch at the top of the draw, the lake and everything around it was in shadow, the only sunlight the pink of alpenglow on the mountain peaks beyond the farther shore. Ty blinked to let his eyes adjust and then he saw, in the blue of the shadows, the flickering orange spark of a fire down by the lake, just a little way back from the shore. He resettled the pack on his shoulders, tightened the waist belt and made his way down the talus.

"Hey," he said as he stepped out of the shadows. "You built a fire ring."

"Hey, yourself," Soren said. He nudged a piece of driftwood farther into the flames. "Yeah. I didn't see no ring anywhere around here, and I figured the lake could use one, just in case folks want to fish here and cook their catch after the lake gets my name. So I built one. That young man'a Kathy's would probably have a fit if he knew—them Forest Service folks don't want to change nothin' unless they do a study and have a meeting first. But I been building fire rings in the Wind River Range for fifty years, and ain't nothin' or nobody died of it yet. Besides, I figured it would help you find me."

"That it did. And it'll keep the bugs off too."

"If this breeze stays the way it is, it will."

Ty shed his pack. "You hungry?"

The old man shrugged. "Ain't done much to *get* hungry. Then again, *you* did enough walkin' today for three men. So if you want to cook somethin' up, go right ahead. I imagine I can have a plate too, once you cook it."

So Ty cooked up the stroganoff while Soren cleared a spot for their sleeping bags. The old man walked over two patches of lake gravel, tossing all the larger rocks to the side. Then he walked over the patches again, kicking with his heels into the pebbles, digging pockets for their hips and shoulders and heels, inspecting his work under the little light clipped to his cap. He laid the ground cloths out, shook the sleeping bags to get the loft back into them, and set them out as well. Only then did he accept a plate from Ty, and he ate in silence, looking at the distant peaks against the darkening sky as he chewed.

Ty broke with protocol, washing the cook kit as well as preparing the meal, and Soren did not object. The old man was already in his bag by the time Ty unzipped his own, and as Ty slid down into the cool nylon, he smiled in the dark.

"I'd forgotten about this," he said. "How you used to dig sleeping spots for us in the sand or gravel. It's comfortable."

"That's the idea," Soren replied. He took his glasses off, their lenses throwing back the red of the dying fire. "Well, I think I'll catch some winks. G'night, Tiger."

"Good night, Soren."

Two minutes later, the old man was steadily snoring.

Orion was high in the sky, the three stars of the sword twinkling in the thin air, when Ty awoke. He scratched his head and looked at his watch: the glowing green dots of the tritium face showed it was just past a quarter of two. A shadow moved between him and Orion.

"I wake you up?" Soren asked.

"No," Ty lied. "I was just looking at the stars."

The shadow moved. "You're a good fella, Tiger. Sorry I woke ya. Go on back to sleep; I just gotta take me a little walk."

Ty nodded in the dark. "Be careful. Don't trip over a rock."

"Not to worry. Got me a light."

The old man's shadow moved away. When it got about twenty feet distant, Ty saw Soren lift his hand and the little light on his cap bill switched on. Ty settled down in his sleeping bag and went back to sleep.

An hour later, he came awake, brushing at a mosquito buzzing near his ear. He sat up and looked over at the old man's sleeping bag.

"Soren?"

Nothing.

Ty peered into the darkness. On Soren's sleeping bag, a lighter wedge showed in the starlight.

Ty reached down into his bag and came out with a small, squat LED flashlight. Thumbing a button at the light's base, he produced a foggy circle of blue-white light, which he played over Soren's bag. The sleeping bag was open, its tan interior the source of the lighter wedge.

Ty switched the light off, waited a moment and then looked at his watch.

"Oh, man . . ."

He sat up and scanned the surrounding darkness. He was making his third pass when he saw it: the briefest play of a small flashlight against the base of the far escarpment, high above the talus slope. Ty took a breath, cupped his hands to his mouth, then lowered them. Sighing audibly, he reached under the hood of his sleeping bag, found his jeans and pulled them on. Then he put on his boots, laced them tight and, flashlight in hand, stood up.

Ty kept the flashlight switched off as he walked, moving slowly up and across the slope of broken rock because there was no moon—only starlight. He kept looking up at the surrounding cliffs and twice again he saw it: a small light shining against the granite base of the rock. Each time, Ty reoriented himself and kept making his way steadily up the talus.

He reached the bottom of the escarpment and looked both ways along its base. The light shone again about sixty feet to the north of him, so Ty went that way, planting his feet carefully, making virtually no sound at all.

He was almost on top of him, no more than ten feet away, when he saw the old man. And there was this sound, a *huh-huh-huh* that sounded something like laughter but was not laughter at all.

"Soren?"

Ty switched on his flashlight, and the old man turned around.

Tears were running down his face.

CHAPTER
TWENTY-TWO

"SOREN? WHAT'S WRONG?"

The old man wiped at his face with the back of his shirt cuff, closed his eyes, shook his head and waved Ty away, his palms out.

"Soren?"

"Go away, Tyler." His voice came out weak, punctuated by sobs. "Leave me . . . leave me be."

"I'll do nothing of the sort. It's the middle of the night." Ty moved nearer. "What's going on?"

Soren's face softened. Then he turned away. "No, Tiger." Soren spoke to the rock face, not to his friend. "No. This here ain't nothing I ever wanted to get you involved in. It sure ain't. You're a good kid . . . a good man. I got no business pulling you any further into this."

Ty swept his flashlight beam around. There was nothing but broken rock, the cliff face, the darkness, and above them, the glowing white pinpoints and fog of thousands upon thousands of stars.

"Pull me any further into what, Soren?"

The old man shook his head again and looked back at the rock. "I thought I could do it. I done it before, didn't I? But that was years ago. And now? Now I just can't."

Ty exhaled, an audible huff.

"Can't what, Soren?" He glanced at his watch. "Come on; it's going on three o'clock."

The old man held his left hand up as if to protest again, but then he dropped it, his shoulders sagging. He looked Ty in the eyes, shook his head, then turned and placed his hand on a slab of rock about five feet high, which leaned against the cliff face.

"It's this thing," he said. "Took me most'a the day to find it. It was mostly buried by rockfall, and I got that all cleared away while you was gone to the camp. But I couldn't move it then. I thought maybe I was too tired. Thought maybe I could come do it now. But I can't."

He kicked at the slab of rock with the toe of his cream-soled work boot. "I been tryin' and tryin' and tryin', and it just won't budge."

Ty looked at the slab, looked at Soren. "That's what you're doing up here? You're trying to move this rock?"

Soren did not answer.

"Why?"

The old man's shoulders sagged even further.

"You'll see," he told Ty. "You'll see."

Ty set the flashlight down, leaning it against a stone so the beam shone on the thick granite slab. He approached the stone, placed a hand on either side of it and pushed—first to one side, then to the other.

It didn't budge.

"You say you put this here by yourself?"

Soren nodded. "Years ago. Years and years. Must've settled in. As I recall, I sort of moved it downhill to get it here."

Ty quit trying to move the slab to the side and instead gripped it at the top, getting his fingertips behind the edge, and pulled with all his might. Finally, it broke loose and slid maybe an eighth of an inch. Letting the slab settle back into place, Ty looked behind him.

"Okay. Soren, you'll want to step over to the side, out of the way."

The old man, now holding Ty's flashlight, did as he was told.

"All right." Ty gripped the top of the slab again and pulled it back—an inch, two inches, six . . . "Watch yourself." He gave it one last tug and then stepped back.

The slab balanced on its edge for a few seconds, then toppled over, striking a low boulder as it fell flat, and breaking in two with a loud crack and a brief scattering of blue-white sparks. There was a momentary rumble as the top part continued downhill, the sound of the crashing rock echoing back hollowly from the other peaks across the black, empty expanse of the lake.

"Wow. You hear that?" Ty looked back, in the direction of the echo.

"Soren?"

But the old man wasn't looking across the lake. He was pointing the flashlight into a cleft in the cliff face, a cleft that had been hidden by the slab, and he was sobbing again.

CHAPTER

TWENTY-THREE

THE CLEFT IN THE ROCK FACE WAS NO MORE THAN A YARD WIDE, and roughly that high as well. A few feet in from the opening were six objects. The largest of them was a pack frame—just the frame, with no pack attached. On its waist belt was a water bottle in a carrier and an old nylon belt pouch, its waterproofing creased and whitened and peeling away at the edges. Next to the frame sat a pair of dusty brown boots, the low-heeled sort that cattlemen referred to as *ropers*. A belt with a rodeo-style buckle was folded and stuck into one of the sagging boots.

But it was the other two objects in that small space that drew the eye. Atop the pack lay a gun belt, the ivory grips and rusted hammer of a six-gun protruding from the holster. And next to the pack, propped up like a broom in a closet, stood a lever-action rifle with a telescopic sight.

"What's going . . . ?" Ty turned to Soren. "Whose stuff is this?"

The old man did not answer. He handed Ty the flashlight

and, bending low, reached into the gap and picked up first the belt and then the boots, dust falling from them and dancing in the flashlight beam as he lifted them. Then, with belt and boots clutched to his chest with one hand, his weathered hiking staff in the other, Soren turned and began to pick his way downhill, the headlamp on his cap bill a blue-white spark in the hollow, encompassing darkness of the cirque.

With the flashlight gripped in his teeth, Ty pulled the pack to the front of the cleft and took the pistol from the gun belt. It was a .44 Magnum Ruger Blackhawk, the old model, and someone had obviously put some money into the gun: the yellowed grips looked to be genuine ivory, and the entire pistol had been nickel-plated. On top of the hammer, where a man's thumb would fall as he cocked the trigger, a small patch of trigger guard on the right side and the once-blued trigger were the only parts that looked rusted, the plating having apparently worn through on the hammer and guard from heavy use. The gun belt was Spanish-tooled latigo leather, dried out now, but it looked expensive. The cartridge loops were full of tarnished brass .44 Magnum rounds, all except for the center loop, which held a longer rifle cartridge of some type.

Returning the gun to its holster and setting it aside, Ty opened the belt pouch, the brittle fabric tearing as he did it. There were only a few things inside: plastic sheet like you'd use as a ground cloth, a cardboard box of .30-30 Winchester cartridges for the rifle, a plastic bag full of what looked to have once been beef jerky, some parachute cord, a hooked-end knife of the type that hunters used for skinning a kill, a wire saw of the kind that survivalists favored, and a map of the southern part of the Wind River Range. A single X was marked on the map, at a trailhead. Other than that, there were no markings at all, no clues to the identity of who'd carried it.

Ty turned and looked down the cirque. Soren was about halfway down to the lakeshore, the bobbing light on his cap marking his progress.

Ty looked at the rifle next. It was a Model 1894 Winchester, a model from the early sixties or before, with the steel butt plate and the forged receiver. It had not fared as well as the pistol; the once-blued steel of the rifle was now gritty with rust, the walnut stock cracked and split from years in the elements. The scope was a Leupold that someone had obviously spent some money on. Ty tried the action, but the lever only moved a fraction of an inch; the insides of the rifle had rusted tight.

Ty put the rifle back where he had found it and, picking up the dusty, cracked gun belt and its revolver and folding them under his arm, set off down the talus after Soren.

The old man was sitting next to the darkened fire pit, the boots still clutched to his chest, when Ty got there. Setting the gun belt aside, Ty leaned over the fire pit, raked the coals with a stick and blew on the red embers until they danced with flame. Then he added kindling, patiently waiting until the fire was going enough to stoke it further with driftwood.

Soren was rocking silently, pitch darkness behind him, the dancing flames reflected in his glasses, hiding all expression in his eyes. Ty took the boots from his lap.

They were a big man's boots, size twelve, and the belt was a big man's belt, well over a yard long. The buckle was tarnished silver inlaid with a bright yellow metal that could only be pure gold, a nice piece of workmanship with a longhorn skull carved in its center. But again there was no inscription, nothing to identify the owner. And there was nothing else in the boots but the belt.

Ty set them aside, next to the gun belt. He looked up; the sky was still a field of stars against a velvet black. Then he turned to Soren.

"Do you want to tell me what this is all about?"

A gray fog of light flared and died very low in the night sky over the saddle, far to the southwest. Soren turned toward it, waited for it to happen again.

"Lightning," he said. "Passin' south of us. But it don't smell like rain, does it? I don't like that. Nope. I don't like it one bit. Trees, grass—everything's way too dry. We're livin' in kindling— rain's what we need, not lightning."

Ty waited.

"So." Soren turned back to him. "Do I want to tell you what this is all about? No, sir, I surely do not. But I have to, Tiger. You seen this much. It's only fair. I have to tell you the whole thing."

Ty nodded toward his backpack. "Air's on the brisk side. Want me to get some cocoa out and brew it up before you start?"

The old man shook his head. "This here ain't your hot-cocoa sort of story."

CHAPTER
TWENTY-FOUR

"I don't know as you remember when I was Sublette County Sheriff," Soren began. "It was back when your daddy was still—well, back when you was just a little shaver. I remember coming to see you when I would get off duty and you could just barely walk. Had to leave my pistol in the truck, on account of otherwise it was all you wanted to see. Don't know if that was because of television, or something just bred into little boys, but you was crazy for guns back then. Come to think of it, I remember reading about you winning all them important matches when you was servin' in the Marines, so I suppose maybe it was something that never went away. Anyhow, I was sheriff for two terms, and then I give it up and let my sub-sheriff run and take over, and he held office until he made retirement age."

Now, I got to tell you, running for sheriff was never my idea. I ain't never been one for politics. Always seemed to me that folks that run for office without provocation done it for one of three reasons—either they figured they could get ahead person-ally while they was in office, or they figured they could get ahead personally once they was done. That or they just wanted to be in the spotlight all the time, which in my book is probably the most dangerous sort of politician of all.

I was none of the three. Leastwise, I hope I wasn't. Like I said, running for office was never my idea, and when folks come to me about it, at first I told 'em I wasn't interested. But as time went by they wore me down. And Miss Edda was on their side, which probably wore me down a lot quicker.

You see, the thing was that the old sheriff was retiring—moving down to Arizona, which is what lots of folks from around these parts do once they retire—and there was this rancher, up-country, near the foothills of the Winds, a fellow by the name of Virgil McLane, and he was not only making noise about running for the office but was being pretty awful free with his money, throwing picnics for just about anybody that could vote, or get registered, legal or not, and cozying up to the folks what owned the newspaper and the old AM radio station.

Well, I figured if a man wants something all that bad, a body just might as well let him have it. Being sheriff ain't no bed of roses, especially when you got to do things like oversee sales of property for overdue taxes—that didn't happen all that often back when I was comin' up, but it happened every once in a while, and I can remember a couple of times it happened to good people who had just fallen on hard times. And let me tell you, you want to be moved to tears, you just watch somebody get moved off a homestead their great-granddaddy carved out with his own sweat and blood.

Now, this was about the time that a bunch of folks around here got in trouble on some oil speculation. Word was that this was one of the main reasons McLane wanted the job. He was hoping those folks would go up the creek financially, and he could fix things so cronies of his got an uneven chance to pick up these folks' land for unpaid taxes, hang on to it until he was out of office and then sell it to him for a song: what they call a "straw man sale." That, plus once I was in the job, I'd learn that Virgil McLane and his kin didn't pay much attention to any law that didn't operate in his favor. He pretty much did whatever he wanted, and if somebody raised a fuss, he'd either threaten 'em or bribe 'em until they shut up, and if that didn't work, he had him some Cheyenne lawyers that could talk the siding right off a barn, and either drag things out until the outcome didn't matter, or confuse the issue so much that by the time they was done, any sane man would swear that McLane was pure as the driven snow, and Santa Claus was the guilty party. I guess he figured being sheriff would help him along plenty in that regard.

Like I said, I didn't pay me a ton of mind to that. If Virgil McLane wanted to carry on like that, why he was the fella who had to go to sleep at night knowing he was that way. As the saying goes, the best anyone can do is lead a horse to water; plenty of folks had tried that over the years with Virgil McLane, and he was still the sort of man you didn't want to share a room with for long.

But there was plenty'a good folks concerned that Sublette

County wouldn't be a fit place to live if Virgil McLane became the law there. And as I said, Miss Edda was among 'em. So I flung in my hat.

I didn't campaign all that much at first. About the most I did was go speak at churches—folks wasn't as touchy then about bringing up public issues in the house of the Lord. But as time went on, and scuttlebutt had it that I was pulling way ahead with the voters, McLane started looking for dirt he could dig up on me. And when he didn't find none—he even got some crony of his in the IRS to audit my tax returns, and it come out that the government owed *me* money—well, he started making stuff up.

He knew that back when I was a kid, I helped Finis Mitchell a couple of summers when he was seedin' trout in some of the up-country lakes. We'd put little trout fry in five-gallon milk cans, tie the cans together two by two and put 'em over packhorses and lead 'em up into the mountains. Horses had to keep moving every minute or the oxygen would go out of the water and the trout would die. But old Finis had this down to a science. There wasn't trout in but five lakes in the Wind River Range when he first started seedin' back in the thirties, and by the time I was helpin' him, he'd given anglers more than two hundred places in the range where a body could fish.

We saw it as a way to help all the fishing guides in the area, and the way we looked at it, we was bein' good stewards of the land. But by the time Virgil McLane and his henchmen got done with the story, you'd have sworn old Finis and I was environmental terrorists or something. McLane said we was introducing species and upsetting the natural balance of things, and that we hadn't done no proper studies first.

Well, this was all years ago. When we put those trout in, it was before the war. Nobody even knew what a proper study was, and besides, the state and the Forest Service had given us their blessing. The state even supplied the fry. You know how Wyoming is; sheep and cattle outnumber people here ten to one. There ain't never enough tax money to do all the things that need doin'. The government figured what we was doing could bring sportsmen to the area and help the economy, and so of course they was all for it. But McLane didn't paint it that way. And then, when he said I had upset the wilderness just so I could come back years later and start that fishing camp up at Big Sandy, when he said I had nothing more in mind than making money, regardless of what happened to these here mountains—well, I don't mind tellin' you, that got my dander up.

Now, I didn't give him back what he was givin' me, although I have to tell you—that was more Miss Edda's doin' than it was mine. No, what we did was we took out a mortgage on the house and bought us some billboards, handed out campaign buttons to everybody in the county, except McLane and his kin, and made up bumper stickers, even hats—I think maybe I still got a hundred of those still sittin' in the root cellar back home.

That got even more people noticin', and the more McLane tried to toss dirt my way, the more I talked about how I was plannin' to make the Sheriff's Department better organized, more able to respond, the extra training I thought we should get so deputies could respond to heart attacks and the like when the folks havin' the problem was too far from the Fire Department. Other folks chipped in to help with the campaign, and that kept me from gettin' in too deep with the bank.

Pretty soon the newspaper and the radio station was talkin' to me. They had to. I was news now. And when they asked me about the lies McLane was spreadin' about me, I just told 'em, "Mr. McLane knows that none of that stuff is true." And when they asked me why he was sayin' it then, I said, "I expect he's sayin' it because he wants to get elected sheriff."

Thanks to Miss Edda's cool head, the more McLane raved, the smarter and more levelheaded I looked to the voters. Election day come, I got seventy-one percent of the vote. And what do you think McLane did? He didn't offer no concession speech; he didn't shake my hand. He demanded a recount. But the election commissioner said, "Soren got seventy-one percent, and that don't leave no room for doubt, Virgil. Besides, you ain't the boss of me, and you can't demand nothin'."

So that was it. I put on the badge.

They say that if you want to see the worst side of your community, you ought to go into law enforcement. And I suppose there's a lot of truth to that. I know that my deputies and I wound up in livin' rooms around the county that I never in my life would have thought we'd be visitin' on official business. Friends' houses, preachers' houses, folks at the head of civic organizations, you name it.

But I also got to see a lot of good in people. I saw people that didn't have nothin'—folks that was livin' paycheck to paycheck and waxin' lean in between—comin' out and pitchin' in when somebody had a house fire, or spending the whole night walkin' a search line when one family's little girl come up missing about a year after I took the office. Found her too. Safe and sound . . . safe and sound.

I guess I should've known when I run that I'd end up out at Virgil McLane's place as well. Not that he ever called me. Neither did any of his kin, although from what I hear, his wife had plenty of reason to call the law, which was probably why she spent so much time out East.

But things must've been better between them at one time, either that or McLane's missus was willin' to tolerate him, because they had a son.

Parker was his name. Parker McLane. And I hope to tell you, that apple didn't fall too far from the tree.

Which was too bad, because this Parker was a good-lookin' kid. I mean movie-actor good-lookin'. Guess you could even say *charming*, because you walked into a room and saw him there, you wanted to like him. *Did* like him until he got the first two or three words out of his mouth. Then you didn't want nothing to do with him.

Lester Sykes, the fella that was sheriff before me, gave me the lowdown on Parker. Just a bad apple, pure and simple, even when he was small. I won't go into details, but some of the stuff Lester got sent out there to the McLane place on, it was the Humane Society that was the complainant. Virgil made it all go away, of course. Either he'd write a donation and the complaint would be dropped, or those lawyers of his would make things look like an accident. But Parker McLane was one of the few human beings I ever met that I could honestly say I thought of as pure evil. It even occurred to me that maybe one of the reasons Virgil had run for office was because he figured maybe he could use the position to keep his boy out of trouble. Like maybe there was a heart inside all his rough and bluff, after all.

Anyhow, by the time I come on the scene, we didn't have no trouble with Parker most of the year, because his momma had taken to livin' back East, and Parker was bein' sent to school out there. Bein' sent and bein' kicked out was more like it, because I guess he went through seven or eight of them fancy boarding schools before he found one that would graduate him. Then he was off to college—out East again—and either the college was more tolerant or his daddy had written a big enough check to *make* 'em tolerant, because he stuck in the one school for a change.

But summers he was back at the ranch, and summers were a different story.

I remember the first time Parker and I bumped heads. I was headed home for supper. It weren't late at all, maybe five in the afternoon, but there was this pickup truck weaving all over the road ahead of me, and it was plain as day that whoever was drivin' was dead drunk. I put the beacon up on the dash and pulled him over, and it was Parker. He didn't have a license—he'd lost it the year before, for DUI—but he told me he didn't *need* no license on account of the truck was a farm vehicle, and he was takin' it over to one of his daddy's pieces'a property to do a job.

Well, that was somethin' he could say just about anytime. His daddy had little ranches and property and pasture all over the county, even a couple across the county line, down Labarge way. So just about any direction a body headed, he was headed toward McLane land, and as far as the law was concerned back then, a farm truck was the same as a tractor or a combine, or whatever. No license required to operate it, and the law allowed use of the roadway to get it from one place to the other.

So I couldn't write Parker for operating without a license, but I *could* decide he was impaired and a nuisance and a menace to traffic, and so I did that. I called me a deputy over to drive the truck and follow me back to the ranch, and I took the boy—he was more man than boy, I mean, he was of age—but anyhow, I took him home.

I could have done a heap worse. The way that kid was driving, it wouldn't have taken any imagination whatsoever to see as to how he could easily have killed somebody in that condition. That, plus public drunkenness is a misdemeanor. And operating impaired is operating impaired, whether it's a farm vehicle or a car. But I figured that gettin' him home would remedy the situation, and besides, his daddy already had a chip on his shoulder as far as I was concerned, and I thought maybe showing Parker some leniency would maybe smooth the waters between us, you know?

But I thought wrong. Old Virgil must've seen us comin' as we pulled up his lane, because he was standin' on that big porch of his when we got there, a six-gun strapped on his hip like he was John Wayne or somethin'.

That in itself don't mean a thing. Wyoming's an open-carry state. You strap a pistol on where folks can see it, and you can go pretty much anywhere you choose, except maybe a courtroom or a jail and the like. But you know that a gun belt ain't the sort of thing that a body wears while havin' dinner with the missus or watching the ball game on TV, so it was obvious that Virgil put the gun on just for us. That, and it was like I said before—he always thought of himself as some sort of old-time Wild West character, and I think he liked the feeling of making other folks uncomfortable.

I didn't, so I left my gun belt in the car. But before I could get two words out of my mouth, Virgil starts in ranting and raving about how I was trying to intimidate his family, and how if a real man had a quarrel with him, he'd come see him face-to-face. Well, that gets my deputy goin', and pretty soon McLane and him is standin' toenail to toenail, and the job's changed—now I'm trying to keep *those* two from coming to blows. Parker ain't no trouble by this point; Parker's barely standing, so he just stumbles on into the house and he's gone.

I got my deputy back into my truck, and I told Virgil to keep his boy off the bottle before he let him near the truck keys again, and that got Virgil mouthing off all over, but I told my deputy to stay put in my truck, and I got in as well. That was about all there was to it, but it was enough to get the bad blood going even stronger between us, as far as the McLanes was concerned, and all I got for my trouble was a warmed-over supper.

I don't know; maybe things would have come out better if I'd just run Parker in to the jailhouse for his own safety. As it was, the chip on Virgil McLane's shoulder sure grew a couple sizes bigger that day.

We'd bump heads again. Or I should say, his boy and I did. You see, Parker had him an appetite for more than whiskey. He fancied himself a ladies' man, and for that matter, he probably was one. Like I said, the boy could turn on the charm and keep it on if he thought it would work things to his favor.

But once he seen a girl three or four times, word was that he would either get all possessive and suspicious, or he'd find something with them that rubbed against his grain, and apparently he'd take it out on them the way folks said his daddy took it out on his momma. A couple of girls went home with black eyes, and one got a fat lip.

Problem was, there wasn't anybody willing to file a complaint against Parker. Most of these girls came from families that had business dealings with Virgil McLane. If you sold feed or farm machinery, or even diesel fuel, Virgil was probably your number-one customer. And the ones who didn't come from families like that, Virgil paid 'em to shut 'em up, and got his lawyers to scare people into thinkin' he'd sue for defamation of character if anything wound up in the papers or in court. So that all got swept under the rug.

Still, Sublette County may have lots of land to it, but population-wise it's a pretty small place. There still ain't any more than seven thousand people in the whole county even now, and back in the time what I'm talkin' about, I suspect it was a lot less than six. Place that small, word travels fast. Maybe it was because nobody his age would have anything to do with him anymore, or maybe it was just another form of sick comin' out, but next thing you know, Parker McLane was messin' around with underage girls.

Now, I know I started courtin' Miss Edda when I was twenty-two and she was just sixteen—fact, we was them same ages when we married—but that was back when folks married younger, and besides, when I say I was courtin' her, that's just what I mean. I was seein' her with an eye toward marryin', and right up until the day we got married we weren't ever alone for one moment. Her momma or her daddy was always right there. I got it in my mind to treat Miss Edda to a restaurant dinner or a movie, I was treatin' her folks too, but we didn't do that all that often. Mostly our courtship consisted of me visiting with Edda and her folks, right there in their front parlor.

That's not how Parker McLane was operating. About this time, he was a twenty-five-year-old man, and he was sneakin' around seeing high school girls—girls sixteen, sometimes fifteen years old. He had his license back by then, and he had him a fancy red Corvette convertible. He'd offer girls rides. Next thing you know, out comes a bottle, he gets 'em drunk and I don't need to tell you what comes after that.

That's three or four laws broke right there, and I don't need no complaint to prosecute somethin' like that. First time I got word of it, I run Parker in, Virgil McLane and his six-gun and his lawyers notwithstandin'. I was ready to throw the whole book at him.

Problem was, again there wasn't anybody willing to testify. Between not wantin' to parade their daughters' goings-on out in front of the community and being scared of McLane money and McLane lawyers, there wasn't a single family willing to come forward and say what had to be said to send Parker McLane on up to Rawlins, where he belonged. I even took to havin' a deputy tail Parker, to see if we could catch him picking up an underage girl, but he got wise to us. Besides, a county our size didn't have but a handful of deputies, and I didn't have the manpower to keep that up for long.

But once I run Parker in a couple of times, word got out around the county, and folks began keepin' a closer eye on their teenage daughters. Same with Lincoln County, Teton County— pretty much everybody learned to stay clear. So Parker began to look elsewhere.

I know he got in some of the same trouble over in Utah, but he didn't have no record, except for the DUIs, and his lawyers was able to dicker the charges down to a misdemeanor, and he never brought none of the girls across the state line, so it never become federal. Still, the next time would've been a different story, so Parker stuck with Wyoming after that, but he moved over to the other side of the Continental Divide, over Dubois and Lander way.

I don't need to tell you that, once you cross these mountains, it's like another world. Sure, Pinedale and Lander may look no farther away from one another on the map than Pinedale and Jackson. But while Jackson and Pinedale folks may see one another all the time, you don't never see anybody from over on the west side of the range unless they got business matters or kin there. That's because there ain't no direct route between the two—you got the highest mountains in the state standing in the way. You want to go from Pinedale to the east side of the Winds, you go to 191 south and then 28 north again. That's a whole lot of drivin'—drivin' up and down, as well as south and north—to get not very far, and most folks don't want to go through the trouble. Ain't much in Lander that you can't get in Jackson, and Jackson's a heap closer when it comes to driving distance.

'Course, Parker McLane knew that too, so he took to drivin' down on Friday nights to Route 28, headin' up to them towns on the east side of the range, and seein' what he could find. And what he found was Lucy Washington.

As we put things together later, Lucy was fifteen years old when Parker McLane and her first met. And maybe I should say in his defense that she didn't look fifteen; she looked older. Not that I ever laid eyes on her myself; pictures is all I ever saw. But even in them pictures I could tell that she was beautiful. And I don't mean pretty in the way that just about any fifteen-year-old girl is pretty. I mean movie-actress beautiful. I guess over Riverton way, where she lived on the reservation, she was famous for it.

Lucy's mother was a great-great-granddaughter of Chief Washakie of the Shoshones. The Shoshone always was a handsome people, but Lucy was even somethin' above that. Folks was tellin' her parents that she ought to get in one of them pageants, win her a college scholarship. That sounded good to them, because she wanted to be a doctor, and they figured if they could get the first four years free, they'd be ahead of the game.

So they had some pictures taken by a professional—of her wearing a fancy ball gown, and another in traditional dress. Even in them still photos, you could tell she had a bearin' about her that most girls don't get until they're college age, if then. She looked smart—clever, but in a regal sort of way. And with her long black hair and those clear brown eyes and high cheekbones, she was a real knockout.

From what we was able to piece together later, Lucy was taking dancing lessons. Not the Arthur Miller kind, but Shoshone dancing, for the dances they do at their powwows. There was talk of making her Miss Eastern Shoshone Festival the next year when she turned sixteen, sort of a way for her to get started on pageants, and she wanted to be able to dance if that happened.

The lady what taught the dancing was outside of town, living on a little ranch, and like lots of Shoshone families back then, Lucy's family only had the one car. So she hitched rides; it was common enough on the reservation. And one day, while she was hitchin', the car that stopped to pick her up was Parker McLane's shiny new red Corvette.

Just the fact that Lucy got in the car with him was something real rare for a reservation girl. Young or old, the Shoshone usually won't get in a car with someone they've never met; they're a sensible people that way. But like I said, Parker McLane could be a charmer when he wanted. And Lucy had somethin' of an independent streak. Folks said it was part of what made her seem older than she was. She was confident.

Anyhow, she got in the car and he drove her out to her dancing lesson. Next week comes, and he drives her out again. And the week after that, he picked her up but she never showed up for her dancing lesson; fact was, she was hit-and-miss about it for the next few months. She begged her teacher not to tell her parents, said she had her a beau. Of course, the teacher said she thought at the time that Lucy was talking about a Shoshone boy.

This is where it gets quizzical. Parker McLane's track record was a new girl every few weeks. That was about all the time it took for him to find a reason to have a fallin' out with 'em. But as far as we were able to put together, he saw Lucy Washington once, sometimes twice a week, over the next six or seven months. And he wasn't going out with anybody else. He even showed up to see her crowned Miss Eastern Shoshone Festival when she got selected—lots of folks saw him there, and while they didn't know who he was, they picked him out easy enough in a state police lineup later on.

And you don't go drivin' no brand-new red Corvette around the reservation without it bein' noticed. First time the tribal police saw him, they thought it might be stolen, so they tailed him and run the plates. When it came up a Sublette County plate, they figured, "Okay, that's just the next county over." So they never stopped him. But the policeman remembered doin' it, and he remembered that the car was registered to Virgil McLane. He also said that was the last time he saw that particular car, but this was late fall. Winter was coming on, and you don't drive no Corvette in the winter—not through the mountains in Wyoming. We figure he kept seein' her, but he switched over to one of his daddy's pickups. And the reservation's like anyplace else in Wyoming; you can't throw a rock without hittin' some old pickup.

Six, seven months go by, and Lucy is sixteen now, and she's told one or two close friends about Parker. Looks as if she was in love with him. Who knows? Seein' as he kept coming back for so long, maybe Parker was in love with her too, or as close to in love as a person like Parker McLane could get.

But after seven months, somethin' happens. Exactly what, ain't nobody sure, leastways nobody who's talkin'. My first thought, trying to piece things together, was that Lucy Washington got pregnant. The chief of the tribal police didn't want to think that way of her. He said she was one of the nicest girls he ever knew; he thought maybe Virgil McLane found out who his son was seeing and just forbade him from going over there anymore. Either way, the same thing happened. Parker McLane stopped coming to the reservation, and that tore Lucy Washington up plenty.

The last few days, we got good details here and there. Lucy told her best friend that she wanted to hear it from Parker, face-to-face, if he didn't want to see her anymore. I guess she didn't want to call him from home, because her father would see the number on the long-distance bill, and the few times she'd tried from a pay phone, old Virgil had answered, and she'd lost her nerve and hung up.

She had her driver's license by then, but no car. Her folks had gone to Laramie for the weekend, and she was at home watching her little brother. About an hour after her parents leave, she takes the brother over to a neighbor's house and asks if they can watch him until about midnight or so. Says she's going to the movies up in Dubois. The neighbor lady says sure, and Lucy walks to the south part of town and hitches a ride out with a fellow from the reservation, a guy that's driving down to Salt Lake to pick up a grandkid who's comin' home from college.

The fella that picked her up knew her, and said he was surprised to see her leaving the reservation. She told him some story about a cousin coming up to meet her from Green River and said she was trying to shorten her drive by hitching down to 191. From there, they was going to meet and drive up and spend the weekend in Jackson Hole.

Fella remembered this, because Lucy didn't have a suitcase. All she had was this little purse. He asked her, "How you gonna spend the weekend without a change of clothes?" And she said her cousin was bringing them, which struck him as odd.

He drove her to 191, but there wasn't no car there. He offered to wait with her for her cousin, but she wouldn't hear of it. So he dropped her off and continued on down to the south. Then, about ten minutes down the road, his conscience started naggin' on him, so he turned around and went back. But when he got back to the intersection, Lucy was gone. And that was the last time anybody from the reservation ever laid eyes on her.

Now, here's the strangest part. The person that picks her up on 191? It's one of my deputies. He'd just sold a quarter horse to a fellow down in Rock Springs, and he was running back to Pinedale with the empty trailer. Fact is, he knew he'd be runnin' close to his shift start, so he had his uniform hanging from the rifle rack in his pickup truck. Lucy gets in, sees that, sees the police radio mounted under his dash, and she asks if she's in trouble. He asks, "Why? You just rob a bank?" And she says, "No—for the hitchhiking." And he tells her, "Maybe in some places, but not here."

Of course, he asks her what she's doing out hitchin' alone,

and apparently she's had a few minutes to improve her story, because she tells him that the motor went out on her daddy's station wagon, and that she was running up to the northern part of the county to get a sedan he'd bought—he was gonna pull the engine out of that one and put it in the wagon. And my deputy asks her who's sellin' the sedan, and she says, "A man named McLane."

Well, my deputy says he thought he knew everybody that was selling anything with wheels anywhere in the county, and he'd never heard that the McLanes had a car for sale. She tells him, "Oh no. They didn't have it up for sale. It was just sitting out in the weeds, behind their barn, and my daddy did some roofing for them a while back and remembered seeing it, because it was the same make and year as our wagon. So when our motor died, he called Mr. McLane and asked if he could buy it, and Mr. McLane said to bring him the money and pick it up." And then she said that her daddy had planned on hitchin' up, himself, to get it, but he was feeling poorly, and it had sounded like McLane wanted the car out of there right away, so she'd said she'd come.

My deputy didn't say anything at the time, but he told me later on that he remembered thinking that sounded just like Virgil McLane. First off, if a fella is without a car and he's bad enough off that he's calling you about one you got going to seed off in a field somewhere, the decent thing to do is just offer to give it to him. And second, if you do sell it, it seems as if just about anyone would drive the car down to the fella what bought it and then let him drive you back home. That way nobody has to hitch across empty country. But Virgil McLane was just inconsiderate enough to take money for it and make a body come get it to boot. He'd do that without batting an eye. So, far as my deputy was concerned, that part of the story rang true.

He was real surprised when he come to find out later on that Lucy was only sixteen. She'd seemed a heap lot more grown-up to him—nineteen or twenty, at least. Like I said, she had that impression on people.

The other thing he mentioned was when they was driving along and he had the police radio on low, listening to the dispatcher, and Lucy was looking out the window, he asked her if she wanted to come to the station and call the McLanes before she went out there, and she said that she didn't need to because she had called them before she left home. That was neither here nor there, but he said that when he talked to her, and she turned his way? She'd wiped her face while she was doing it, and he could have sworn she'd been crying.

They get to Pinedale, and my deputy drives her up to the north part of town. She asks how to get to the McLane place, and he says she should keep followin' 191 out for a while, like she's going to Bondurant, but take the second dirt road to the right and follow it north across the Green River and that would lead right to the McLane ranch. He even remembers her taking out this little beaded purse, made of deerskin, and asking if she could give him something for gas, but he told her not to be silly—he'd been goin' her way, and it hadn't cost him a dime.

Then, after he'd come in and changed into his uniform, my deputy said he'd started feeling mighty foolish, because while that girl wouldn't have had any trouble at all getting a ride on 191, that dirt road was another story. You could wait there for

hours and not see a car heading up that old two-track. So as
soon as he started his shift, he headed out there, got to the dirt
road and took it north past the first ranch. But there wasn't no
sign of her, so he'd figured she must've gotten lucky and caught
a ride. Then he got a call and he turned around, and the way
we pieced it together later, he was the last person to see Lucy
Washington alive. Leastwise, the last person other than the one
that made her disappear.

Midnight comes and goes and back on the reservation the
neighbor gets concerned that Lucy hasn't come back to get
her brother. She goes next door, but the house is dark; nobody
answers. She knows Lucy's folks are in Laramie, but that's all
she knows. By one o'clock, she's really worried, so she calls the
tribal police.

The police chief later told me that he'd thought Lucy was just
late coming home from the movies. He offered to send someone by to pick up the little boy, but the neighbor lady said no,
he was already asleep in bed, and she'd keep him for the night.
Then the chief called again in the morning to see if Lucy had
shown up, and when she hadn't, he began calling around to see
if anybody'd seen her. Word gets out that she's missing, and
when the fellow who'd given her a ride down 28 gets back to
the reservation, he hears it and calls the chief to let him know
that he'd taken her over to 191.

That puts her heading on up into Sublette County, so the
chief of the tribal police calls our office to let us know that it
looks as if he's got a teen runaway. I took the call, and I asked
him to send me a picture, so he puts one of her pageant pictures
on the wire. And while it's coming off the teleprinter line by line,

my deputy looks down at it and says, "Hey! I know her. I gave her a ride yesterday. She was heading up to McLane's."

Well, I don't need to tell you that my heart started sinking right there. I called the reservation's chief of police back right away and asked if there was any chance Lucy knew Parker McLane. He had some of his officers there in the ward room with him, and he asked 'em, and the one remembered running a tag on a red Corvette a few months before that come up registered to a McLane in Sublette County. And as soon as he said that, I told him that I had grave fears about his missing teen, and that I figured we had better take the investigation up a notch, right away.

I told him what I knew, and even though there wasn't no criminal conviction against Parker McLane except that one misdemeanor in Utah—weren't no *arrests* except for that one, now that I mention it—he agreed that this put a new light on things. Seeing as he was the one what opened the investigation, he told me he was calling the FBI office in Denver to ask if they would assist. And seeing as I was the closest law enforcement to 'em, I told him I would send deputies up McLane's way to pick Parker up so he wouldn't go anywhere before the FBI got there.

Lucy Washington had already been missing better than twenty-four hours by this time, and while I'd never had reason to suspect Parker McLane of murder before, this girl wasn't falling into any of Parker's old patterns. I was powerful worried she was dead already.

I tell you what, Tiger. In that one single day I learned to hate that job. Things back then wasn't the way they are now. These days, the Sheriff's Department and the reservation both got their hands full with dope rings—them what-they-call-its . . . meth labs. Back when I was sheriff we never had more than five or six prisoners in the jailhouse, and half of them would've been fellas wising up about being more punctual on their child support. But just two, three years ago, the county built a new jail, designed to hold fifty, and there's some folks complaining *that* won't be big enough by half, ten years from now.

Back then, about the most serious thing my office had ever handled was a couple of kids from up Jackson way that was running down here on Saturday nights, when all the ranch hands was off in town, and stealing cattle with a stock trailer. Domestic disturbances, bar fights—that was about as rough as things ever got. And now I was picking up the son of the fella what run against me for my job, and I was pretty sure it would turn out I was picking him up for murder.

Except it never come to that. Oh, the FBI came up, and they questioned everybody. They put Parker McLane in a lineup, and lots of the Shoshone picked him out as having been at their festival, but there ain't no law against that. A few people came forward and said they'd seen Lucy Washington riding in his car or truck, except his lawyers was quick to point out that, on the day she went missing, quite a few people in Pinedale saw her in my *deputy's* truck, and *he* sure wasn't being given no third degree.

So that's how it went. After a couple of weeks, even the FBI had run out of questions to ask. Parker McLane's lawyers had made this big show at first of saying he had nothing to hide, and how they was wantin' to clear him of suspicion so we could get on with findin' the girl. But now they was makin' noise about filing a writ of habeas corpus, and I knew we wouldn't have no answer if they did, so we cut him loose, even though I felt certain he had murdered that girl. Lucy Washington had just vanished without a trace. We couldn't even call it homicide because we didn't have a body . . . didn't have a single person that had so much as seen her in harm's way.

Officially, she was missing. That was all. And that was the way it was when I wrapped up my second stint in the office, and Lucas Baxter, my sub-sheriff, run for the open slot. He ran unopposed, and people said that was an indication of how much esteem the folks of the county held me in. But I knew in my heart of hearts that a defenseless young girl had been killed on my watch, and it vexed me something powerful that not only could I do nothing about that . . . I couldn't even prove it ever happened.

No. Don't say nothin' yet. I'm just gettin' to the part I need to tell you.

I'd thought I was gettin' ready to retire about the time Miss Edda and her gang drafted me to run for sheriff. Now that I was done with that, I figured it was high time I got doin' the things retired folks do. I started that little postcard business. I took Miss Edda shoppin' all the way up to Jackson Hole anytime she wanted. I took you fishin'.

But every once in a while, I got it in my head to do somethin' a little right, probably on account of I never got to do that *big* back when it was my job. There was a couple times I heard about folks comin' up here into the Winds to shoot elk out of season, out of the rut, when the herds hung close together. So I'd get up here before them, chase the herd out of whatever valley they was in, and leave the poachers with nothin' to shoot.

And one week—this was just about the time you went off to join the Marines—I was in the hardware store down in Green River, and the owner there was a fella I knew and he had him a little sporting goods section, fishing and hunting gear, in the back. This was in the spring, late March. The snow was just startin' to melt down in the low country, and this fellow at the hardware was tellin' me as he had a customer come in there earlier in the week buying a couple boxes of .30-30 rifle cartridges and a brand-new Leupold Gold Ring scope. Wouldn't tell me who it was that had bought 'em, but I figured he didn't need to tell me what he had already, so I didn't press it.

Now, you know there ain't no open season for nothin' besides turkey in the spring, and you sure don't use no rifle to hunt turkey. So I start askin' around, and it turns out one of the ranchers that had an airstrip and his own plane had been flyin' over the Winds a couple times the week before, and he'd said he'd found a whole bunch of bighorn sheep holed up here on the slopes next to Cirque Lake, and one of them had a spread on his horns that you could see, even from way up in the air, was real Boone and Crockett material.

Bighorns, of course, ain't like elk or deer. They don't shed antlers at the end of every rut, because they don't have antlers like a deer or an elk or a moose. They got horns, like a cow, and you get an old ram, he might have him an enormous spread on his horns, and there's folks that would like to have something like that on their wall, even if they can't claim it as a record on account of it was taken out of season.

A ram in the spring ain't nothing like a ram in rut. Late winter and spring, rams'll sometimes get together in bachelor flocks and stay that way all the way until summer. But they aren't as aggressive, and they aren't as wary as they are in the rut, and stalkin' 'em goes from hunting a wild animal to shooting, well, a sheep.

So I put two and two together and figure that somebody must be goin' after those bighorns, and I look at the weather on TV and see they're callin' for rain mixed with snow for two days, and then it's gonna let up after that—on a Tuesday, it was—and be clear. Anybody lazy enough to poach sheep in the spring ain't gonna go hiking in the rain. But you know me, there ain't no bad weather as far as I'm concerned; there's just weather, and I'll walk in anything that's mild enough not to blow me over. So if Tuesday's the earliest this bird's gonna show, I figure I can come on up here on the Monday night, chase them sheep away up over the saddle notch down yonder, head back to my truck and leave whoever it is wants to poach 'em with nothin' left to shoot at.

I drove in to Big Sandy trailhead that Monday morning, parked my truck—it was the only vehicle at the trailhead—and headed on up here, pretty much the way you and I come yesterday. I was a lot more spry before my hip broke, and I covered ground pretty quick. I got up to the notch, up top of the draw by late afternoon, glassed the end of the lake, and sure enough there were about ten rams there, and one of 'em had horn tips better than a yard apart.

But I couldn't just run down there and shoo 'em off, because if you spook sheep, they don't just run away. They climb. Them bighorns are mountain animals, and when you frighten them, they head for high ground unless they don't see any other alternative. That's good strategy for a critter tryin' to get away from a catamount, but it don't do no good against a rifle.

So I had to get up on this ridge here, behind us, and make my way down until I was just above 'em. Then I got me two flat rocks and clapped 'em together—sounded just like a shot.

Well, that got the bunch of 'em moving, and I followed from the ridgeline, and when they slowed down I clapped them rocks back together again. I did that four times and all but one of 'em skedaddled over the saddle notch down the cirque. But one didn't. He decided he was gonna climb up the far cliffs instead. And wouldn't you know it? He was the one with the big spread.

I couldn't leave the job half done like that. And I couldn't just stand under him and make noise. That wouldn't do nothin' but force him up higher. So I had to find a gully I could follow up, traverse over to a place where I was above him but still on the lake side and then see if I could make him jump down and bolt for the saddle.

But the doing of it turned out to take a whole lot more time than the telling of it. By the time I'd gotten a considerable ways above that old sheep, the sun was startin' to go down. Then I had to traverse over to a spot where I was sure any noise I'd make would scare him off in the direction of the saddle and not deeper into the cirque. And I hadn't come prepared for climbin', mind you. The most extreme thing I come geared for was a bit of muddy walking.

I got close above him and them horns looked even bigger. To get horns like that, a ram would have to live a heap'a winters, and that takes a pretty smart animal. I was close enough I didn't even have to clap no rocks together. I just yelled, "Git!" and off he went, down the rocks, and he hightailed it for the saddle.

By now it's dusk, and I don't want to be stuck up on that cliff in the dark, so I headed down as fast as I could, still bein' careful. What's the saying? "Make haste, slowly"?

Yet even as I'm comin' down, I'm worried about that old ram. He'd slowed up considerable as he was goin' over the top of that saddle. And that got me thinkin' that maybe he wasn't planning on going all that far. I mean, there was a reason them sheep was holed up in here. They had a break from the wind, they had forage they could get to under the snow, and they had cliffs all around that they could climb to get clear of most critters comin' after 'em. Smart old ram like that, he's not gonna want to get too far away from that sort of easy livin'.

So of course now I'm worried that maybe he's gonna sneak back in here, come dark, and be waitin' here when that poacher shows up. So I hiked on up to the top of the saddle. By the time I got there, it was full dark with the stars out just like they is now. I moved down a ways and found me a spot out of the wind, but not so sheltered that I couldn't hear it if one of them sheep come scrabblin' up the scree.

I didn't have no sleeping bag—not even a ground cloth. But I had me a goose-down jacket and some mitts and a stockin' cap, and I put those on. Then I emptied out my rucksack, took off my gaiters and my boots, and stuck my feet in the rucksack and pulled it up around my legs as high as it would go, and that way I made myself as snug as I could and settled down to spend the night.

Sure enough, about half an hour before dawn, I hear rocks sliding, and there in the starlight I see that old ram and about five of his kin comin' up the scree field. So I chucked a few rocks in their direction and yelled at 'em, and as the rocks were comin' from above, they took off back down the way they come.

They made one more try just afore sunup, but this time I pulled on my boots and chased 'em until they was all the way down, in the trees. Then, after I came back up here to fetch my rucksack, that's when I made my mistake. I hadn't gotten all that much sleep, so I sat down and decided to close my eyes for a bit. Next thing I know, I wake up and my watch says it's two hours later.

Well, I was callin' myself every name I could think of as I trotted up over that saddle. Last thing I wanted to do was to run into the poacher whose day I'd just spoiled.

But that's what I done. I didn't see him at first on account of a lot of this cirque was still in deep shadow, but when I was about halfway down from the saddle, he stepped out into the light on the trail down by the edge of the lake, and I could make him out: a tall, stocky fella wearing a cattleman's hat and a six-gun, bare pack frame on his back, and carrying a lever-action rifle. By this time he'd seen me, so there wasn't nothing to do but keep coming the way I was coming.

It wasn't until I got about seventy yards away that I realized it was Virgil McLane. And he must have recognized me about the same time, because I could see his face take a set, if you know what I mean. So I walked on up and stopped about five, six feet away from him—just far enough that there wouldn't be no mistake that I was tryin' to shake his hand, because I had no intention of doin' that. He didn't say nothin', so I said, "Mornin', Virgil."

And he said, "Morning, my foot. What you doing up here, messing in my business, Andeman?"

I guess it was plain what both of us had been up to. A man don't carry a rifle and a bare pack unless he's planning on shooting something and packing it out—or at least packing out the head and cape, in this case. And as for me, the sun was on that slope leading up to the saddle the way I'd just come. You could see the tracks them sheep had left going up it the day before. It was pretty obvious I'd come in to scare 'em off.

So I said, "Ecclesiastes, Virgil: 'To every thing there is a season.'" Then I pointed at his rifle with this old walkin' pole of mine and I said, "And you know good and well that this here ain't the season for that."

Well, that cattleman's hat that he was wearing put his face in shadow pretty good, but even so, I could see him redden up. He was pretty steamed. Then he laughed—and not the kind of laugh that says anything's funny—and he says, "I can't believe you. You drive all the way out from Pinedale and then walk all the way up here just to spoil things for me? What—you got nothing better to do?"

I told him, "Seemed like a good use of time to me. And I

think that old ram would agree. The world ain't yours to do with as you please, McLane. There's rules. There's laws."

McLane says, "Laws?" and laughs again.

That's when he starts in: "Oh, that's right. You're Wyatt Earp, the Law West of the Winds. Real good at running in my kid whenever you took a mind to. Of course, when the one time came that a *real* sheriff was needed around here, you couldn't solve a crossword puzzle, let alone the crime."

Now I'm startin' to feel my face get hot, and McLane must have seen that, because he leans forward and says, "What did you think I was going to do, Andeman? Let that little red whore show up and threaten me with the half-breed kid she was carrying? Let my only son marry her? Or let her bleed us dry askin' for money? You think I'm gonna put up with that for one single minute? I'll tell you what, the place I dumped that little tramp's body, the FBI can hunt for a million years, and they ain't ever gonna find her."

Well, I'm so mad, I'm shakin' now. And that's when McLane pulls that six-shooter you got in your hands there, aims it right between my eyes and says, "And now that you heard that, I guess there ain't no reason to let *you* live either."

CHAPTER

TWENTY-FIVE

SOREN FELL SILENT, AND THE DARKNESS BEYOND THE FIRELIGHT grew so quiet that you could hear water lapping against the stones on the shore, even though there wasn't a breeze blowing. Somewhere up near the saddle, a stone fell, and the rattle and click of rolling gravel sounded for several seconds before finally fading dead away.

Soren was gazing at the fire, the light of it dancing on his glasses. He looked like a man whose thoughts were miles and years away.

Ty cleared his throat. "Well, I guess I can take it he didn't shoot you."

"Never had the chance," Soren said, shaking his head. He picked up his old staff with his right hand and lightly tamped the big burl at the top of it into the open palm of his left. "I had me this stick. Soon as he had that gun pointed at me, I gave him a swing. I didn't even think. I just lost my temper."

"Lost your . . ." Ty laughed. "Soren, I think you're entitled to do that if the man's pointing a gun at you. Sounds as if you saved your own life."

Soren looked down, turning the staff in his hand. "I didn't save no life. Took his; that's what I done."

The old man shivered back a sob.

"Soren," Ty said while leaning forward. "That man was going to shoot you."

Soren shook his head.

"Well, how do you figure that?" Ty asked. "He was pointing a gun."

"You've got his gun just the way it was when he was pointing it at me. Look it over."

Ty pulled the nickel-plated revolver out of its holster and laid it on his lap. "What? Because it's not cocked? He could have done that in a heartbeat."

"No." Soren's voice was elevated, irritated. "Not the hammer. Look at it the way I would'a seen it. Look from the front."

Slowly, with the caution of a man conditioned to respect firearms, Ty turned the muzzle of the gun so it was pointed over his shoulder, then tilted it so the firelight was falling on the front of the revolver.

"Barrel's not blocked," he said.

"The cylinder," Soren told him. "Look at the chamber that would've come up if he'd have cocked it."

Ty turned the pistol so the firelight fell into the chamber, the top one on the cylinder to the right of the barrel. "There's . . ." He turned the gun and brought it nearer to his eye. "There's paper in there."

"Money, probably."

Ty looked up.

Soren held his hand out, and Ty gave him the gun. The old man turned it in his hand, holding it carefully, like some ancient relic.

"These Blackhawks, they're real popular around these parts. A couple of my deputies had 'em, brought 'em to the range for practice. I shot 'em many a time. And I knew that, back before they changed the design, you didn't want to leave the hammer down on a loaded chamber on one of these old guns, because the firing pin was right on the hammer. You drop a gun built like that, it can go off when it hits the ground, hurt somebody. So most folks that owned them carried 'em with one chamber empty, and let the hammer rest on that; same way cowboys used to carry their six-guns back in the olden days. And a fella like Virgil, all wrapped up in the lore of the Old West like he was, would've known that, back in the day, cowboys used to carry their buryin' money in the empty chamber—a ten-dollar bill or a twenty, although, knowin' Virgil, in his case it was most likely a hundred.

"Like I said, Ruger changed the design thirty, maybe forty years ago, and offered to refit any of these old guns to the new design, free of charge, so you could carry 'em safe with all six chambers loaded. But some folks had gotten used to it, or didn't want to bother, so they just carried 'em the way they always had."

Soren patted the gun and wiped the barrel with the side of his thumb. He looked up.

"The trainin' the state police gave us when we was workin' for the Sheriff's Department—they showed us to look for things like this, size things up in an instant. 'Threat assessment.' That's what they called it. And I could tell at one glance that either Virgil had messed up and left his hammer sittin' on a live round, rather than an empty chamber, or maybe he'd done it intentionally, just tryin' to scare me—he was mean, that way. But it didn't matter to me, Tiger. I didn't care if that gun was comin' up on an empty chamber or not. It didn't matter one bit. I swung this old stick, and I hit him right here"—Soren touched his temple—"and I could see it in his eyes, soon as I did it. The way they looked like he was starin' at somethin' a million miles away. He was . . . he . . ."

The old man turned and peered up into the darkness, back up the cirque, to the saddle, invisible in the night.

Ty leaned forward and put three fingers under the revolver's cylinder. Soren opened his hands and let him take the gun back.

"I don't much care whether the chamber coming up was hot or cold." Ty turned the gun in his hands, the firelight dancing in the nickel finish, and then set it aside. "The man pulled a gun. You had every right to defend yourself."

Soren sniffed, his face still turned away.

"I mean that, Soren."

"You don't know." The old man turned back, his cheeks streaked with tears. "You don't know what it's like."

Ty crossed his arms, raised his head.

"I know you think you do, Tiger. But this is different. There was other things I could have done. I didn't just kill that man; I murdered him."

"Not first degree."

"No. But murder is murder."

Ty leaned the boots to the side so he could see them better in the firelight. Dust fell from the creases.

"So. Are you going to tell me why all these things wound up in that fissure up there on the cliff?"

Soren took a breath. Let it out slowly. "Yeah." He swallowed. "But I gotta warn you, Tiger; this right here is where it gets worse."

CHAPTER

TWENTY-SIX

"I'd had plenty of first-aid training back when I was guiding," Soren explained, "and even more when I was sheriff, and I knew right away that no amount of CPR was going to bring Virgil McLane back. He was gone. And as he lay there on the ground, I looked at him, at what I'd done, and all of a sudden I could see what was going to happen if I went back and said what had happened: an investigation, and probably a trial—definitely a trial if the investigators did their jobs right—and Parker McLane getting his daddy's lawyers after me once I was in prison and taking the house out from under Miss Edda. Even the thought of Miss Edda having to go to the store and have everybody stare at her because she was the wife of the fella that used to be sheriff and now was a murderer . . . I tell you, Tiger, I got woozy just thinkin' of it."

And I'll tell you now what really scares me. It's how, once I made up my mind to cover it up, how methodical I got about it. First thing I did was to go gather up some timber from down the lake, by that place where we got us our firewood this trip. I got it, and I made me a travois, and I rolled McLane's body onto it, and then I picked up my end and started dragging.

I was a little younger then, and a lot stronger. Like I said, I hadn't broke my hip yet, so I was still doing a lot of hiking, lots of trips up here into the Winds. And there was snow all the way up the saddle; as long as I was careful about kicking steps into it before I put my weight down, McLane dragged pretty easy.

I took him up over the saddle, on down into the woods beyond. Going downhill was even easier. I drug him a good ways, looking as I was going, and pretty soon I began to see bear sign, which is what I had my eyes open for.

I was finding scratch marks high up on the trees—grizzly bear, not black—and there was some fairly fresh scat.

Now, not many folks know it, but grizzlies are scavengers, especially in the spring, when a momma might wake up out of hibernation, have cubs on the way and not have the energy to fish. So I drug old Virgil off into the woods, far away from any trail, and set him down right near that bear sign.

I knew that bears and coyotes could take all the flesh off a body in a week or two. That, and scatter the bones. And there's plenty of other critters that'll come along and gnaw the bones away as well. It's why you don't see dead deer and elk and whatnot all over this country; the forest cleans up after its own.

But there wasn't nothing going to eat up his rifle or his six-gun or his pack frame, so I heaped all of them on the travois. Then I started thinking about searches I'd done for lost hikers, and what we'd found. The leather things—boots and belts—always seemed to survive for years and years, so I took them too. To tell the truth, blue jeans have a way of standin' up to the elements too. But there just wasn't no way I could bring myself to pull the pants off the body of a dead man, so I left them and hoped that, what with the location being out of the way, the animals that took care of everything else would tear the jeans up enough that there wouldn't be nothing left to find.

The hardest thing was going through his pockets, getting out his wallet, his keys, anything that could identify him in case he got found before the critters took care of him. I had to pretend I was back on duty, back in law enforcement and gathering evidence, just to get through that part. I took his hat too, then drug the travois back up over the saddle. The snowpack was deep enough that I didn't worry about tracks; any sign left by my drag would be long gone with the spring thaw.

But I begun to run out of gas by the time I crested that old saddle again. I guess I'd been operating on adrenalin before, and that had left me. Virgil McLane was not a small man, and I was tired. Even pulling the empty travois was all I could do. I knew I couldn't carry McLane's things out plus my own, and besides, I didn't know what I'd say if I run into somebody on the hike out and they was to ask why one man was carrying two men's things. Chucking it into the lake seemed like the thing to do, but it was too early in the season. The lake was still iced over, slushy ice, and there weren't no way to get to deep water.

So I looked in them cliffs up there and found me that cubbyhole, saw there was a good-size rock I could roll into place in front of it, and put everything up in there. This wasn't even noon yet. Just think of that; I'd killed a man and hid the evidence, all in the same morning. I found that map in McLane's things, saw the X where he'd left his truck by the trailhead, and knew right away where that was. Then I rolled the rock into place and come down here—maybe not right here, but real near it—busted up the travois, then burned it and the hat. By the time I got done, it was early afternoon and the sun was already melting all them tracks over the saddle. The fire was down to ashes, and I scattered them. You couldn't even tell that a soul had been here.

That just left the truck. I couldn't leave it near that trailhead; I was afraid it would tell searchers what part of the Winds to look in. And then I remembered that hardware fellow down in Green River. He knew that McLane was fixin' to poach sheep up here. That settled it for me; I couldn't even leave that truck anywhere *near* the Winds.

So here's what I done: I hiked out to McLane's truck, started it up with his keys, saw that he had nearly a full tank of gas, and I drove it out. Didn't know where I was going at first, but I made me a plan while I was driving. I went all the way to Salt Lake City, stopped in a Denny's on the way, and used their pay phone to call United Airlines. I made a reservation in McLane's name for that night's flight out to San Francisco. Made it first class, because I figured that was how McLane traveled, and I paid for it over the phone with his credit card. Then I put his wallet in a paper sack and tossed the sack in the dumpster behind the Denny's. After that, I drove to the airport, put his truck into long-term parking and left it there.

It was a throwed-together plan, but it was a throwed-together plan that worked. I had me a fright about a day or two later, because Lucas Baxter, who'd followed me as sheriff, called me up. Turned out he was just letting me know that McLane had gone missing—his wife had reported it. Guess she'd called home and the help didn't know where he was. Lucas was wondering if I had any ideas how to go about searching for him. I was just glad he phoned me up rather than stopping by, because I was white as a ghost until I figured out he was just looking for my help.

The only help I gave Lucas was reminding him of what he already knew. I told him that he couldn't really treat it as a missing person report until Virgil had been gone for ten days. That's procedure. I told him that Virgil and his missus wasn't on the best of terms anyways, and that it wouldn't be out of character for him to take off without telling her. But then I reminded him of what should happen next if the ten days went by without a sign of McLane—check phone records, look at his mail, and check his credit card receipts.

Of course, once they done that, they found the airline reservation. Couple days later, they learned that the ticket hadn't been used. Something like that happens, you start looking from the departure point back, and it didn't take long to turn his truck up. So it looked as if old Virgil had fallen into some mischief on his way from the parking lot to the terminal, and that's where the investigation centered.

Nobody noticed that he had a six-gun and a rifle missing. I guess that's because he had plenty of both back at his house. The only one that might have caught something like that was his son, and that boy was drunk half the time, and probably even drunker still now that the ranch was just one court hearing away from becoming his. That was how the will was set up: stocks and bonds to the widow, with the ranch and cash in the ranch accounts to the son.

In fact, Parker McLane come to some grief over all that. Seeing as he was the one that benefited the most by his daddy disappearing, the investigation turned on him. They searched his car and found some cocaine, and he did a little jail time for it before his lawyers won an appeal because of a technicality with the search warrant.

Time passed—a year, and then two—and Parker finally got a circuit judge to declare his daddy dead, and once that happened, all interest in the case seemed to just blow away. McLane's missus was probably relieved that Virgil was dead, his son was busy trying to make the ranch disappear, one whiskey at a time, and the help didn't care so long as they still got a check at the end of the month. There didn't seem to be one person on earth who cared what had happened to the man, and so the investigation died for lack of evidence.

That only left all the stuff that was up here. I thought I'd come back late some spring, once the ice had melted but before hiking season, and I'd deep-six everything I'd hid. Except I broke my hip that winter—slipped on a stinking sidewalk, of all things—and I couldn't go nowhere until I got my surgery. Even after it, I wasn't in much shape to go nowhere, but I was worried less and less about what I'd left up here. I figured that if nobody had found anything in five years, why would they find it now?

But then some of my friends in the legislature got them the idea of naming this lake after me. I tried to talk 'em out of it, but they thought I was just being humble.

You can see my concern. I'm thinking that this place gets in the papers, on the TV, and pretty soon, hard to get to or not, people are going to come up and have a look. It would have only been a matter of time before somebody would get curious about that rock up there and find what I left here. So that fixed it; I had to come back.

CHAPTER

TWENTY-SEVEN

"BUT YOU COULDN'T COME BACK BY YOURSELF," TY SAID. HIS voice was low, almost a whisper.

The old man shook his head. "Not up here. I just wasn't sure I could make it anymore. Not on my own. So I . . ." Soren sniffed, dabbed under his glasses with his fingertips. "So I wrote to you, Tiger. I took advantage of your good nature. I knew you'd come if I asked you."

"I'm glad you asked."

"Not me."

"I promised you I'd come. Remember that? A long, long time ago."

"I remember." Soren nudged the empty boots with the toe of his own. More dust fell away in the firelight. "But not this way. It ain't right. You never bargained for none of this."

The driftwood popped in the campfire, popped and then hissed, as if something damp had been released in the heat. High above the saddle, more shooting stars—three of them this time—streaked white across the night sky and burned away to nothing.

Ty took the revolver from its holster again and thumbed the hammer. It rasped back to half-cock, but when he tried to turn the cylinder, it wouldn't budge. Rust, or grit, or both had long since cemented it in place.

"You know," he said, not looking up, "all you really needed to do was turn this cylinder so it was coming up on a live round. Maybe cock the hammer. Better still, put it in McLane's hand and fire off a round, leave some residue on his hands. Do that, and you would have sealed the deal on self-defense. You wouldn't have had to worry about a trial. Man like McLane, they probably would have given you a medal."

Ty looked up. Soren was nodding.

"I thought of that," the old man said. "But this here is still Sublette County. My old jurisdiction. Lucas Baxter's jurisdiction. Case like this, Lucas would have investigated himself, not assign it off to a deputy. There would have been questions. Lots of questions. And I couldn't see me sitting there and telling the man I'd put in that job some made-up story about being shot at."

Soren laughed and then sniffed again.

"Ain't that something? I could kill a man, hide the evidence, leave a false trail behind me . . . I could commit murder, but I couldn't bring myself to lie to a friend."

"It wasn't murder."

"It weren't nothing else. I'll tell you that right now."

"Soren, it was justice. McLane asked for it. He deserved it. He killed that girl."

The old man looked up, tracks of tears wet upon his cheeks.

"No," he said. His voice faltered, even on that one short word. "No, sir. McLane didn't kill her. He most certainly did not."

CHAPTER
TWENTY-EIGHT

"BUT, SOREN . . ." TY LEANED FORWARD, TRYING TO SEE THE OLD man's eyes behind the reflection of the campfire on his glasses. "You just told me that McLane confessed to murdering that girl."

"Lucy. Lucy Washington."

"Yes. Didn't he say out loud that he killed her?"

"Said it. But he sure never did it."

Ty raised his hands, palms up. "Then why would he . . . ?" Ty dropped his hands. "How do you know that?"

Soren nudged the empty boots again.

"When I was in the hospital, mending up after my hip replacement, I had all sorts of people stopping in to see me: Emma's kin, mine, folks I took fishing, deputies from the Sheriff's Department. And I guess that don't surprise me. This is big country, but there ain't all that many people stay here year-round, so if you live here long enough, you get to know all of them."

Ty nodded.

"But the one visitor that did surprise me was Jack Hightower, who come by one night just before the end of visiting hours. You see, Jack got elected sheriff in Teton County about the same time I become sheriff in Sublette. But Jack was a lot younger, and he stayed on. Guess he was about fifty by this time. Anyway, he come by in his uniform, and I said, 'Well, Jack, this is a surprise. Didn't expect you to run all the way over here.' And Jack says, 'It's not just a personal visit, Soren. It's also business. I have something I need to tell you. We found us a body on the Forest Service land last week.'"

Ty whistled.

"I hear you," Soren said. "I was thinking exactly what you're thinking. I even asked him, 'Here in the Pinedale District?' Hightower then looks at me funny and says, 'No. Over in Jackson District, my neck of the woods. And I knew you'd want to know about it right away. You should also know that the body was skeletonized. We identified her by the dental records.'

"Well, the *her* threw me, and I must have shown it, because Jack says, 'It's that girl, Soren. Lucy Washington. That one you were looking for all those years ago.'"

Ty held a hand up, shoulder high, palm out.

"I know, I know," Soren said. "Just because she was over Jackson way doesn't mean anything. McLane could have dumped her there. But he didn't."

"How could you know that?"

"Because of what Hightower told me next."

Soren began searching around by the fire ring. Immediately Ty went to his pack, got a water bottle and handed it to him.

The old man smiled briefly, drank and wiped his lips on his flannel sleeve.

"Hightower told me that they didn't really find the body so much as they was led to it. Three girls was missing from up by Crater Lake, in Oregon, and they were all about the same age, young and slender and pretty, and they were all hitchhiking when they went missing. So the sheriff up there called in the feds, and they put together a sting—set some pretty young FBI agents out hitching on the highways, and lo and behold, after a week, one of them gets picked up by a fella in a pickup that pulls a gun on her.

"Like I said, she was an FBI agent, so he didn't have the gun for very long, and they had other agents tailing the truck once she was picked up, and they took this fellow in and questioned him, and he broke pretty soon and showed them where he'd put the bodies. Then, after he did that, he says to the agents, 'Well, I suppose you want to know where the rest of them are too.' "

" 'Rest of them'?" Ty said.

Soren nodded. "Turns out this fellow was a traveling farrier, went around shoeing horses on the rodeo and horse-show circuits. And as he drove from place to place, he'd stop by national parks and forests—touristy places where an out-of-state plate wouldn't raise no eyebrows—and look for young girls, college girls, out seeing the country and hitchhiking from place to place. Then he'd pick them up and he'd ... well, I guess you can figure for yourself what he did. And after that, he'd kill them, but he wouldn't just dump their bodies on public land. He'd bury them, and rock them over so nothing would get uncovered by animals. He'd done this all over—the Tetons and Yellowstone, Grand

Canyon, Yosemite, Rocky Mountain, Crater Lake, Glacier. If it was a park west of the Mississippi, he probably killed him a girl or two right near it. But nobody picked up on the pattern, because all their families knew was that they was out sightseeing. The only reason they noticed them girls missing by Crater Lake was because they had jobs in the area and was hitching to work.

"As for the rest of them, the proximity to national parks was something that only became clear once the killer led the agents to the bodies. And that was the other strange part—he didn't have nothing written down, yet he remembered where he'd buried every single body, knew what each victim looked like, even remembered what they was wearing."

Ty shook his head. "And when he said 'pretty young Indian girl' . . ."

Soren nodded: short, quick nods.

"Jack Hightower knew right away who the victim was. But he didn't say nothing until the coroner confirmed the identity. After that, he came and saw me, because he knew how it had frustrated me that I'd never been able to close the case."

"So that was it? It was a random thing?"

Soren nodded. "I never said nothing to my deputy, the one who had picked her up, but if he'd dropped her off there half an hour later . . . why, that girl would probably still be alive today."

The two men sat silent for a moment. Then Ty straightened up.

"What about McLane?" he asked. "Why then did he say he did it?"

Soren lifted his hands a few inches, let them fall back to his

lap. "I've asked myself that same question every night since—"
he paused, nodded at the boots—"since this thing here happened. And some nights I think he was saying it just to get my
goat; other nights I think he was trying to frustrate me, the way
I'd frustrated his poaching. Some nights I think maybe it was
Virgil McLane's idea of a joke. It was like he was wired wrong,
you know? Other times I think he was saying it . . . I don't know,
just to be saying it."

Ty huffed. "Well, it's not fair. It doesn't make any sense."

"That's something you notice when you get to be my age—
ain't none of it fair. And a lot of it doesn't make any sense."

High above the shadowed mountains, meteors streaked
across a star-dotted sky.

CHAPTER
TWENTY-NINE

ITS FEET EXTENDED, THE EAGLE DESCENDED TOWARD THE LAKE, back-pedaled once with its wings, broke the water's surface and then flapped heavily away, a small trout wriggling in its talons. The bird beat several times against the thin mountain air, rising gracefully into the blue morning sky.

Beneath it, a man's boot, the left half of a pair of brown leather ropers, arced through the air, small stones spilling from its open top as it tumbled. It hit the water and disappeared with a splash.

Ty stood and watched the ripples spread across the calm lake. Then he wrapped the cracked and dry leather belt around its faux rodeo buckle, tucked it into the toe of the second boot and filled that one with rocks from the lakeshore. With the underhanded arc of a man tossing a heavy horseshoe, he launched this boot as well, then watched it land in the darker blue of deep water.

He picked up the pistol, the gun belt wrapped stiffly around its holster.

Soren's thin, weathered hand gripped Ty's wrist.

"No." The old man had come straight from his sleeping bag, no boots over his red-toed socks, no John Deere cap over his tousled white hair. "No, Tiger. Don't."

Ty hefted the six-gun and its holster in his captive hand. "It's what you came here for, Soren. What *we* came here for."

The old man firmly shook his head. "Dragging you into this weren't never my intention."

"I don't mind being drug in. I'm glad to help."

Soren worked his lips. "But I ain't glad. Don't you see that? Not about having you involved. Not about carrying it anymore. In a way, I'm glad you know now because it's woke me up. It's high time this thing ended. I'm turnin' myself in."

Ty hefted the gun again.

"You're not going to tell anyone about the empty chamber, are you?"

Soren nodded, just as firmly as he had shaken his head. "I'm going to tell Lucas Baxter. And I'm going to tell him everything, same as I told you."

Ty sighed.

"You don't know what it's like." Soren's voice was high and shaky, and tears now edged his eyes. "It's like a canker, Tiger. Like this big, hurting sore that only gets worse. And it's been eating me up for years. I can't hold my head up no more. I don't care what they do to me. It can't be no worse than what I done to myself."

Ty looked at the revolver. "What about Edda?"

Soren removed his thick glasses, wiped at his eyes and then put them back on. "I imagine Miss Edda would be pleased to finally have a man for a husband again. Now, let's take that six-gun and put it up in the cliff and cover it up again, best as we can. I've already disturbed Lucas Baxter's crime scene enough as it is."

After he'd returned the gun to its hiding place, Ty caught a couple of trout to fry for a late breakfast, although there was little beauty to the way he did it. He simply looked for the rising fish and cast to the spot. It was easy to see that he was fishing for utility, not for sport.

After the cook kit had been cleaned and returned to its two stuff sacks, Ty looked around at what had to be carried back—the two sleeping bags and the ground pads, the fishing gear and jackets.

"I think I'll empty out and repack," he said.

"Well, give me something to carry too," Soren told him. "You toted everything up here. I may be old, but I ain't helpless."

The second pocket on the pack yielded an unfamiliar rectangular shape. Ty pulled the object out and turned it over before he recognized it.

"Here," he said, handing the pocket-size Bible to Soren. "You can take this."

Soren looked at the little, worn Bible. He glared back at Ty. "Edda put you up to that, didn't she?"

Ty shrugged. "She asked me to take it along. It was my idea to bring it up here."

Soren tapped the cover of the book in Ty's hand. "Do you know what I was doing the last time that Bible was in my pocket?"

Ty shook his head.

"I was killing Virgil McLane with this here hiking stick of mine. Killing him dead. What do you think of that?"

Ty was silent for a moment.

"I think," he finally said, "that you're still carrying the staff."

CHAPTER

THIRTY

THE TWO MEN STOPPED FOR A BREAK AN HOUR OUT OF CIRQUE Lake. Ty, who wasn't even perspiring, just stood at first, taking a little of the weight of the pack off his shoulders by leaning back against a rock ledge. But when he saw Soren mopping his brow, Ty shed the pack, found a water bottle and sat down next to the old man.

Soren drank and then handed the water bottle to Ty, who took a perfunctory sip before giving it back to Soren. The old man drank again, recapped the bottle and leaned forward to return it to its place on the pack. He sat back, patted his bib pocket, took out the little Bible with a motion that seemed almost automatic and leafed through the pages. Then he looked up, blinked and closed the book.

"Mind if I borrow that?" Ty asked.

Soren handed him the little book.

Ty leafed, a few pages at a time, through almost the entire Bible, went back to the contents page, checked it and then turned to the Psalms. He went forward several pages, found something, followed it with his fingertip, then looked up and said, "Mind if I read you something?"

Soren grimaced. "Do I have a choice?"

"No."

"Well . . ." Soren made a *carry on* motion with his hand. "Thank you for asking, anyhow."

Ty found his spot again on the page.

" 'Have mercy upon me, O God,' " he began, " 'according to thy lovingkindness: according unto the multitude of thy tender mercies blot out my transgressions. Wash me thoroughly from mine iniquity, and cleanse me from my sin. For I acknowledge my transgressions, and my sin is ever before me.' "

Ty looked up from the little book. "Your King James Version, here, might be a little more obtuse than what I've read before, but the substance is still there. I'd say that about covers your situation, doesn't it?"

Soren leaned, his elbow on a rock, middle finger under his nose, index finger pointing up along his cheek. He looked at Ty over the tops of his glasses.

"What?" said Ty.

Soren leaned back and crossed his arms. "You seem to be forgetting that, even though I haven't carried it lately, I've read that book once or twice. I've pretty much memorized the Psalms."

"And?"

Soren nodded at the Bible. "You want to read to me? Read the next verse."

Ty shifted the book so the light fell more directly on the page. " 'Against thee, thee only, have I sinned, and done this evil in thy sight . . .' " He glanced Soren's way and went back to the reading. " 'That thou mightest be justified when thou speakest . . .' "

Ty looked at Soren again.

" 'That thou mightest be justified when thou speakest,' " Soren concluded, " 'and be clear when thou judgest.' There you go."

Ty closed the book and handed it back to him. "What do you mean, 'There you go'? I'm not even sure what that says."

"Well, I am." Soren looked down at the Bible. "It tells me that, when a man's done what I've done, the Almighty is absolutely within His rights to find that fella guilty."

Ty crossed his arms. "What is this, Soren? Some new sort of pick-and-choose faith? Are you trying to tell me that verse says your goose is cooked?"

Soren held the little book in his right hand and rapped its back cover lightly against the knuckles of his left. "No," he finally said. "I'm just being ornery. I guess about all I can say is that my goose *deserves* to be cooked."

"And?"

"You know good and well what *and*."

Ty waited.

"And I am washed clean from my sin, like that verse says. On account of I'm a Christian. On account of Jesus paying the debt for me. Just the same as He paid for you."

Ty shrugged. "Well, I can accept that. Can you?"

Soren slipped the Bible back into the bib pocket of his overalls.

"I can," he said. He leaned on the staff and got unsteadily to his feet. "But I also know that sometimes something other than heaven has to be answered." He looked down at Ty. "You talked to that investigator about that old Muslim you shot. And your commanding officer gave permission for you to stay off of that patrol that your friend got killed on. You did right; you submitted to earthly authority. You've got to let me do the same." The old man tapped his staff on the ground. "Let's get goin'. We're gonna want to hit Clear Lake early enough to catch us some dinner."

As they closed in on the camp, they heard the horses before they saw them—the whinnies and nickers of animals reassuring one another in unfamiliar surroundings. And as they made the turn for the rise up to their tent, they could see the four-horse pack string—three chestnuts and a bay—tied off on a line run from tree to tree. Hanson, the wrangler, was removing a duffel from one of the packs.

"Hello, boss," the wrangler called as the two men came up the trail. "I was afraid I was going to miss you two. How's the fishing?"

"Hey, Hanson," Ty said. "It's going good. The bears around here are probably starving, we're eating so much trout."

Hanson lifted the duffel. "Here's the cure for that. I brought your provisions. Want me to hang 'em for you?"

"Thanks, but I can do it." Ty glanced at the duffel. "That looks like a lot more than eggs and bacon and butter, Hanson."

The wrangler grinned. "The Thriftway had a deal on rib eyes, so I got you a couple and some baking potatoes and enough tinfoil to cook 'em; figured you might be getting tired of fish about now. And don't you worry, boss. My girl got her steak and baked potato Saturday night. So did I." He turned Soren's way. "Mr. Andeman, Kathy up at the lodge sent you a sack of those muffins you liked at breakfast the other day, along with a squeeze tube of orange marmalade."

"Well, thank you," Soren said. They were his first words since they'd sighted the pack string. "Tell her that's very kind."

"Will do."

Ty picked up the duffel. "Hanson, if you've got the time, we were going to wet a line and get us some trout for dinner. You're welcome to join us."

"Thanks, boss, but I've still got one more camp to provision."

"How about coffee, then? Won't take me but five minutes."

"No thanks, boss. I finished off a thermos on the way up here. If you don't mind, though, I'll walk with you while you put your supplies up in your bear hang."

Ty cocked his head. "Okay. Sure. Come on along."

They walked into the pines, and Ty waited until they were out of sight of Soren before asking, "What is it, Hanson? What's on your mind?"

Hanson walked with his hands in the hip pockets of his jeans, looking down at the ground as he walked. "Bobbie Bridger was up at the lodge last night, boss. Said the fire hazard was real high and that there were already a couple of burns in the southern part of the range. Under control last he heard, but he said to tell everyone I saw to keep a weather eye to the south and to watch your open flames."

Ty stepped over a fallen pine trunk. "Yeah. We figured the

lightning would touch something off. That all you needed to tell me?"

Hanson shook his head.

"Well, go on, then."

Hanson glanced at him and then down at the ground. "Bobbie and Kathy had . . . words, boss. I was trying not to eavesdrop, but I was carrying plates into the kitchen and I could hear them. Your name came up. The only part I heard clear was Bobbie telling Kathy that maybe she should have stuck with you, and Kathy saying that maybe she should have. So I don't know if you want to be or not, but it sounds like you might be in the middle of something."

They got to the bear hang, and Ty gave the line a pull to release it.

"I appreciate the warning." He held the bag open while Hanson handed him items from the duffel. "Never mind the steaks and potatoes. We'll take those back for supper. So, did Bridger and Kathy smooth things over this morning?"

Hanson shook his head again. "Never had the chance. Right after that, Bobbie lit out for Big Sandy Lake. It was why he was up to the lodge in the first place; that little black bear up there, the last year's cub? He's been getting pretty bold up around the campsites. Some folks cut their trips short on account of he's gotten to be such a nuisance. Bobbie had driven in to the lodge to use the trailhead. He camped at Big Sandy last night and might be there the next couple of nights as well. You know—keep an eye on things and see if that bear needs relocation."

"Better down there than up here, it sounds like."

Hanson winked. "You caught my drift just fine, boss."

CHAPTER

THIRTY-ONE

TY WOKE AT DAYBREAK TO A SCENE ALMOST IDENTICAL TO THEIR
first morning in—with Soren sitting on a log next to the camp
stove, cooking breakfast. The smell of bacon frying touched his
nostrils. Ty pulled on his jeans, unzipped the mosquito netting
and sat in the tent doorway putting on his boots. "Now, that's
the way to wake up," he said.

Soren turned. He looked more relaxed, more at peace, the
smile sitting easily on his face.

"If you was gettin' your beauty rest, you'd better go back to
sleep!" The old man laughed at the old joke and forked bacon
into a billy-pot lid, then broke a couple of eggs into the frying
pan, the bacon grease sizzling as they hit. "I'll have breakfast
ready in a couple. Sure is a cracker of a morning, ain't it?"

"It sure is," Ty agreed. He put his hands to the small of his
back and stretched, looking up at a blue sky unmarred by jet
trails. He turned and sniffed for a moment, as if he smelled

something else besides the bacon. Then he went to get the water bag to make coffee.

Soren was just sliding fried eggs onto plates when a voice rang from down on the lakeside trail: "Hello the camp."

The two men looked down, and Soren smiled when he saw the familiar green Forest Service jacket. "Hey," he called. "You're just in time for breakfast."

"Thanks, but I've got to get up the trail," Bridger said, taking his peaked cap off and wiping his brow with his sleeve. He kept his pack on. "Got a call on the radio this morning. That burn down south has flared up again, and it's jumped a couple of ridges. Looks like it's headed this way."

Soren stood, gazed south and said, "Don't see no smoke."

"No, sir," Bridger said. "The wind's keeping it to the lee of the range right now. But it burned this way overnight, and it could be here by noon, especially if the wind shifts, and the forecasters are saying it will. I've been asked to tell all the camps along here to break and head back to the trailhead."

Ty looked around at all their things.

"I know you horse-packed in," Bridger said. "Hanson was going to bivouac up at the last camp yesterday and come down this morning. I imagine I'll run into him on the trail. Anything you don't want to carry, just cache it here and I'll ask him to pick it up on his way out."

"How much time do we have?" Ty asked.

Bridger gazed southward. The sky remained a perfect robin's-egg blue. "You'll have time to finish breakfast and strike camp. But I wouldn't dawdle. If that burn gets some wind behind it, it'll be coming on fast." He glanced at his watch. "I'd best roll.

Before I go, I wanted to ask a favor. There's a young couple camped at Big Sandy, and they were out hiking when I got the call. I put a note on their tent, but I want to make sure they know to get out. Could you swing by there for me, tell them to strike camp and leave right away?"

"Sure thing," Soren said, nodding emphatically.

"Well, okay." Bridger put his hat back on. "I'd better get on up the trail."

He started walking toward the lake and Ty trotted after him.

"Hey, Bob?"

The ranger turned.

"Hanson was . . . well, he overheard something at the lodge the other night. I didn't want to—"

Bridger waved him off, his mouth set straight, his face red.

"Later, Perkins," he told him flatly. "I've got a job to do."

Ty started to speak again, but Bridger shook his head. "I'll send Hanson," he said gruffly. "Meanwhile, you two had better strike camp."

THIRTY-TWO

THE MAN AND THE WOMAN WERE BOTH SLENDER AND FIT, BOTH in their twenties. He was in jeans, a CBGB T-shirt under his day-pack; she wore khaki shorts and a buttoned shirt tied off above her midriff. Their boots still looked new, and they appeared surprised to see visitors.

"Hi," the man said. He stuck out a hand to Ty, who shook it. The woman hung back. She had close-cropped, streaked blond hair, and she was pretty.

"Bob Bridger, the ranger who was camped here last night, asked us to look in on you," Ty said.

At that, the woman brightened. "We thought he'd still be here. He said he was going to hang around and see about that bear."

The man nodded. "Truth is, last night is the first full night's sleep I've gotten since we got here last week. But wouldn't you know it? The bear didn't come around."

Ty pointed south, where a low gray cloud of smoke was now

visible through a far pass in the range. "The Forest Service is fighting a burn that's jumped some ridges. Could be here soon. He asked us to see that you got out."

The woman shaded her eyes and looked south. "That's pretty far away."

"Could be here before you know it," Soren told her. "Them fires get moving, you can't outrun 'em."

The woman smiled at the old man. "Well, then I guess we'd better get packed."

The two tenderfoots struck camp with the lethargy of people who had only loaded backpacks in their living room. Ty gave the man a hand taking down the tent, and when the woman began rolling up the sleeping bags, Soren said, "No, missy—you stuff 'em . . ." and he showed her how.

They were in the middle of doing all this when they heard a grunt and all looked up at the same time. The woman made a little piping sound.

There, not twenty feet away, was a male black bear, his head lumbering left and right as he squinted at the four people.

"You folks stay real still," Ty said under his breath. He reached for a stone on the ground, but before he could pick it up, Soren was on the move.

"What do you think you're doing? Go on now," the old man told the bear.

"Soren . . ."

"This critter's been babied too long," the old man said. He leaned on his staff and waved his free hand. "Go on! Get out of here!"

The bear crouched a little and then took a step toward Soren. It rose up on its back feet.

"No you don't!" Soren moved closer to the bear, swinging his staff. The burl on the end thunked off the big animal's hide and it growled and lifted a paw. Then Soren swung hard, and the staff connected with the bear's ear. It swayed, turned, fell back to all fours and took off running for the tree line, bawling in fright as it ran.

Ty and the two tenderfoots watched it run, its large furry rump bouncing as it flew across the clearing.

"Way to go, Soren! I guess you showed him a thing—" His eyes wide, Ty stopped in midsentence.

Soren was on his back on the ground, clutching his left shoulder, his face contorted in pain.

THIRTY-THREE

TY DROPPED HIS PACK AND KNELT NEXT TO SOREN. THE OLD man's eyes were screwed tightly shut. His hat had fallen off and, despite the coolness of the morning, his forehead was beaded with sweat.

"It hurts," he half groaned, half whispered, right hand clutching his chest. "O Lord. It hurts."

"Did the bear get him?" the woman asked. "I don't see anything."

Ty looked up at the young couple. "He's having a heart attack. Are either of you trained in first aid?"

The woman shook her head.

"I . . . I sell cars," the man stammered, as if that would explain everything.

Ty put a hand to Soren's brow. "All right," he told the couple. "I'll have to stay here with him, then. I need you two to get to the lodge just as fast as you can. Leave your things. We'll get them out later. Tell Kathy we need whatever we can get up here—a helicopter and medic if she can get them, a four-by-four if we can't. He needs a hospital, and he needs it five minutes ago."

"We'll make good time," the woman promised. She tugged at the man's sleeve and the two of them started toward the trail at a trot. The tops of the trees rustled as the breeze picked up.

Ty got a first-aid kit out of the backpack, ripped open a small bag and shook out a white tablet, which he put in Soren's mouth, and then he held the water bottle to the old man's lips. "This is aspirin. It'll help," Ty explained.

He pulled a down jacket out of the backpack, put it under Soren's head and shoulders and placed the backpack under Soren's knees to elevate his feet. The couple had left their sleeping bags nearby, so he shook one out of its stuff sack, opened it to its full length and fluffed it out.

"Old man, don't you die on me," he said as he laid the sleeping bag over him.

Soren chuckled and then winced. "I may not have any choice in the matter, boy."

"You ever have heart trouble this bad before?"

Soren shook his head. "It feels like it's been saving itself up for this one."

He closed his eyes, gritted his teeth and then opened his eyes again. He reached out from beneath the sleeping bag and clutched Ty by the wrist.

"Tiger, you tell them what I done. I ain't dyin' with this behind my lips. You tell 'em what sort of man I was."

"Tell them yourself," Ty said, wetting a bandanna and laying it on the old man's brow. "We're going to get you out of here."

"You bet." Soren's voice was flat. "Boy-ee, would you look at that eagle? He's way up there, ain't he?"

Ty looked up. There *was* an eagle—it was too small to see what kind—wheeling on a rising thermal, a good thousand feet above them. When it turned edge-on, it nearly disappeared, but when it came around and both wings were out, it became visible again.

"He's looking for critters," Soren said. "Things running away from the fire."

Ty sniffed. The air held the scent of smoke—not the woodsmoke of campfires but the smoke of sod and dry pine needles and tree roots burning along with the trees. It was the sort of smoke that told you to take to your feet.

"You just rest easy," he told Soren.

"I ain't planning on gettin' no exercise."

The old man had another heart attack about an hour after the first, and Ty gave him another aspirin. Soren's face was gray now. He looked as if he had run too far, for too long, and when Ty told him to go to sleep, he did so without protest. Little flakes of soot began to dot the sleeping bag as the smell of smoke grew heavier.

Ty looked toward the lake.

"That burn reaches us, I'm going to have to drag us both into the water," he said. "It won't have to be for long. This is all just grass around here. It'll burn past pretty quick. You understand?"

But the old man slept on. Ty shaded his mouth with his hand to keep soot from falling into it.

Half an hour later, Soren woke up. He had color in his face again, and he smiled.

"Hey, Tiger."

"How are you doing, Soren?"

The old man nodded. Then he opened his eyes wide and looked at the sky.

"Look at him," he said, his voice clear. "Would you look at him, Tyler? He's just like . . . he's more than . . . Ain't he somethin'? Beautiful."

Ty followed the old man's gaze. All he could see was a sky partially veiled by thin smoke and, just above them, gray flakes of soot wafting like snow.

"What are you looking at, Soren?" Ty kept searching the sky. "The eagle? Where is he?"

The only sound was the soughing of the pines and, somewhere far off, the *whump whump whump* of helicopter blades.

"Soren?"

Ty looked down. Soren's eyes were shut. His chest had stopped rising.

Ty touched the old man's neck, kept his fingers there a moment and then touched the other side. His shoulders sagged.

"Old man, where have you gone?"

CHAPTER

THIRTY-FOUR

THE DOOR HAD OPENED ALMOST AS SOON AS TY HAD KNOCKED, enveloping him at one and the same time in the heady smell of baking and Edda Andeman's tearful hug. For one long minute they stayed that way, Edda sobbing and Ty holding her while a fat, gray long-tailed cat rubbed and twined amongst his ankles before walking on into the kitchen.

"No you don't!" Edda broke off the hug and, wiping her eyes with her apron, she scooped the cat up and held it in the crook of her arm. The cat seemed accustomed to being held that way; his purr thrummed between them like an old electric motor.

"Billy here has kitchen privileges, but not while I'm baking," she explained, scratching the old tom behind one ragged-edged ear. "And he knows that, but he likes to test the boundaries now and then. Which is a cat thing. Or a male thing. Or both."

Kissing the cat on the top of its head, she set it out on the back stoop, pulled Ty inside and shut the door. She looked at the back door again.

"I keep thinking that he's going to walk in here any minute."

"I know." Ty put a hand on her shoulder. "It's hard."

She squeezed his hand. "You still like that cinnamon nut roll I make?"

"That's the silliest question I've heard all year."

Edda smiled. "Want coffee with it?"

"Please. Soren was letting me make the coffee up in the Winds, and while he never said anything about it, it's not my finest achievement."

The two of them paused for a moment, as if time could not go on while Soren's name still hung in the air. Then Edda poured the coffee, placed a slice of the roll on a bread plate and set them on the kitchen table, nodding for Ty to sit.

"Tell me something, Tyler," she said as she pulled out a chair to join him. "How was it, at the end? Was he in very much pain?"

Ty stopped stirring his coffee, set one fist within the other and leaned on them, his knuckles tight against his lips. "Yes," he finally said as he sat up straight. "It was a heart attack, Edda. A bad one. Brought on by the exertion, I guess. I'd have to say it hurt quite a bit."

Edda sniffed, dabbed her eyes.

"Well, thank you," she said, not looking up. "I appreciate your honesty."

"Except at the end," Ty added.

"The end?"

"Just before he . . . just before. Edda, he was looking up, right past me, and he was happy. I think he saw where he was going. Do you think that could possibly be true?"

The old woman smiled. "I know it could be, Tyler. I know it is."

They were quiet for a moment again, and then Ty leaned forward and took a small black book from his hip pocket and laid it on the table between them. The gilt letters on its cover were nearly worn away, but Edda traced them with her fingers as if they were new and freshly printed.

"Did he carry it?"

"I took it out of his bib pocket after . . . after I closed his eyes."

She nodded, thin-lipped. "Did he read it?"

"We both did. I think we about wore it out, that last day."

Edda looked at him, eyes bright, face stern. "Tyler Perkins, don't you be telling me stories just to make me feel better."

Ty leaned on his hands again. "Edda, if that was my intention, then I wouldn't have told you he was hurting."

She looked at him, searching his eyes.

"Well." Edda picked the little book up. "All right then."

She kissed the worn black cover and held the Bible to her chest.

Ty picked at the roll, eating it in small bits with the motions of a man who wasn't really tasting what he was eating. As he sipped his coffee, Edda looked up at him and cocked her head. She looked younger, sitting that way.

"All right. Tell me the rest."

"Pardon?"

"You're holding something back. Tell me about your trip."

Ty set the coffee cup down. "We . . . fished. We camped."

Edda closed her eyes, shook her head. "Tyler, I have known

you ever since you were eight years old. I've heard you talk about every single trip you ever made into the mountains with that husband of mine. I know how you think. And I know there's something you're not telling me."

Ty said nothing.

Edda put her hand on his.

"Dear, the only thing that could possibly hurt me is if Soren had another woman waiting for him up in them mountains." She smiled. "And now that I think about it, that might impress me more than it would hurt me. But I doubt that's the case. Tell me; you'll feel better."

Ty rubbed his forehead. "You're sure you want to hear?"

"I'm positive. Never been surer. Tell me the rest."

So Ty told her. He started with the night that Soren announced his intention to walk up to Cirque Lake, and he continued through to the part where he had awakened in the night to find the old man gone. He told about trying to throw the evidence into the lake, about Soren stopping him. He recounted the old man's determination to make a clean breast of it, the tears, the testimony they had made to each other and the solace he had felt when he'd made it.

He left nothing out, and when he was done, he sipped at his coffee, and the look on his face must have told Edda that it had gone cold, because she took his cup to the sink, poured it out and fixed him a new cup, steam rising from its rim.

"Soren was going to let the authorities know what he had done?" She asked it matter-of-factly, the way a person might ask about the weather.

Ty nodded.

"Well, then." Edda stood. "Amen. Would you excuse me just a moment?"

She crossed the kitchen to where an old-fashioned black rotary wall phone hung next to the door that led into the dining room, picked it up and dialed a number from memory.

"Hello, Loretta," she said after a moment. "It's Edda. . . . Why, thank you, I appreciate that. . . . Yes, I'll miss him too. . . . We're thinking Saturday morning. Delbert said he'd have something in the paper tomorrow. . . . No, I don't need a thing, but thank you. But I did have a reason for calling. Would the sheriff be in, please?"

Ty's head snapped up. "Lucas Baxter?" He'd barely said the name, but he mouthed it pronouncedly so Edda could see it.

She nodded.

"Edda, no," Ty said, rising from his seat. But Edda held up a hand to him, palm out, then put her finger to her lips.

"Hello, Lucas. It's Edda Andeman," she said into the receiver. She listened for a moment and then said, "Actually, yes—there is something. Would you mind very much stopping by the house? . . . No, it's not any sort of emergency. We just need to talk. . . . On your way home would be fine. And come hungry; I made nut roll. . . . Quarter past five? . . . Fine. I'll see you then."

Ty stood. He looked ready to burst, but held his piece until Edda hung up the phone.

"You don't have to do this," he said when she had. "No one has to know. I can go back up to that lake tomorrow, take all that stuff and throw it in deep water with the rest of it. I shouldn't have let Soren stop me."

Edda returned to the table, set her hand on his shoulder and pressed until he sat back down.

"I'm very glad that he did," she said, retaking her seat. "I'm more than glad. I'm relieved."

"Relieved?"

She nodded.

Ty looked her in the eyes. "You knew." It was a statement, not a question.

Edda smiled. "You know, Tyler, one of the things I've always loved about you is how you are always ready to give the benefit of a doubt. But you're a bright young man. When Soren told you his story, you must have wondered how he got both his truck and Virgil McLane's back from two different trailheads that day. And you must have known that Soren couldn't possibly have taken that truck to Salt Lake City by himself. I mean, he couldn't very well have just taken a bus back home; someone he knew might have been on it, or someone might have seen him getting off. So he needed a confederate. But you didn't want to think it was me. Did you, dear?"

Ty seemed to deflate. Edda sliced another piece of nut roll and put it on his plate.

"I know it seems out of character to you, dear. But it was very much in character; I loved him. And if it helps matters any, I didn't know *whose* pickup truck that was the night we moved it. It didn't belong to anyone we knew socially, not to anyone in our church. But other than that, why, everyone in the county has one of those old trucks, it seems. There's too many to keep track of."

She motioned toward Ty's coffee cup, and he shook his head.

"I'd best tell you the whole story," Edda said, stirring her own cup but not sipping from it. "May I?"

Ty nodded. Three times.

"Please," he said.

CHAPTER

THIRTY-FIVE

EDDA LOOKED OFF TOWARD THE CORNER OF THE KITCHEN CEILING, then refocused her attention on Ty. "Did your mother ever tell you that Soren and I once had a son?"

He nodded. "She said he died young."

Edda shut her eyes. Opened them. "James. His name was James. And the day I went to the doctor and found out I was pregnant, Soren said, 'Well, look at you. My little mother.' And those were our names from that time on. Soren called me Mother, and I called him Papa.

"But James, poor little thing, he was born with a bad valve in his heart, the sort of thing that today they fix right away, but back then they wanted to wait until he was bigger. My, that frustrated him. He wanted to go into the mountains, don't you know. Go fishing with his papa. And when he was five, and the doctors said he was big enough, he was the one who was campaigning for the operation: 'The doctors are gonna fix my heart, and I'm gonna fish and climb Gannett Peak with Papa.'

"Except the operation didn't go well. We'd known all along that was a possibility, but we'd just felt certain that the Lord would use the doctors to make James strong. But he picked up an infection while he was recovering in the hospital, and it weakened him horribly—weak, and dehydrated despite the IVs, and he just never had the chance to catch back up. We were at the hospital over in Cheyenne so much that it was practically like we were living there after a while. And the last night, after we'd been told there really wasn't any hope, and after we'd prayed, we were just sitting there by the bedside, watching our poor little boy struggling to breathe under that oxygen tent, and then finally he stopped struggling, and Soren looked at me and said, 'Mother, I think he's gone.' "

Tears spilled down Edda's cheeks as she looked down at the table and folded her hands.

Ty reached across the table, put his hand on hers. "Edda, I'm so sorry."

She wiped her face with the flats of her fingers and smiled.

"Don't be," she said. "I was just thinking that Soren and James are together in heaven now, and all I've got here is the cat!"

They both laughed.

"The only reason I told that story, Tyler, is because that night was the last time Soren called me Mother. I went back to being Edda, and he became Soren again. It just hurt less to do it that way. But all those years later, when Soren got back from the Winds, he came here into this kitchen, he kissed me on the cheek and hugged me tight, and then he said, 'Mother, I'm in a fix.'

"I said, 'Papa, what's wrong?' But he wouldn't tell me. Said it was best I didn't know, but he needed my help."

Edda went to the cupboard, moved aside an oatmeal box and brought out a Mason jar filled with rolled currency and a little change.

"We call this our rainy day money. You know, money for when you need something right away but can't depend on getting to the bank. And Soren came over here and he got the money that was in this jar then, every bit of it, and he stuffed it in his overalls pockets, and he said, 'Best get your coat. The sun's goin' down, and we've got a long night ahead of us.'

"Well, he was right about that. It took us over an hour to get out to that trailhead, and when we did, like I said, there was this pickup truck I didn't recognize, and Soren's getting out these keys I'd never seen. I started crying right there, but Soren shushed me and said, 'Now, Edda, we're gonna fix this thing, you and I, and everything is going to be just fine. I'm gonna drive that truck and you're gonna drive mine, and you just follow me. It'll be a ways, but just follow me.'

"Well, I thought 'a ways' would be Green River, but when we crossed the Utah line, I didn't know *where* we were headed. We were almost all the way through Salt Lake City when we stopped at a Denny's and Soren ordered a couple of hamburgers, because it was past midnight and we'd never had our supper. He left the table for a few minutes, and the food came while he was gone, but I didn't want to eat. I was worried sick. When Soren came back, he said, 'Eat up, Mother. If you don't touch it, they might remember us.' Just the thought of why he didn't want *them* remembering us made me even more upset and I wanted to cry again, but I knew I shouldn't, so I ate, and he ate, and then we left.

"And when we got outside, Soren pointed down the road and said, 'The airport's right down there.' Which I knew, because we'd gone there before to drop off some missionaries who had visited our church. Soren gave me his watch. 'Wait here twenty minutes,' he said, 'and then drive to the airport, to the sign for arriving flights, and I'll be standing there. If I'm not there at first, drive around and come back.'

"I did just what he said. I had a little cry while I waited and then I drove to the airport and I cried again when I saw him standing there, because something inside me expected I might never see him again. Then we drove home—it was nearly sunrise when we got here—and we went to bed. We were exhausted.

"But nothing happened the next day, or the day after that, or the day after that, and I started thinking of everything that had happened that night as if it were a bad dream. I convinced myself we were okay. Then Lucas Baxter called, and Soren went white as a ghost, and when he hung up the phone and I asked him what was wrong, he said, 'Virgil McLane's gone missing.' And I knew right away what had happened."

Edda looked up at the ceiling again, then closed her eyes and chuckled.

"What?" Ty said.

She opened her eyes and looked at him. "Oh, I was just thinking . . . how long have you and your Angela been together now?"

"Together? We've been married a little over five years. But together? Only a little over one, really. I was deployed a lot."

"That's hard."

He nodded.

"Well then, maybe you know and maybe you don't . . ." Edda clasped her hands. "Have you gotten to the point yet where *you* isn't *you* anymore? Where *you* becomes the two of you?"

"Angie has. She thinks of us as . . . you know, *us*. Me? I mostly think of her."

"Men do. For a while at least. Actually, to some extent, they always do. But trust me, after a while you'll get to the point where the thought of there being a future that does not contain the two of you together, of being apart from each other, becomes unthinkable."

Ty's eyes opened wider and Edda added, "Don't worry; I'm not going to poison myself and leave the cat motherless. But the thought of Soren being taken away from me . . . it scared me silent. As for Soren, he was worried about scandal, and people shunning me, and me losing this house, and who knows what else. And it tortured him, I know, because he was a man of great character, and it hurt him to act otherwise. He didn't think he had a choice, and neither did I. We loved each other, and our first instinct was to protect."

Ty rested his chin on his fist. "That's beautiful, in a way."

"Maybe in a play, it would be. But in reality, if you have to live it? It's just wrong."

Ty ran his hands back along the top of his head, the close-cropped hair springing up behind them. "Edda, you helped Soren. You crossed a state line. That's federal. If you say anything, you're taking on a lot of risk."

She sipped her coffee thoughtfully. "I've thought of that many times before, Tyler. And if what I have done merits punishment, then I'm ready for that. But frankly, I think Lucas

Baxter will be able to clear things so that doesn't happen, not just because we're friends but because this way he can close a case. As for Parker McLane, he's a libertine and a lecher and a drunkard, but he's not vindictive. He's not his father. In fact, I think he and his mother might sleep better knowing for sure that Virgil won't ever come walking through the front door again."

"Soren won't get that lake named after him."

Edda smiled. "Probably not. But he knew that when he made his decision to go public with this. I think we honor his memory best by respecting his wishes, don't you?"

Ty got up, walked to the kitchen door and looked out the window for several long seconds. Then he turned back to the old lady.

"The way I look at it, Edda, what Soren did, what you helped him with after the fact, it all may have been wrong, but it wasn't . . . well, it wasn't evil. Virgil McLane's dead, and a case can be made that, under the circumstances, Soren might have done something else, something that left Virgil alive. But McLane's family doesn't care that he's gone. His community doesn't care that he's gone. Most people around here are probably glad. That leaves only two parties that could possibly be offended: Virgil McLane and Jesus Christ. And Jesus has already forgiven the sin, and there's no way to ever make this up to McLane. So if that's the case, why open this back up? In one day I can go back up there, get rid of that stuff in the cliff and put this behind you forever. Why not let me do that?"

Ty opened his hands, dropped them. Edda cocked her head again, picked up the little Bible and joined him at the door. She looked out the window, then up at Ty.

"Because that's not true, Tyler. Virgil and Jesus weren't the only two offended. Soren was. And I was. We became chained to a lie. And now it's reaching out to wrap you up as well, and your Angela, if we let it, because a husband's troubles are a wife's sorrows, don't you know?"

Ty said nothing. But after a moment, he nodded his head at that.

Edda looked out the window again. "Every night, for months and then years, Soren was tormented by the place where he'd put us. He stopped reading this book, because it reminded him that our silence was wrong. The only reason I still read it was because I believed that sometime, somehow, we would have the opportunity to be open about this. And now that opportunity is here. In fact . . ."

She leafed through the little Bible, found a passage, followed it with her finger and then held the book out to Ty.

"Read this for me, dear. Out loud. Right here—verse thirty-two."

Ty read, " 'And ye shall know the truth, and the truth shall make you free.' "

Edda tapped the page.

"This may not be what Jesus was talking about there when He said that, but it doesn't matter. It still applies. Truth is freedom, and lies enslave us. Soren wouldn't want us to live chained to a lie. Don't you see that?"

Ty turned to the window, the edge of the book touching his chin.

"Yes," he said, not turning back. "Yes. I suppose I do."

CHAPTER
THIRTY-SIX

Stafford, Virginia

DRESSED IN BOXERS, SWEAT SOCKS AND A MARINE CORPS T-SHIRT three sizes too large for her, Angie sat atop the covers on the queen-size bed, four pillows behind her, a study Bible and a yellow highlighter to her left side, a book of sudoku puzzles and a pencil to her right. She turned the page on the paperback novel she was reading, scratched her head, mussing thick auburn hair that already looked slept in, then turned back and reread the same page.

She kept her place in the book with her finger and looked up. Headlights traced lines through the blinds on the streetside window, lines that traveled across the far wall and then vanished.

Slipping off the bed, she padded down the hall, through the

kitchen and toward the front entryway. She lifted a slat on the sidelight blinds, gasped, fumbled with the lock and ran out the door and down the walk, practically colliding with Ty as he was locking his pickup door.

"Hey." He smiled down at her, sizing up how she was dressed. "I guess it's a good thing I didn't come home during daylight."

She wrapped her arms around him, put her cheek against his chest. "I'm so sorry about Soren."

"Me too." He stroked her hair.

"How's his wife?"

"She's missing him. But she'll be okay. How's *my* wife?"

"She missed you." Angie held him more closely. Lifting her face, she whispered, "She loves you."

Ty kissed her, and kissed her again.

"I love you, Angie." He whispered it in her ear.

She squeezed him, and Ty squeezed back.

TOM MORRISEY—the author of five previous novels including *In High Places*, as well as numerous short stories—is a world-renowned adventure-travel writer whose work has appeared in *Outside*, *Sport Diver*, and other leading magazines. He holds an M.A. in English Language and Literature from the University of Toledo and an M.F.A. in Creative Writing from Bowling Green State University. Tom lives with his family in Orlando, Florida.

www.tommorrisey.com

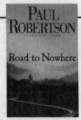